Outlaw Tales

Texas circuit-riding Baptist preacher John Morgan Young, named for Confederate general John Hunt Morgan, sits on the rocky overlook above Turner Falls in southern Oklahoma, photographed in the 1930s before the rush of modern development. The falls were once called Honey Creek Falls, then the name was changed to Turner's Falls to honor pioneer settler Mezeppa Turner; finally the name was shortened to Turner Falls. These Arbuckle Mountains, near the border of prosperous Texas, were once the hide-out for Belle Starr and Jesse James. Above the falls is a cave that afforded excellent protection from the weather and gave a commanding view of the approaches to it. It served, at least in legend, as a prime Jesse James stopover.

Outlaw Tales

Legends, Myths, and Folklore from America's Middle Border

Collected and Edited by
Richard Alan Young
and Judy Dockrey Young

August House Publishers, Inc.
LITTLE ROCK

Published by August House, Inc.,
P.O. Box 3223, Little Rock, Arkansas, 72203,
501-372-5450.

Printed in the United States of America

10 9 8 7 6 5 4 3 2

LIBRARY OF CONGRESS CATALOGING-IN-PUBLICATION DATA

Outlaw tales : legends, myths, and folklore from America's middle border
/ collected and edited by
Richard Alan Young and Judy Dockrey Young. — 1st ed.
p.   cm.
ISBN 0-87483-195-4 (pbk.: alk. paper) : $10.95
1. Outlaws—West (U.S.). 2. Peace officers—West (U.S.)
3. Folklore—West (U.S.). 4. West (U.S.)—Social life and customs.
I. Young, Richard Alan, 1946– . II. Young, Judy Dockrey, 1949– .
F596.088 1992
398.2'0978—dc20   92-2274

First Edition, 1992

Executive editor: Liz Parkhurst
Project editor: Ed Gray
Design director: Ted Parkhurst
Cover design: Wendell E. Hall
Typography: Lettergraphics / Little Rock

This book is printed on archival-quality paper which meets the
guidelines for performance and durability of the Committee on
Production Guidelines for Book Longevity of the
Council on Library Resources.

AUGUST HOUSE, INC.   PUBLISHERS   LITTLE ROCK

To George David Hendricks, Ph.D.
on the occasion of the Fiftieth Anniversary
of the first edition of his landmark book
The Bad Man of the West

*George D. Hendricks, author of **The Bad Man of the West** and the editors' cousin, recalls his grandfather Hendricks in the 1880s:*

In the 1880s my grandfather Hendricks was working for Sanger Brothers department store in Dallas, Texas. He is the man after whom I am named, and he worked collecting bad accounts. He traveled to all parts of Texas—cattlemen from all over charged purchases at Sanger Brothers when they were in town on a drive—and he met all sorts of people, let me tell you.

He sometimes collected up to $1,500 on a single round and word had gotten out about the fact that he might be carrying cash-money. He carried a six-shooter to protect himself. On one such trip a doctor, not having the cash—there was a depression on still—paid his bill with a horse and saddle. Grandfather saddled the horse and was leading it back to Dallas. He stopped for the night to camp and tied both horses to the same tree.

He was sitting by the fire when a voice behind him called out in a rough staccato, "Reach for the stars! I've got you covered!" Luckily for Grandfather the spare horse pawed the ground behind the robber just at that moment. He stood, turned to face the robber, and smiled as he raised his hands. He looked the robber straight in the eyes, then let his eyes wander over to the second horse.

"No need to shoot him, Johnny," he said to the thin air. "We'll just take him in and collect the reward."

Knowing there was a second horse, the robber turned to face his imaginary opponent. When he looked back, Grandfather was gone.

The robber turned about, with his back exposed, trying to spot his intended victim when Grandfather spoke from behind his own horse. "Now drop that gun or I'll shoot!"

Grandfather came out from behind the horse, his six-shooter drawn, with the dead drop on the outlaw. The outlaw obeyed and dropped his gun.

It's "the oldest trick in the book," but I guess the outlaw hadn't read "the book." ❧

Contents

BEADLE'S HALF-DIME Library

$2.50 a year.   Entered at the Post Office at New York, N. Y., at Second Class Mail Rates.   Copyrighted in 1882 by BEADLE AND ADAMS.   February 7, 1882.

Vol. X.   Single Number.   PUBLISHED WEEKLY BY BEADLE AND ADAMS, No. 98 WILLIAM STREET, NEW YORK.   Price, 5 Cents.   No. 237.

LONE STAR,

The Cowboy Captain; or, The Mysterious Ranchero.

A ROMANCE OF WILD LIFE IN TEXAS.

BY COL. PRENTISS INGRAHAM,

AUTHOR OF "CRIMSON KATE," "GRIT, THE BRAVO SPORT," "BISON BILL," "GOLD PLUME," "LITTLE GRIT," ETC., ETC.

"NOW, PARDS, READY! ONE! TWO! THREE!"

Many of the legends of the 1880s had their start in the "dime novels," which corresponded roughly to modern comic books, or in this case, Beadles Half-Dime Library for February 7, 1882 (Vol. X, No. 237), Lone Star, the Cowboy Captain, or, The Mysterious Ranchero: A Romance of Wild Life in Texas by Col. Prentiss Ingraham.

Foreword

THE BAD MAN OF THE WEST (by George David Hendricks, illustrated by Frank Anthony Stanush; The Naylor Company, Publishers, San Antonio, Texas, 1942) was the first book that attempted a panopticon study of all the major outlaws of the West and attempted to analyze what made them who they were.

Of all the outlaws, some two hundred fifty, assessed in his study, the median birth date for the men was 1850; most of them went into the War Between the States as teenagers. Ninety-five percent of them were from the Old South and their median death date was 1885—probably due to middle age setting in and a loss of nerve, of eyesight, of hand control, and someone faster on the draw gunning them down, usually in a fair fight.

Most of them were ex-Confederates. Many were guerrillas at one time and most had fought under William Clarke Quantrill. After the war many couldn't cope with peacetime—they suffered from what we now call post-traumatic stress disorder; they found civilian life too dull; they longed for the hero's welcome they had received when they had victoriously returned home. Many of them lost family in the fighting and longed for revenge; many lost their homes during the War, or in the depression, or due to tax increases levied by carpetbagger governments; most saw their prewar way of life destroyed, leaving them rootless and desperate. Many tried honest labor but found it did not pay the emotional or financial rewards raiding had. Some went renegade as Union guerrillas were pardoned for their crimes and depredations during combat, but Confederate guerrillas were charged as murderers or criminals for acts no more violent than the Union's.

Others became *desperado* (Spanish: "without hope") when institutions took their land or homes: banks, most of which were based on Union money and run by pro-Union men after the war; railroads, which grabbed up land for back taxes and forced Southerners to move out so Northern settlers could move in; and Union sympathizers, many of whom had used questionable legal means to steal land from Confederates gone to war.

To the utter amazement of Unionists, carpetbaggers and even law-abiding former Confederates, the ex-guerrillas-turned-outlaws were often supported, hidden, fed, and encouraged by down-and-out Southerners. It was as if the South were still fighting the Union Army and the "rich Northern interests" in the banks and railroads.

Many famous lawmen were ex-Confederates and many criminals were ex-Union men, but the pattern of Union/lawmen and Confederate/guerrilla/outlaws was a common one.

Dr. Hendricks' book employed sources from oral folklore, newspaper accounts, old-timer interviews, government records, and other documents. Many old-timers were still living in the 1940s who knew the central characters personally. They are gone now, to the Last Roundup, but the clippings are still in scrapbooks, the great-grandchildren remember some of the stories, and the newspapers and documents are on microfilm for bleary-eyed researchers.

This is where we, the collectors and editors of this anthology, come on the scene, a new, next generation to pass along the stories of the American Middle Border.

—Richard Alan Young
HARRISON, ARKANSAS
November 1, 1991

Introduction

WORKING AS PROFESSIONAL STORYTELLERS out of Silver Dollar City, a craft and entertainment theme park in the Missouri Ozarks that re-creates the Middle Border life of one century ago, we have come across many outlaw tales. As Ozark folklorist Vance Randolph pointed out, Ozark men and boys consider outlaw tales as one of their prime storytelling genres, and women and girls tell family folklore that, in this area, often includes scrapes with bushwhackers or jayhawkers, guerrillas, and outlaws. While ghost and scary stories are the tales most often requested of an Ozark storyteller, second in popularity is a tie between tall tales, which are usually humorous, and outlaw tales, which are usually "thrilling" but may by humorous as well. From our winter home in Harrison, Arkansas, and our summer home in Stoneridge (Stone County), Missouri, we have ranged far and wide across the Middle Border lands to collect narratives and track down fragments or story leads. While our choice of themes for this, our fourth book of stories, seems logical to us, we feel a need to explain our choice and introduce the reader to the genre of tales anthologized in this collection.

First, we feel close to the outlaw legends, especially those about Belle Starr. As a boy in Texas in the 1950s, Richard heard Belle Starr stories from his father and grandfather, and his family visited Belle Starr sites, like the cabin at Devil's Den (Oklahoma) outside Tishomingo, and the Outlaw Cave or Jesse James Cave above Turner Falls in the Arbuckle Mountains. As a girl in Oklahoma in the 1950s, Judy, whose family had lived in Indian Territory before statehood, lived outside Wagoner, home of

Belle's son Ed Reed, and her father told stories about growing up on a sandbar in the Canadian River, not far from Younger's Bend where Belle and Sam Starr had their home. Were the stories we heard fact or fiction? So much time had passed that truthfulness no longer mattered—this was the stuff of legend!

Why another book on Western outlaws when there are literally hundreds on the market or in libraries? Many of the books are now out of print and some are jealously guarded by private collectors and not available to the general public. Many of these books are outdated as researchers use modern techniques to cross-reference outlaw data. For example, Glenn Shirley, in his biography of Belle Starr (*Belle Starr and Her Times,* University of Oklahoma Press, Norman, 1982) reveals from careful research that the idea of Belle not marrying, or marrying in non-traditional ways, is a myth. He found marriage licenses for her and Jim Reed in Collin County, Texas, evidence that she and Bruce Younger (not Cole, as legend claims) were in fact married in Kansas in 1878, and records of her legal marriage to Sam Starr in the Cherokee Volume 1-B, 297, of "Marriage records..." for 1880. Microfilmed census records and court records, computer-cross-referenced in the last two decades, and centrally located, give researchers the ability to look at a broad range of historical sources not available to the average author of the late 1800s and early part of this century. There are still new revelations to be found, "new" old photographs to publish and newly retold stories to retell in print.

These are "outlaw tales" because they tell of the deeds, homes, hide-outs, treasures, lives, deaths, and descendants of outlaws. Some of the stories deal with lawmen and their descendants, but only because these brave officers had dealings with the outlaws. As every adult who as a kid in the '40s or '50s or early '60s watched black-and-white television shows and "B" grade Westerns at the local theater knows, our heroes were always the lawmen, but it was the outlaws who stole the show. (In Richard's neighborhood in Abilene, Texas, an old haunt of John Wesley Hardin, kids at play drew straws and the losers had to be the lawmen.)

These are "tales," and *tales* isn't an exact folklore term. To begin with, storytellers and storyholders, historians, folklorists, anthropologists, sociologists, and literary critics all deal with tales, and define the genre differently, depending on the purpose of the tales. Some tales are *myths:* classical myths are ancient stories set at the beginning of time that explain psychologically and in a pre-scientific way origins of things and sources of human behavior; myths in this collection are stories believed by the tellers but patently and demonstrably untrue in the light of research. Some of these tales are *legends:* the word legend actually comes from the Latin verb *legere* which one Latin dictionary defines as "select, gather together, read." Yet legends are usually transmitted orally. Legend could be defined as "a story coming to us from the past, believed by the teller but not historically verifiable," or, perhaps, "a half-true story from the past." Legends are first told orally, then set down in writing by some collector or academician, then reborn and told again when admired by readers of a new generation. Some of the stories in this collection are legends because they are told as truth about bigger-then-life people and events, but either difficult to substantiate or, better yet, from the yarnspinner's viewpoint, impossible to either prove or disprove.

Some observations about legends from the storytellers' viewpoint (as opposed to the folklorists' viewpoint): legends tend to have at least one truthful element, even if it's just the name of the geographical feature that is to be explained (e.g. "How Cannibal Plateau got its name"), the name of the bigger-than-life central character (e.g. "Belle Starr and the Mock Stage Robbery"), or some feature of the narrative that is a historical fact, much embroidered upon by years of retelling. Generally speaking, a story isn't a legend until enough time has passed to make it difficult to verify the details, forcing the listener or reader to rely on the credibility of the narrator. When legends are reduced to writing do they become a separate but unnamed genre— literary legend? Literature? They are quite distinct from oral narratives when they become frozen or fixed on the printed page, while their oral counterparts live on and continue to change subtly with each retelling.

There is also the problem of *mock legend*, written by a fiction writer to earn money. This is the case with Paul Bunyan and Pecos Bill, according to research by J. Frank Dobie. It also seems to be true for Alton Meyers, who wrote an article about Belle for the *Police Gazette*, and who may have written or helped write the often-inaccurate *Bella* [sic] *Starr, the Bandit Queen*, published by Richard Fox in July 1889. (The first notice of publication of the small wire-sewn paperback pamphlet was in the *Police Gazette*, and had her name spelled correctly.) Writing furiously against a deadline, shortly after Belle's murder, the author of *Bella Starr* did include many facts, but used heresay, innuendo, and apparent outright fabrication to finish the book and sell as many copies as possible through sensationalism. "Real" legend, we would assume, comes from minute inaccuracies or embroidering upon an orally transmitted narrative. Mock legend comes from haste, greed, desperation—emotions writers know all too well. Of course, writers may deliberately write mock legend as a sub-genre of fantasy, according to fantasy author and editor Lin Carter, but that is not the type of mock legend to which we refer here.

Some of these tales are *folktales* of a sort. They are not necessarily anonymous in their authorship and certainly not timeless or placeless as folktales often are. But they are believed regardless of their verifiability, are handed down orally from one generation to the next, represent the mores of the people who tell and retell them, and pit good against evil—often in unconventional interpretations, e.g. the James boys against the "evil" bankers who are merciless to victimized war widows.

Most of these stories are *family folklore*, that is, someone in a family, extended over time, experienced or heard of an event and told their version of that event to upcoming generations in that family, who subsequently shared the tales with us. Why do families offer us their stories? Sometimes pride in family accomplishments, or vanity, if the tale is demonstrably false (something we never question when we hear a story for the first time), often in an attempt to preserve the story and keep it from dying out in a world where so many people find their only entertainment by pushing a button on something electronic.

But in true folklore these stories are not myths, not exactly legends, and not quite the same as folktales. In many cases what they resemble most is the class of stories now known as "urban legend."

Before they were studied or written about extensively by folklorists from Richard Dorson to Jan Harold Brunvand, before, say, the 1970s, Americans did not have a name for *urban legends.* But we told them with great vigor! As folklorists were beginning to seriously work with urban legends, in the 1960s, half of this collecting/editing team, Richard Young, was in college at the proverbial "small college in the Midwest," the University of Arkansas at Fayetteville. There, among his storytelling buddies, they shared both the standard urban legends (now known by names like "Drip, Drip, Drip" or "The Hanged Boy," "Hook-Arm," "Pond of Snakes," and "Call from the Downstairs Phone"—surely you recognize some from their conventional titles), but also outlaw legends as well. They called them "chain stories," because, like chain letters, the stories are passed from one teller to a dozen listeners, who subsequently pass them to a dozen more listeners, etc. Also, except for the family folklore element in some of the stories, the tales functioned like chain letters in another way: just as chain letters called for the sender to add his name at the bottom of a list and drop the top name off, so chain stories became the oral property of the teller in the minds of the listener and previous tellers in the chain of retelling were forgotten.

Even the family folklore falls victim to this when Grandpa says he *knew* the man who saw Jesse James and the grandson grows up saying the grandpa *was* the man who saw Jesse James.

Another urban legend characteristic is that such tales are retold in a new generation as if they had happened recently; this is a kind of temporal compression. That same compression occurs in family folklore when the teller says, "Grandpa knew Jesse James as a boy," but when asked for grandpa's birthdate the collector is given the year 1883. Since Jesse was shot by "the dirty little coward" Bob Ford in 1882, it must have been *Great-grandpa* who knew Jesse as a boy. Or maybe it was Great-grandpa's *neighbor* who knew Jesse ...

This brings us to stories we have affectionately labeled "The Big Three." We frequently hear these three claims: Great-grandpa danced with Belle Starr at a barn dance, Great-grandma knew the widow to whom Butch Cassidy gave the gold to save her home (or was that Jesse?), and finally, I am the illegitimate descendant of Jesse (or sometimes Frank) James. We do not doubt these stories when we hear them. Some of them may be true. But we have left out of this collection many fragmentary and non-narrative versions of the above "Big Three" stories.

One term we use throughout this book is the phrase "the Middle Border." From its very beginnings in the 1780s the United States had fairly clear borders on the east (the Atlantic), the north (Canada), and the south (the Gulf or Spain's claim line). But in the West, the border running north-to-south across the middle of the continent was constantly moving. In the 1790s and early 1800s that boundary was the Mississippi; in the 1850s it was near the 95th West Meridian at the western edge of Missouri and Arkansas; in the 1880s it was near the 107th West Meridian near Santa Fe, Denver, Laramie, and Deadwood. It was that imaginary line east of which there was civilized society and organized law enforcement, and west of which (discounting the well-settled California coast) there was wilderness and a lack of organized law enforcement. The lack of settlers and subsequent lack of agriculture and large cities precluded a tax base large enough to support a system of law enforcement and courts; yet in that area were fortunes to be made in buffalo hides, cattle drives, gold and silver prospecting, and in providing those non-essential services (liquor, prostitution, gambling) that men in a nearly womanless society, on a vast plain where monotony often reigned, so desperately wanted. Here is the explosive formula: great wealth gotten easily, lost easily, taken easily, mixed with liquor and lack of law enforcement. Money, liquor, guns. Some other Western aficionados would say "money, liquor, cards, and guns."

It is in Kansas that we can see most clearly the movement of that elusive Middle Border. As the railroad moved its westernmost railhead farther toward the Rockies, year by year, a new cattle town became the wild-and-wooly west of Hollywood films: Abilene, Hays, Ellis, and on the Santa Fe Route, Dodge City. The outlaw fringe also moved west. The outlaw activity of the 1870s is largely in Missouri, Arkansas, and Texas; in the 1880s, Kansas, Oklahoma, West Texas; by the 1890s, Colorado, New Mexico, Arizona, and northward in Wyoming and the Dakota Territory. By the time Butch Cassidy's gang was robbing trains in Wyoming, Oklahoma was almost ready for statehood. The Middle Border moved westward, ever westward, and our image of the Wild West moved with it.

The outlaws and lawmen are the folk heroes of that era. From the 1700s we idolize Washington, Jefferson, Franklin; from the early 1800s we adore Daniel Boone, Davy Crockett, even Mike Fink the keelboatman. From the War Between the States we honor Lincoln and Grant, Jeff Davis and Robert E. Lee, courageous adversaries regardless of our regional background. Suddenly, in the 1880s, there is an explosion of folk heroes: Wild Bill Hickok, Wyatt Earp, Bat Masterson, Seth Bullock, Bill Tilghman. On the reverse of that coin are Jesse and Frank James, the Youngers, the Daltons, Sam Bass, Bill Longley, John Wesley Hardin, Billy the Kid, and especially the colorful womenfolk like Calamity Jane, Poker Alice Tubbs, Belle Starr, Rose of Cimarron, Cattle Annie and Little Britches.

Not all of these bigger-than-life characters are represented in the tales collected here; these are the best stories that have come to us over the years.

It would be hard to determine which outlaw or lawman had the largest number of legends to his or her credit. Surely Wild Bill Hickok, Jesse James and Belle Starr would be among the leaders as the stuff of legends. But what does an outlaw legend consist of? Often it is no more than a single fact (or item of information that is believed as fact, although unverifiable). Sometimes an outlaw legend is one small event or one personality trait that is described by a storyteller. Here are examples of legends that the collectors of this anthology have heard:

Belle's Spyglass

Belle Starr actually rode sidesaddle because it allowed her to keep look-out ahead and behind without appearing suspicious; she always carried a spyglass hanging from the off-side (right side) of her saddle, and used it to spy out movements of cattle, horses, and marshal's posses from promontories carefully selected across Indian Territory. Her favorite promontories were outside Inola. On one, a stone lookout tower was built. On another, a graveyard sits today.

This short narrative contains no line of action, just suppositions about Belle's tactics. It would be impossible to verify this legend.

Duel on the Empty Grave

Clay Allison once got in an argument with another tough hombre, and proposed that the two of them shoot it out in proper fashion. The two dug a grave and stood at opposite ends of the hole. Allison said a short, loud prayer. Then they drew and fired; the other shootist was the victim. Allison covered him over in the grave into which he had conveniently fallen.

Other versions of that story include such details as a card game, a last drink of whiskey before the prayer, and other details. George D. Hendricks, Texas folklorist and historian, confirms that this duel actually took place in New Mexico, perhaps at Taos.

Another Belle Starr legend says that Belle had a son, perhaps by Sam Starr or perhaps by Bill (Jim July) Starr, who was given the name Bandy. An article on page 3 of the Fort Smith *Southwest American* of April 20, 1911, reads:

Starr Must Serve Life Behind Bars

OKLAHOMA CITY, OKLA., APRIL 18—Bandy Starr, son of the famous Belle Starr, woman outlaw, must serve his life sentence for the murder of Ed Cordell at Wilburton in 1909 ... Starr killed Cordell at Coal Chute No. 1, two miles east of Wilburton, Dec. 22, 1909.

None of Belle's biographers record the birth of such a son. Since Starr was a common Cherokee name, the young murderer may have simply sought to enlarge his reputation by making a claim to the more famous branch of the widespread Starr clan. In spite of the lack of evidence, legend says Belle had two other sons besides Ed Reed, the Bandy mentioned above, and one other whose name varies with the stories.

Another sample legend is:

Belle's Love Child

Belle Starr had an illegitimate child by Cole Younger, and named Younger's Bend after him, who was the first of her many lovers.

This fragment contains many falsehoods. Belle was never in love with Cole Younger. The child she bore (Pearl) was not Cole's. Cole himself denied it (after Belle's death, when there was no reason for him to lie to protect her reputation) and Pearl denied it in essence by using calling cards that read Pearl Reed while living in Fort Smith later in her life. (These cards are preserved in an album at the Belle Starr home, a structure moved from its foundations at Galesburg, Missouri, to Red Oak II, a reconstruction of Midwestern town life built by artist Lowell Davis outside Carthage, Missouri.) Glenn Shirley points out from his research that Pearl was known as Pearl Younger rarely, and because of Belle's marriage to Bruce Younger, Cole's cousin in Kansas. Furthermore, Younger's Bend in the Canadian River already bore that name when Belle moved there with her Cherokee husband Sam Starr.

We have omitted from this collection most of the fragmentary or non-narrative legends that we have heard through the years (similar to the ones above). This collection is an attempt to present the most interesting, most tellable, most thrilling or most humorous, and most intriguing stories we have been told. While some of the tales are very personal, and clearly identified with one teller only, most are stories we have heard from many tellers (even tellers who claim the stories to be personal, e.g. "My grandfather was the sixth man at the Coffeyville double-bank robbery. He held the horses for the Daltons." Just for the record, there was no sixth man at that robbery; no one was holding the horses. All five robbers were killed or captured. Nevertheless, we have met no fewer than three families who claim that their ancestor was that sixth man, and of course, the ancestor in question is three different men).

What stories *have* we retained among the hundreds we have heard? Each story in this collection has one or more of the following elements:

- *Sentimental value to the collectors, as a story coming down through our Middle Border families,*
- *Folkloric value because it is rare or unique among the many outlaw stories we have heard,*
- *Historic value because the events in the story are verifiable, or,*
- *Storytelling value because the narrative can be told by anyone who loves to hear and tell outlaw stories.*

We have endeavored to credit all our stories, except where anonymity has been requested, and we trust that readers and storytellers who retell these tales will courteously credit the tellers who shared their stories with us.

We now share these stories with you, and hope that they will find new life in a new generation of readers and yarnspinners.

—Richard and Judy Dockrey Young
SILVER DOLLAR CITY, MISSOURI

Belle and the Stuff of Legends

THE MIDDLE BORDER'S MOST FAMOUS WOMAN BECAME THE OUTLAW SWEETHEART OF AMERICA, THE "FEMALE JESSE JAMES."

The outlaw about whom we have heard the greatest number and variety of legends, most of them either patently untrue or both unverified and unverifiable, is the lady born Myra Maybelle Shirley. She later married Jim Reed in Texas and her two children, Pearl and Ed, bore his name. After Jim was shot she later married Bruce Younger—not Cole, as legend has it—in Kansas, for some reason of propriety, and then abandoned him at their apparent mutual consent to marry Sam Starr in the Indian Territory. After Sam was shot she is presumed to have married Bill July, who was adopted by Tom Starr (Belle's father-in-law) under the name Jim July Starr. He did not change his name at her whim, as legend says, but rather because of his adoption by Tom Starr. With so tangled a record of marriages one can see that her whole colorful life could easily be, and is, equally tangled and difficult to research.

The first story isn't legend at all, but fact, and serves to give the reader a glimpse at how legend has enhanced this already remarkable woman's life.

Portrait of Belle

The most widely known photograph of Belle Starr was taken on the streets of Fort Smith, Arkansas, to take advantage of the good light in front of the photographer's shop. Belle was in town awaiting trial on a charge of horse stealing, the only class of crime with which she was ever charged, and she had asked permission to pose for a photograph. The jailer consented and sent along Belle, her beautiful mount, her pearl-handled pistol, unloaded, and a deputy United States marshal on his horse to accompany and guard her. When the photograph was taken, Belle was mounted with her horse sidelong to the camera, her pistol, riding crop, and sidesaddle all proudly displayed. To the right side of the image on the large glass negative sat the deputy marshal astride his horse, the animal's head to the photographer. In the prints Belle ordered the deputy was cropped out.

When S.W. Harman published his famous book about Judge Isaac Parker's court at Fort Smith, *Hell on the Border; He Hanged Eighty-Eight Men* (Phoenix Publishing Company, Fort Smith) in 1898, he had the entire negative printed. He then hired someone to paint out the street and shop, replacing them with a supposed Indian Territory scene that more closely resembles a desert in Arizona. He furthermore had the face of the deputy painted over and replaced with an artist's rendering of the face of Sam Starr, of whom no photographs were known to exist![1]

Prominent Western researcher and author Glenn Shirley, whose biography of Belle is the most authoritative, states that of the more than one hundred narratives about Belle found in, or heard orally based on, the Indian-Pioneer Histories of Oklahoma, not one event ever made it into the contemporary

This is the most famous photo or Myra Maybelle Shirley—later Myra Reed, Myra Younger, and Belle Starr—taken on the street in front of Rhoeder's Photographic Gallery, Fort Smith, Arkansas, May 23, 1886, while Belle was in town answering a charge of larceny (horse-stealing). Deputy U.S. Marshal Hughes, to the photographer's right, has been cropped out.

newspapers. Some of the narratives are clearly hearsay, but many of the events are simply so small or personal that newspapers would not have printed them had they been reported. From the Indian-Pioneer Histories come the following narratives, with commentary.

Belle's Black Disguise—I

Belle Starr's story has been told and retold many times of late, but this is the only authentic account ever written of her first arrest [by a relative of the participants]...

L.W. Marks was then [in the 1880s] a young deputy United States marshal riding for the greatest criminal court in the world, at Fort Smith, Arkansas, which was presided over by "Hanging Judge" Isaac Parker...

Marshal Marks' first encounter with Belle Starr occurred when he was ordered to look out for her when she got off the train at Muskogee [Oklahoma]. She was said to have a large sum of counterfeit money in her possession. He and his posse were on hand when she alighted from the train and [they] followed her closely to the cabin of a Negro family on the outskirts of town, where she completely vanished into thin air. Both men [it must have been a small posse!] saw her enter the house and followed immediately behind her. Yet a thorough search failed to find her. There was only a sick Negro woman asleep in bed and an old Negro attendant, shawl over her head, smoking a pipe in the chimney corner.

Sometime later Marshal Marks was given a writ for the arrest of Belle and Sam Starr for horse stealing. They were reported headed for the Osage Hills which was then...a safe and favorite rendezvous for desperados. Perhaps spurred by his former failure to capture Belle, Marshal Marks made a more determined effort to arrest her and her husband, but he was often confused by the conflicting reports of the people [whom he questioned] along the way; sometimes it was a man and a boy he was trailing, sometimes a man and a woman. Finally he came to where they had stopped for the night with a Negro family away out west. The marshals camped too and concealed themselves near the watering hole.

Presently Sam Starr and a Negro boy came leading the horses to water. The officers arrested and disarmed Starr, chained him to a tree [a common practice in those days] to look as if he were just standing there, then sent the Negro boy with a message to Belle to come down as Sam wanted her. The ruse worked, and she hastened down. She being a woman, the marshals did not want to use violence, so they hid behind trees on opposite sides of the path and stepped out as she passed by, each taking an arm.

She was disarmed on each side [of her two visible pistols]. Under the drapery of a pannier overskirt was a six-shooter and concealed in the bosom of her dress were two derringer short pistols. She fought like a tiger and threatened the officers with death, "if I ever get out," and she meant it, too.

In those days transportation was slow and tedious. Marshals, to make their trips, had to take wagon outfits and camping equipment, traveling overland picking up offenders of the law along the way. A trip lasted for a month or six weeks.

Belle Starr was the most exasperating, desperate prisoner the marshals had ever dealt with. She would drop knives, forks, blankets or anything she could reach as she rode along in the wagon. The loss was not discovered until the article was needed. Her one object in life seemed to be to irritate and annoy those having her in [their] charge. Because of her sex the officers were as considerate and forebearing as possible, until patience ceased to be a virtue or even safe.

The outfit was camped near Muskogee at the old fairground [one night]. Here the prisoners were left under guard while the marshal and his posse went in pursuit of other criminals for whom they had writs. Just as they were returning to camp for dinner they heard a shot and saw Belle running around the tent in hot pursuit of the guard, a smoking revolver in her hand.

She had been alone in her tent eating her dinner when the side blew up [in the wind], disclosing the guard seated on the outside with his back toward her, his pistol in his scabbard. It was but the work of an instant for her to seize the pistol. She intended to kill the guard, liberate the other prisoners, her husband, and herself. Unfortunately for the success of her plans, in attempting to rise she had placed the barrel of the gun on the ground, discharging it and jamming it so badly it would not work. The timely arrival of the officers saved the day. She cried with disappointment and rage when she was disarmed. Thereafter, for the safety of the others, she was chained [just as the male prisoners were].

At Fort Smith Sam and Belle Starr were convicted of horse-stealing [the trial began February 15, 1883] and Judge Parker sentenced them to one year in the penitentiary at Detroit, Michigan. It so happened that the same young marshal, L.W. Marks, was put in charge and deputized to deliver the sentenced convicts to the pen in the regular prison [railroad] car "Old Ten Spot." Belle and Sam were among the number and when she realized she was actually sentenced and on her way to prison she became more talkative.

One day she asked Marshal Marks if he remembered chasing her into a Negro's cabin at Muskogee. She then bragged of how she had outwitted him—she said the officers had followed her so closely she had taken refuge in this strange cabin where she saw a sick Negro woman asleep in the bed. [Belle had] spit on her hands, rubbed them in the soot of the chimney, then over her face and hands, drew her shawl over her head, picked up a pipe off the mantle, dipped it in the ashes, then crouched down to smoke, answer their questions and watch the search.[2]

Belle's Black Disguise—II

I lived near the range of Belle Starr, a noted outlaw. I remember one time the law was after Belle and she stopped at a Negro cabin; she made the Negro woman hide her. She dressed in a black dress with a white apron and shawl, blackened her face, and when the law came in she was rocking in a chair with a cob pipe in her mouth.[3]

One can see the slow development of legend as the details of Mrs. Marks' narrative become condensed into this shorter, more summary version, told by Mrs. Gertrude Cooper of Sentinel, Oklahoma. The versions we have heard vary slightly in details but seem to be clearly based on the event described by Mrs. Marks.

Another famous Belle legend deals with her use of psychology in a robbery. Glenn Shirley states this story is false, that Belle never participated in this robbery, but the legend persists in the **Indian-Pioneer Histories** *(Volume 104, pages 84-85) and in the oral tradition. Here is the version we heard at Red Oak II outside Belle's old hometown of Carthage, Missouri, where her childhood house has been moved and reconstructed:*

Belle and the Indian Child

My favorite Belle Starr story is the one where Belle rides to the town where the Seminole tribal payroll is about to be issued from the government. Belle comes riding into town on her fine horse and suddenly she rides up beside an Indian child, picks him up and sets him in front of her on her horse as though she's going to give him a ride. Then the people start getting worried because she looks like she's going to ride out of town with the boy, kidnapping him. All the people start following her and she rides slowly out of town. Everyone has followed her out into a field where she just puts the boy down and laughs and rides away. When everyone gets back to town they find that Belle's gang has robbed the bank of the tribal payroll.[4]

This legend is one of the most popular about Belle, even though she never was known to participate in a bank robbery and the robbery of the Seminole Nation payroll was not done by Belle Starr or any gang that could be considered to be hers.

Obviously, the stories about Belle Starr were "told and retold," and much of what was told was hearsay. For example in the **Indian-Pioneer Histories** *(Volume 20, page 481) Jack B. Corbell told Charles H. Holt on November 19, 1937:*

Jack Corbell's Story

Belle Starr, the woman outlaw of those days, was known generally in those parts [near Briarton, outside Eufaula] or in the northeastern part of the territory. She married a man by the name of Reed and it was believed by many people that one of her sons killed her to collect the reward.

Of course, there was no reward offered for Belle Starr at the time of her death for she was under no indictment, and her biographers only know of one son, Ed Reed. The legend (or even "outlaw urban legend") element appears in the brief sketch in the words "it was believed by many people" and in the apparent acceptance of Bandy Starr as being Belle's son, in spite of the fact that his age would indicate she had died before he was born.

Some of the legends about Belle that are provable fiction may stem from confusion of Belle with other notorious or famous women of the time. Some legends state that Belle was killed during flight from a crime scene; perhaps the retellers of this story have Belle confused with another woman outlaw. The Fort Smith **Daily Herald** *for Thursday, August 1, 1878, carried this story, which may have become confused in the minds of the public with Belle's death in 1889:*

Female Horse Thief Shot

A lovely woman died in her boots on the banks of the Arkansas River two weeks ago. For several weeks the pioneers of Costella County Colorado had been harassed by the depredations of horse thieves. Finally a posse of frontiersmen took to the saddle in pursuit. They struck the trail, pushed on rapidly, and after a long ride overtook two thieves. Shots were exchanged and the desperadoes were killed. One of them was a woman dressed in a rough, loose suit of men's clothing, with a heavy pair of rawhide boots drawn up, and her pantaloons tucked in the spacious bootings. Her face, in the cold pallor of death, showed a complexion that had once been light and rosy, eyes of a fair hazel color, and hair that was cut short concealed by the slouch hat she wore. She was about twenty-two years of age.

This description fits so closely with some of the false oral legends and especially the incorrect published versions of Belle's death known in Europe as to lead the authors of this collection to believe this newspaper account is the source of those legends.

Another patently false legend states that Belle would take outlaws in at Younger's Bend and then turn them in for the reward. This is quite obviously another lady outlaw:

Lou Bowers

Bob Hutchins was shot in the leg by Lou Bowers, a lady outlaw in southern Oklahoma, who used to let criminals hide out at her place in the Arbuckle Mountains, and then turn them in for the reward in such a way that they never suspected her.[5]

Which legends can the modern audience believe to be based on fact? The earliest legends about Belle deal with her riding a long distance, outrunning Union militia to warn and save her Confederate guerrilla brother Bud. This event apparently really happened. Another time, however, the Union militia caught up to John Allison "Bud" Shirley and he was shot.

The killing of Belle's brother, Bud, a member of a Confederate bushwhacker organization, by pro-Union militiamen is often cited as the reason Belle turned later in life to crime as she stayed in the company of former Confederate guerrillas who had turned to crime in the post-war depression. Here is a rare firsthand account of the killing of Bud:

The Killing of Bud Shirley

I was present when Bud Shirley of Carthage [Missouri], brother of Myra Shirley who later became Belle Starr, was killed at Sarcoxie [a few miles from Carthage]. I had lived in Sarcoxie and knew all about the town and guided the group of our [pro-Union militia] men who went into town that night to catch some guerrillas said to be sleeping in a house there. We went up by the old mill and tied our horses there, then went on foot around to the other side opposite from Cave Springs, then into the town and surrounded the house. The bushwhackers came out running and while a good many of us were shooting we always thought it was Gilbert Schooling who killed [Bud] Shirley. Schooling took careful aim at Shirley but held his fire until the bushwhacker started to jump a plank fence; then he fired and Shirley fell dead on the other side.[6]

After Bud's death, Belle, then called Myra Maybelle, rode to Sarcoxie and saw the body being loaded onto a wagon. She is said to have grabbed Bud's pistols off the body and fired at the pro-Union militia, who had removed the percussion caps rendering her efforts ineffectual. It seems more likely that the militia would have taken the guns rather than left them on the body, but this is the second legend, chronologically speaking, about Belle, and one of the most popular.

Other legends about Belle include details about her favorite black horse on which she often jumped over tables of men drinking or playing cards in rowdy Indian Territory saloons. Actually Belle's favorite horse was a fine black mare named Venus, but she also often rode a sorrel gelding. The black-horse-jumping-the-table motif seems to come from another famous horsewoman, not at all an outlaw. Mabel Tompkins and her black jumping horse, Sky Rocket, appeared in Buffalo Bill's "Wild West" Exhibition touring the country in 1898. Mabel would jump Sky Rocket over a table of card players set up in the arena just for the stunt. She wore a black riding habit and rode sidesaddle, both as Belle Starr did, and she lived in Oklahoma. Stories of Mabel's exploits could easily have become confused with those of Myra Maybelle Shirley, Belle's christened name.

Finally, there were other women outlaws in the 1880s, some operating in Indian Territory or Oklahoma Territory. Any robbery or larceny committed by a woman could easily be attributed to Belle once the story had passed through about three tellers and the details had become blurred.

Another source for legends about Belle is the simple act of exaggeration. The folks who tell outlaw stories are naturally liable to add details or exaggerate the details already there to make a better or more tellable story. They may even do this unconsciously over a period of years with no deliberate effort to obscure the facts. This is just one of the consequences of oral transmission in a society that has no cultural taboo against embroidering stories.

Belle Rides By

One hot summer day the court of Judge Isaac Parker was in session. Even with all the windows open it was sweltering in the courtroom. One of the jurors was looking out a window to the east hoping for some air, when he suddenly lost all interest in the lawyer droning on about his client's moral character. He stood up and looked out the window. A moment later another juror joined him at the window and pretty soon half the jury box was on their feet at the window.

At first Judge Parker had thought the man stood up to spit out the window, a common practice, but when half the jury was on their feet the judge rapped his gavel loudly.

"What do you jurors find so interesting outside that window?" he asked.

"Your honor," said the foreman from the window. "Belle Starr is riding into town."

Without a moment's hesitation the judge rapped his gavel again and said. "This court will be in recess for five minutes until Belle Starr passes." Virtually everyone in court except the lawyers and the accused went to the high windows and watched Belle ride by on her magnificent racehorse, followed by her daughter, Pearl, on her steed. When they were out of sight up Garrison Avenue, everyone sat back down and court was reconvened.[7]

The citizens of Carthage, Missouri, Belle's birthplace (actually she was born close to the once-thriving village of Medoc, outside Carthage), first learned of Belle (whom they had known as Myra Shirley) when she was on trial for horse-stealing at Judge Parker's court. The following article appears in the June 3, 1886, **Carthage Banner:**

Belle Starr, a noted female bandit who is on trial at Fort Smith, Arkansas, charged with complicity in various robberies, claims to have been born in this city some thirty years ago. She does not give her maiden name but says her father who was a confederate moved from this place to Texas in 1863. She now lives on the Canadian River in the [Indian] territory and is married to a Cherokee Indian. Her place is a famous resort for outlaws.

While some time would pass before Carthage learned who Belle was, it is interesting to note that she was already being billed in the press as a "noted female bandit," and that her home at Younger's Bend was a "resort for outlaws." This clearly shows that the legendary things told about her after her death were already being circulated during her life.

One of the Big Three stories we have heard is known as "I danced with Belle Starr." Here are two fine examples of that type:

I Danced with Belle Starr—I

What would I say was the most thrilling thing I can remember doing back when this country was Indian Territory? Well, I'd say it was the time I danced with Belle Starr, the famous woman outlaw. Not that I was in love with her, you understand, but it was just the idea of seeing her and dancing with her. What did she look like? She was a darn good-looking woman, that's what. She was a fine figure of a woman; graceful as you please and confident. She was wearing a gun strapped around her waist the night I danced with her. *(Extract from an interview with George Washington Smith by James Russell Gray, Vol. 59, pg. 294 of the **Indian-Pioneer Histories of Oklahoma**, December 15, 1937.)*

Another such incident was told by James Robert "Bob" Hutchins, who later became fairly friendly with Belle, but who was the lawman who shot her fourth husband Jim July. Hutchins was from north Texas and fairly well-known in that area. The story was told to us by Texas folklorist George D. Hendricks:

I Danced with Belle Starr—II

Bob Hutchins took his sweetheart to a dance in Whitesboro, Texas, and saw Belle Starr there. He danced with her (it was customary to change partners from time to time) and found her to be attractive with dark eyes and long, black hair. He assumed she was Indian and asked about her heritage. She told him she was part Cherokee [perhaps she meant by marriage] and spoke both Cherokee and Chickasaw. Bob was part Chickasaw and they spoke to each other in that language. They later became friends—as friendly as they could be on opposite sides of the law.

This was the way Hutchins told the story in his memoirs and he was simply not aware that Belle was not part Indian and probably misconstrued something she said.

*In Volume 21 of the **Indian-Pioneer Histories of Oklahoma**, pages 79 and 85, there is an interview with Herman H. Cowen made September 9, 1937, by Charline M. Culbertson for the Works Progress Administration's Writers' Project:*

"It Will Soon Be Daylight"

[Belle Starr] was personally known about the community and attended all the dances and affairs held thereabout. She was at all the dances which were held two and three times a week and I have danced with her many times. She usually caused no trouble at these dances. Only one night she was at a wedding supper and hot coffee was spilled on her. She kicked over the table and everyone ran for the outside. In a short while she came to the door and asked if anyone intended to dance as it would soon be daylight.

The first time I saw Belle Starr she was dressed like a man, and could not be told from a man when she and [her] companion rode up close to another [man] and myself where we were tending some cattle for a man between Webber's Falls and Muskogee. She ate dinner with us that day and went on her way.

In about a month she returned, dressed as a lady, and it was then that I knew who she was. Her husband, Sam Starr, was killed at a dance after his horse had been shot from under him a few days before. He, thinking it was done by Frank West, walked up to West at this dance and told him he had heard he was the man that done the shooting. Sam fired one shot at West who fell back, pulled his gun, and shot Starr. Both died and Belle Starr ordered that both bodies be brought into the house and carefully laid out. Then she said in her own peculiar way, as if nothing had happened, that if the people intended to dance it would soon be daylight.

It is impossible to tell from this narrative whether Mr. Cowen saw these events firsthand or is repeating what was already becoming legend. What is possible to tell is that the stories in the Indian-Pioneer Histories became most of the Belle Starr legends we hear today. No one can say for sure whether this happened by people who read the Histories spreading the stories, by people who were interviewed spreading the stories orally as well as in their written interviews, or by the stories spreading naturally in the oral medium and entering the interviews told as if the interviewee experienced them personally when he had not.

Belle's dress was legendary. In the Indian-Pioneer Histories, her neighbors tended to say she never dressed as a man, whereas people who met her when she was far from her home at Younger's Bend claim she was often dressed as a man. Is it familiarity versus unfamiliarity, or did she dress as a woman near her home and as a man when on the scout? Popular legend says she frequently dressed as a man.

Belle's marksmanship was legendary as well. Here is an extract of an interview in the Histories:

Belle's Marksmanship—I

In the summer of 1886 I attended a picnic at Fort Smith, Arkansas. During the entertainment the notorious Belle Starr, who was there from her ranch in the Indian Territory, offered to give an exhibition of her ability to handle a six-shooter and her offer was accepted. For some reason the law was not after her at that time. She shot from her horse, over her shoulder, and in every position used in that time. I never witnessed better marksmanship exhibited by any person in my life and I have seen many.[8]

This is how Sterling Price "Tom" Glass, the bass drummer in the Carthage Light Guard Band, described meeting her, reworded by the interviewer/historian:

The Carthage [Missouri] Light Guard Band...won two...competitions in the fall of 1886—the first at Springfield [Missouri] and the second at Fort Smith, Arkansas. The...band...received the $400 grand prize at the Fort Smith fair.

While in Fort Smith the band saw the noted Belle Starr and S.P. "Tom" Glass, one of the band members, talked to her and solved the mystery of who she was at the time she had lived in Carthage.

Belle was one of the performers at the fair. The talk was that she was under a two-year sentence for outlawry as a result of her recent trial, but, being deemed trustworthy, was permitted to give a riding and shooting exhibition just the same.

W.J. Sewall, a cornetist in the band at that time, remembers her as a dark, leathery-faced woman of remarkable agility and horsemanship.

Riding a horse bareback at a full gallop, she broke clay pigeons or glass balls with rifle fire while in motion, varying this performance by leaping from the animal while it was moving full speed, breaking more glass balls or clay pigeons from the ground with her rifle, then leaping back on the horse as it galloped past her again, still at full speed, and continuing her firing.

The bandsmen were much impressed and Tom Glass, whose parents had lived in Carthage before the Civil War, sent her a note telling her who his parents were adding that he had heard she had lived in Carthage.

Immediately after she received the note she came over and chatted with him, telling that she had been Myra [May]Belle Shirley when a Carthage resident. She remembered his parents well and it was not unlikely that she remembered Tom's birth in

1861. She might even have remembered he was not "Tom" at all, but "Sterling Price."

Mr. Glass had been born in the period when Major General Sterling Price, commander of the Missouri state guard, was the outstanding southern hero to all Carthaginians of non-Union sympathy. It was natural that a newly born Carthage boy should have been given his name. But later in the war when the Glass family had taken refuge at Springfield [Missouri], a Union-held town, Sterling was not at all a popular name. To avoid possible arguments with the neighbors, the boy had been dubbed "Tom" and bore that name to his death, though always officially S.P. Glass.

After the band returned to Carthage the old hometown knew well enough about the gun-woman's Carthage background. During the rest of his life Mr. Glass, "the man who had talked to Belle Starr," was called upon to answer questions of the curious concerning that day's chat.[9]

Another legend is the Belle Starr diary. Most biographers of Belle's life say she did not keep a diary. But Tulsa attorney S.R. Lewis (in his interview for the Indian-Pioneer Histories, Volume 33, pages 217 and 220, done September 24, 1937, at Tulsa by interviewer Effie S. Jackson) claimed that after Belle's death, Oklahoma writer H.F. O'Brien reported that he went to Belle's home seeking a diary Belle was known to possess. "In her last records," according to O'Brien, "she told of robbing a young minister, McKinney..." exonerating him of the suspicion that he had secretly pocketed money belonging to the Choctaw Nation and claimed it to have been stolen by Belle Starr. Did such a diary exist?

*A reporter for the **Dallas Morning News** wrote in the June 7, 1886, edition:*

> Belle related many incidents of her life that would be of interest and says she has been offered big money by publishers for a complete history of it, but she does not desire to have it published just yet. She has a complete manuscript record and when she dies she will give it to the public. She spends most of her time writing when at home.

The first book about Belle Starr was **Bella Starr the Bandit Queen**, published by Richard Fox, publisher of the **Police Gazette**. That pamphlet's author claims to have used Belle's diary in the preparation of his manuscript, but historians discount that because of the many false claims in the pamphlet and because "having the diary" was a standard literary trick of the day to circumvent research and attention to fact.

Is there another possibility? Is it just possible that the manuscript did exist, that Belle did write it, that the **Bella Starr** author did have it and use it, and that all the fantastic legends about Belle, in all their incredible impossible glory were written to enhance her memory...by Belle herself?

It's a thought!

The Indian people, just like their European-American counterparts, were divided on Belle Starr. This remarkable account is taken from an interview with Jake Longtail of Vinita, Oklahoma, who spoke very little English. (Volume 78, pages 325, 335 of the **Indian-Pioneer Histories** of Oklahoma.) WPA writer James Carseloway interviewed his friend Longtail on February 12, 1938. The interviewer said, "I...am giving it to you, as nearly like he gave it to me as it is possible to write it." The well-respected Indian told:

Longtail's Story

Belle Starr tough, just like man. She scout, ride horse all night. One night she come my neighbor's house, way in night, and say want stay all night. My neighbor put-it horse in barn, then go in, and she say 'My name Belle Starr. They are after me, but can't catch me.' Next morning my friend ain't slept much; afraid come them officer, and arrest him too. He get up 'bout 4 o'clock; can't sleep, and pretty soon here come Belle Starr. She say, 'I want pay you for my stay-all-night, your house,' and hand-it ten-dollar bill. My friend say, 'Don't want no money.' But she just walk out [leaving the bill], get horse, and leave, 'fore daylight.

Another incident, this time with a "white" woman telling, is almost identical to the story told about Calamity Jane. Mrs. George Bassler, then of Leavenworth, Kansas, told a WPA writer (in Volume 77, pages 96-97a of the Indian-Pioneer Histories of Oklahoma) about a run-in with Belle:

Belle at the Phoenix Office

...I had had some experience in a printing office [and] I went to the [Muskogee] *Phoenix & Times-Democrat* office...Mr. Frank Hubbard was the editor...I was there five years...One day while working by my window, someone said in a trembling voice, "Here comes Belle Starr."

I looked up to see just outside my open window the most notorious woman of all Indian Territory. She was not bad looking, but most peculiarly dressed. She had on a divided skirt and a man's shirt. Her dark hair hung in braids over her shoulder and on the end of those braids were tied rattles from rattle snakes. She carried a gun in her belt and with her hand on this gun said to me in a very gruff voice, "Where is 'Doc' Bennett?"

I told her in a small voice that he was out of town. As she drove off she muttered that it was a good thing for him he was not there. An article had appeared in the *Phoenix & Times-Democrat* about her which she had resented and she had "come to get him."

Another body of legends that has grown up around the life of Belle Starr is the false notion that she "lived in sin" with various lovers. This is patently false. She may have met Quantrill, but they were never lovers; she did meet Cole Younger, but they were also never lovers, as Cole himself pointed out numerous times. She bore a child by Jim Reed, but married him in a legal ceremony as recorded in Glenn Shirley's biography of Belle, not some outlaw horseback parody of a wedding as legend says. She married Bruce Younger in Kansas after Reed's death, and married Sam Starr in Indian Territory shortly thereafter. Her marriage to Bruce was legal, as recorded in Shirley's book, and her marriage to Sam was legal under

Cherokee law even though she was still married to Bruce under U.S. laws.

After Sam's death, she was most likely married to Bill July, whom Tom Starr renamed Jim July Starr after he adopted the young man. There is no evidence to link Belle with any other "lovers," but there is a photograph of Belle with the outlaw Bluford "Blue" Duck. Glenn Shirley reports that Belle's lawyers were also defending Duck, and asked her to help his cause by being photographed with him and thereby draw public opinion toward him. The photo clearly shows through Belle's body language that there was no relationship between them. (See the cover illustration.)

After the Civil War, Belle was married to Jim Reed and after he was shot resisting arrest for the first stagecoach robbery in history, she supposedly stormed around Dallas as an angry widow.

Morgan Young's Story

Belle used to ride up and down the streets of Dallas like a man, gambling in the saloons and smoking cigars. She had a fine jumping horse and she would ride into the saloons and jump over tables to win bets with other rough characters.[10]

This kind of story is not substantiated by the newspapers of the day, but residents of the community of Scyene, outside Dallas, where the Shirleys lived, wrote a letter to the governor of Texas complaining about Myra Maybelle and her outlaw associates. If none of the rowdy stories are true, why did the people of Scyene write such a letter? Could the rowdy legends be true, but not have been deemed worthy of journalistic comment at the time?

Belle's jumping horse may have been mythical, but her horsemanship and love of horseracing were real.

Walker Powell's Story

Belle Starr was a great lover of horseflesh, and she loved to race, as all the Indian people did. She had one of the fastest horses in the Indian Territory. A man from Siloam Springs, Arkansas, challenged her to a horse race. Belle had a young, slight Indian jockey, and she instructed him to hold the horse back in the race. She bet five hundred dollars on her horse, matched by the race fan from Siloam Springs. Hundreds of people had gathered for the race, and the horse from Siloam won the race handily. Belle smiled and paid the five hundred dollars. She challenged the man to another race for another five hundred dollars, saying her horse hadn't gotten a good start. Again, at a sign from Belle, the Indian boy held her horse back and the horse from Arkansas won. Once again she paid the five hundred.

She said to the man, "I'm so sure that my horse can beat yours, I'm willing to bet five thousand dollars that my horse can beat yours tomorrow."

The next day Belle told the jockey to race like the wind. The race was on and Belle's horse left the horse from Arkansas in the dust. The man had to pay the five thousand dollars as graciously as Belle had paid him the day before. Belle took her horse and went back to the Indian Nation.[11]

From the **Fort Smith Weekly Elevator** *of February 8, 1889, comes this account of Belle's death:*

Belle Starr Murdered
Shot From Ambush By Unknown Parties

On Sunday evening last the notorious Belle Starr was shot and killed near her home by unknown parties. She was riding along the road alone when her assassin fired on her with a shotgun, the wad of the shot striking her in the face.

As she reached for her gun the assassin fired a second time putting a load of buckshot in her back, and she fell from her horse. The frightened animal ran away and the alarm was soon given, but up to this time, so far as we know, there is no clue to the murderers.

Her husband Jim Starr, alias Bill July, was here [in Fort Smith] attending court as a defendant in [illegible] case and received the news by telegraph Monday evening. He at once left for the scene and will likely be heard from in due time...

In the **Fort Smith Elevator** of February 15, 1889, in the second column at "U.S. Court Proceedings," Jim Starr was quoted "almost in his own language" describing the killing as he believed it to have happened, and naming E.A. Watson as the killer.

Who killed Belle Starr? That mystery has haunted researchers and Belle Starr aficionados for a century. Here are some of the theories, both reasonable and far-fetched:

Glenn Shirley in his definitive biography of Belle Starr, **Belle Starr and Her Times** (University of Oklahoma Press, Norman, 1982), offers excellent evidence that E.A. Watson, a neighbor, killed Belle to keep her from revealing that he was wanted for murder in Florida, making him a fugitive after she had sworn that she would not harbor (in this case, lease land to) any more fugitives. Watson was acquitted of the charge at the time but Mr. Shirley shows evidence that he was in fact guilty.

Charles W. Mooney's mother told him that his father told her that Pearl Starr told him that Belle Starr told her Eddie Reed (her son) did it. (Is that complicated enough?) Pearl is supposed to have revealed this to Dr. Mooney, Belle's family physician, at Eddie Reed's funeral. Mrs. Mooney told her son this in 1934 and he wrote a biography of his father containing that theory of Belle's killer. Mr. Shirley discounts this by pointing out that Eddie was never a suspect at the time and had an alibi. The issue is clouded by the fact that Pearl swore at Watson's trial that Belle died without telling her anything (Pearl was at her side on the dirt road as Belle died), but the legend that Belle whispered her killer's name to Pearl stems from the news article in the **Fort Smith Elevator** of February 15, 1889, page 2, column 3, line 26 that reads:

Belle spoke one or two words to her [Pearl] and then expired.

The issue of a dying statement to Pearl is hopelessly clouded by the many versions issued in the press. For example, the Carthage, Missouri, **Carthage Press** of Thursday, February 14, 1889, reported in part:

Watson is a white man, thirty-two years old, who came to the [Cherokee] Nation a year ago from Florida. He had quarreled with Belle Starr and threatened her life, and she accused him of the crime before dying.

The very short article bore the dateline "Fort Smith, Ark., Feb. 9" and may reflect an interview given by Jim July in an attempt to further the case against Watson, who was eventually acquitted.

Deputy U.S. Marshal James Robert "Bob" Hutchins, who shot and arrested Belle Starr's fourth husband, Bill July, also known by his adopted name, Jim July Starr, claimed that before he died of his wounds in Fort Smith Jim July called for Hutchins in order to make a confession. Hutchins maintained throughout his life that the confession would have been that Jim July killed Belle. This is contradicted by the fact that Jim July was in Fort Smith so soon after Belle's murder that the fact alone almost constitutes an alibi and by the fact that Jim July was not considered a suspect at the time although Watson stated at one time that July had borrowed from him the gun that killed Belle. It is also contradicted by the article written by a "writer being well-acquainted with Jim Starr" that appeared in the **Fort Smith Elevator** *January 1, 1890, stating that:*

He [Starr] said he had something to say to Captain J.H. Mershon [one of two men who had posted his bond], and would talk to no one else. We [the reporter and the doctor in attendance] then informed him that Captain Mershon was absent in Texas and he [Starr] would probably have no opportunity to see him (his medical case having been pronounced "hopeless.")

Jim July never asked to see Hutchins and the article gives no hint that what Starr had to say was in any way a confession.

Bill Wade of Muskogee claimed his aunt was married to Will Vann, who told her one of the Crittenden brothers who were "on the scout" saw Eddie Reed kill Belle, which prompted Eddie

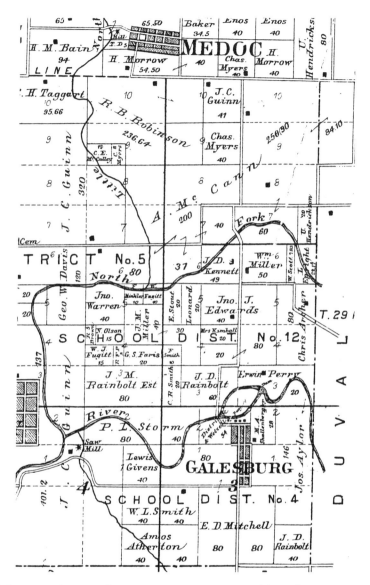

The 1895 plat map for Jasper County, Missouri, Township 29 Range 33, showing the loop island in the Spring River at the town of Galesburg, now largely a ruin, south of Medoc, often given as Belle Starr's home. The house sat at the loop in the river, marked in 1895 as Erwin Perry's tract. The house is represented by a black square.

to kill the Crittenden brothers in Wagoner, Oklahoma, while he was a deputy U.S. marshal there.

A.J. Robinson of Topeka, Kansas, claimed in 1911 his grandmother, Nannie Devena, confessed to him that she had killed Belle Starr by mistake, lying in wait to shoot a neighbor who had beaten her [Nannie Devena] in a labor dispute.

Some authors propose that Jim Middleton killed Belle Starr in revenge for the death of his brother Tom Middleton, whom some suspected of being Belle's secret lover while she was married to Sam Starr, and who was murdered (presumably) by Sam. Oddly enough, when interviewed on May 10, 1937, by the WPA Writers' Project, James Middleton (still living at Briartown) stated:

> I became acquainted with Sam Starr and his wife, Belle Starr, when I first came to the Indian Territory [in 1885] as I rented a place from them the first year I was here, and all our business transactions were always satisfactory, and during my four years acquaintance with them, until she was killed in 1889, I never saw anything in her life that caused me to think she was a bad woman. (*Indian-Pioneer History Collection*, Volume VII, pp. 203-205; Oklahoma Historical Society Archives, Oklahoma City, Oklahoma; interview by James S. Buchanan.)

C.W. West suggests Belle Starr was killed by a deputy U.S. marshal, but offers no evidence or motive, in his book **Persons and Places in the Indian Territory.**

After many years of hearing and collecting Belle Starr stories, many or which we left out of this collection, the editors stood in the reconstructed Belle Starr cabin at Red Oak II outside Carthage, looking at the Hood's Sarsaparilla calendar that hung in the cabin the day Belle died. She had marked out February 1 and 2, but never came home to mark out the 3rd. We had a feeling of incompleteness, of the mystery never solved. Belle Starr will live on; the controversies and investigations will continue; this is the stuff of legends.

Wild Bill: The "Prince of Pistoleers"

"WILD BILL" HICKOK WAS THE CONSUMMATE WESTERN HERO: A GOOD MAN AND A BAD MAN AT THE SAME TIME, A VERY HUMAN CHARACTER WHO SYMBOLIZES THE MYTHIC WEST.

James Butler "Wild Bill" Hickok was a legend in his own lifetime and came to be known as the deadliest gunslinger in the West. He wore buckskins much of the time, and with his long frontier-style hair, elegant moustache, 1851 Colt Navy model pistols with ivory handles often stuffed into a red sash, he was a perfect model for the Easterners' image of the Plainsman. He wore his pistols butts-forward for the older-fashioned twist draw, sometimes called the cavalry draw (not a cross-draw), but he frequently outdrew men with shorter-barrelled pistols in leather scabbards. Many of the stories about him deal with the rare times he didn't outdraw an opponent.

*There are something on the order or two hundred separate Wild Bill legends but only about two dozen are confirmed by the research of modern biographers, including Joseph G. Rosa, author of **They Called Him Wild Bill**. In some cases reporters simply invented stories; other times stories grew naturally out of proportion. Still other times both heroic and cowardly deeds attributed to Hickok were actually done by some of the dozen other people who at one time or another called themselves "Wild Bill."*

*Hickok began his career as a scout and spy for the Union in Southwest Missouri and Northwest Arkansas during the War Between the States. Howard Hickok said that his uncle Jim was given the name "Wild Bill" at Springfield, Missouri, after an incident at nearby Rolla just after the war. Hickok lost an election for city marshal of Springfield but became a living legend the same year as a very inaccurate article in **Harper's Weekly** glorified his exploits as a scout and spy. Wild Bill was appointed deputy U.S. marshal at Fort Hays, Kansas, and served off and on as a cavalry scout, often with William F. "Buffalo Bill" Cody. Henry M. Stanley (of "Dr. Livingston, I presume?" fame) continued the literary legend.*

Hickok was elected sheriff of Ellis County at Hays City but was never certified by the governor. At Hays he "buffaloed" most miscreants instead of firing shots. Abilene, Kansas, made James Butler Hickok its city marshal in 1871 but released him from duty when he had essentially cleaned up the cattle-drover violence on Texas Street and the city council decided to ban the cattle drives and concentrate on local agriculture instead. After a very brief career on stage with Texas Jack and Buffalo Bill (two fellow scouts made famous in the press of the day), Wild Bill went west to Cheyenne, Wyoming, and on to his death at Deadwood, South Dakota.

Many contemporary newspaper writers described James Butler "Wild Bill" Hickok, but this particular description, written many years after the meeting it pertains to, is a good example of the many such descriptions of the great scout:

Alanson Haswell's Description

My great-grandfather was Alanson M. Haswell, a Springfield realtor and newspaper writer who came to be regarded as the town's historian around the turn of the century and afterward. Early on he was hired by the railroad to scout and determine the value of various plots of right-of-way land and to sell off at a commission land not needed by the railroad company. He met James Butler "Wild Bill" Hickok in the winter of 1872 and talked with him more than once into the spring of 1873. He later wrote for the local newspaper and described Bill thus:

> In many ways he was the most remarkable of the old-time plainsmen; he had served in the Springfield [Missouri] region as a Union scout during the Civil War. He must be some thirty-five years of age, a magnificent specimen of physical manhood, tall and straight as an arrow, with his light brown hair hanging down to his shoulders under his broad-brimmed hat. He was a figure to attract attention anywhere. Like others of his profession, he had led a rather dissipated life and was beginning to show the marks thereof. But he was still in the prime of his strength and was one of the most kind-hearted and jovial men I ever met. No one would have imagined to look upon him that this genial man could have killed so long a list of men, but the circumstances of his life were such that time and again nothing saved his life but his marvelously quick use of a revolver. From all I have heard, there was never a case where it was not a justifiable shooting.[12]

The Killing of Dave Tutt

One afternoon three of us young fellows were standing at the southwest corner of South Street on the Square when Wild Bill came along. We all knew him and he stopped to chat with us. We asked him to tell us about some of his war experiences [as a Union scout], and he suddenly straightened up and said:

"It was just after the war was over that I shot a man standing in the very spot we're standing in at this moment."

Of course, we then begged him to tell us about it and he did. These aren't his exact words but the substance of it was as follows: After the close of hostilities, Wild Bill was in Springfield and he met another old scout by the name of Dave [Davis] Tutt [who had scouted for the Confederacy] and the two men had spent much time together. They spent some time playing poker in the back room of a saloon [where Tutt had the gaming concession]. The luck was all against Wild Bill and he lost steadily; both men were somewhat under the influence of liquor and correspondingly reckless. At last, when Bill had no more money, Tutt proposed to play him for his gold watch against one hundred dollars. (The watch had been given to Bill by his mother and was his most cherished possession.) The fire of gambling was in Bill's veins, and stipulating that he would have the right to redeem the watch in case he lost it, the game went on.

In a few minutes Tutt had again won and the watch was his.

Hickok got a loan of a hundred dollars and was trying to redeem the watch but could not find Tutt. About noon the following day he was terribly surprised to receive word from Tutt that not only would he keep the watch but at three o'clock he would wear it and walk across the public square so everyone could see how little he feared Wild Bill. At first Hickok thought the message to be a joke and said as much, but at the appointed hour Wild Bill was on the square on the corner of South Street. Tutt appeared in front of the old courthouse. Tutt carried his pistol and the watch in plain view and just as he reached the center of the square he whirled around and fired at Wild Bill, who up 'til then he had not seemed to notice.

Hickok had stood as still as a statue with his hands on his vest pockets; now he let go his pockets, drew his pistol, cocked it and fired in less time than Tutt took to turn and fire an unscabbarded gun. Tutt's shot went wild but Bill's struck Tutt in the chest and he went down with a bullet through his heart. Wild Bill walked over, bent down, and "redeemed" the watch, thus settling the controversy as to which was the better shot.

Bill was arrested but the coroner's jury found that it had been justifiable homicide.

Wild Bill told us boys that day that after the deed was done, of all the men he'd shot, he regretted killing Tutt most of all. But, he added, "It was him or me and he was pretty damned quick."[13]

Getting the Drop on "Wild Bill"—I

Alanson M. Haswell met Wild Bill in the winter of 1872 on Bill's last visit to Springfield. He apparently did not witness this event but heard of it from eyewitnesses and wrote of it in the Springfield newspaper in 1915:

In the winter of 1872, Wild Bill proved he had lost none of his old-time cunning. One of the "gilded youth" of our city became angry at Hickok for some wrong, real or imagined, and had repeatedly said that he would shoot Wild Bill on sight. On the day in question Bill was standing at the bar of a College Street saloon talking with the bartender. The young man who had made the threats was sitting at a table to the scout's back.

Quietly rising to his feet the reckless youth drew his revolver and holding it within an inch of the victim's head, pulled the trigger! The pistol went off, but in that infinitesimal fraction of a second between the act of raising the weapon and the explosion of powder Bill's hand had swept around, taken the gun by the barrel, and twisted it toward the ceiling and out of the young man's hand. The bullet struck the ceiling.

Bill smiled quietly, handed the pistol back to its astonished owner, and said, "Next time don't cock your gun so close to a man's ear."

He then turned his back and resumed his conversation with the bartender.[14]

Getting the Drop on "Wild Bill"—II

While there is no corroborating evidence, an event in Springfield, Missouri, was apparently actually witnessed by Alanson Haswell and has never been mentioned in any of Wild Bill's biographies. The period of 1872-1873 in Springfield is regarded by Hickok biographers as a "gap" in his known life.

When "Wild Bill" Hickok came back to Springfield in 1872 and 1873 he spent a lot of time in the saloons on Commercial Street. One day he had had a little too much to drink and came out onto the street and began shooting out the new kerosene street lanterns one by one. Down the street came John B. Stokes, a quiet little man and the city marshal of North Springfield.

Stokes was to all appearances one of the last men you would pick out as being fearless; his appointment as city marshal had been considered something of a joke. But now he stepped up to the exalted but half-drunken man known all over the West as the fastest draw and surest shot.

Laying a detaining hand on Wild Bill's shoulder he said, "Here, Bill, give me that gun."

The request struck the scout dumb with amazement and Bill's long trail of half-drunken companions scattered in all directions. The fun was over and now no one doubted that Stokes would be shot dead instantly, or at the very least, a gunfight would start at once.

"Say, old man," said Hickok. "Who the devil are you?"

"I'm the city marshal," came the reply. "Now give me that gun and do it quickly!" The officer's old pistol was suddenly poked into Wild Bill's ribs. The scout did not shoot.

"Well, I'll be damned," said Bill, and he gave Stokes his gun.

At that time the jail for North Springfield was six-foot-by-eight-foot inside dimensions, built of solid oak joists, 2-by-8s laid flat on each other, locked at the corners and well-spiked together with iron spikes. Marshal Stokes escorted Wild Bill to this tiny "log" structure. On seeing the jail Bill again thrust his hand into a vest pocket. The crowd that had followed him scattered again, expecting him to draw a derringer. Marshal Stokes seemed to be of the same opinion for he thrust his rusty old pistol into Bill's ribs again.

Instead of a pistol it was a fat wallet that Bill drew from his breast pocket. He handed the wallet to Stokes and said, "Here, Uncle, there's two hundred dollars in that wallet. Just hold it until morning, and I'll come up and pay my fine." Stokes let Bill go on his own recognizance and the next morning the new town justice of the peace, J.J. Barnard, fined Bill Hickok ten dollars for each of the five street lights he had spoiled, and a twenty dollar fine for disturbing the peace.

Hickok laughed, "Well, Judge, you sure set your fine by the size of my 'pile.' You can bet I'll stay in [Springfield's] Old Town the next time I get on a tear!"[15]

A Ride Home

My grandmother, Edith May Thomas, was the daughter of Wylie Shellers Thomas, a federal marshal out of Springfield, Missouri, just not long after the War Between the States. They lived in [the village of] Arcola [Missouri] at the time. One day grandmother, as a young girl, was walking home from school when a tall, finely dressed man on a fine horse rode up alongside her. The gentleman stopped and asked if she wasn't the daughter of Marshal Thomas. She replied that she was and he said, "Little Lady, I know your father well. May I offer you a ride to your house?"

She accepted and he lifted her onto the horse and they rode to her house. After she had thanked the man and he had departed, she described him to her father.

He said he did indeed know the gentleman well. It was the man they called "Wild Bill" Hickok.[16]

Wild Bill's Coroner's Jury

Charles S. Hunt, Casper, Wyoming, storyteller and folk-historian, and owner of The Powder Horn, said this about "Wild Bill's" coroner's jury:

C.M. Sheldon was my uncle, and that was the oldest of the Sheldon family, which was my mother's maiden name. C.M. Sheldon was the foreman of the coroner's jury that investigated the death of Wild Bill Hickok in 1876. The coroner's jury were just citizens, appointed by the coroner, and then they elected C.M. as their foreman.

Wild Bill had been playing cards and didn't have his back to the wall they way he usually did. He even asked twice for one of his friends to change places with him, but they hadn't finished the hand and gotten around to changing seats yet when he was shot from behind by Jack McCall.[17]

The interior of the most famous saloon in the West, the Long Branch, named for an amusement area at Atlantic City. The Long Branch was the top attraction on Front Street in Dodge City, Kansas. It was narrow with a high storefront like all the saloons—and there were several—on Front Street. (Courtesy of the Boot Hill Museum and Library, Dodge City, Kansas)

Saloons and Spittoons

"THE PLACE AND THE TIME AND THE SPIRIT
THAT NEVER WERE ANYWHERE ELSE BEFORE
NOR SINCE NOR EVER WILL BE AGAIN."
(from page v of the 1942 edition, *The Bad Man of the West*)

Seneca, Missouri

One of the things misunderstood today about the American frontier is the way the frontier moved slowly westward. We think of Arizona or New Mexico as being the "frontier," but the actual frontier was wherever civilization stopped and lawlessness and unorganized territory began. For a while that dividing line was the little town of Seneca, Missouri.

Southern and southeastern Kansas was largely open country and the northeast corner of what is now Oklahoma was Indian Territory. Seneca was the home of one of the Indian Agencies and the last stopping-off point before travelers left society as they knew it. Seneca was a larger town than Tulsa; in fact, people used to come from Tulsa by wagon to load up with supplies because Seneca was the end of the railroad line at that time. The railroads had not yet negotiated permission to push across the Indian nations.

Wanted men from the East would ride the rails to Seneca and from there enter the sparsely populated areas of Kansas and the Indian nations. The main street was wide-open as Dodge City, only on a smaller scale, with saloons and bawdy houses and outlaws.

As soon as the railroads went into Indian Territory, the "frontier" moved west and Seneca settled down and forgot its past.[18]

Ice in Their Drinks

Crime in America, especially in the Eastern states, is very much the same as it is in other countries. But in the Far West there is more recklessness in dealing with human life...

"Property" is safe, for the citizens hunt down with extraordinary energy marauders whose object is simply plunder. Ordinary robbers and gangs of burglars are speedily and summarily suppressed. It is otherwise with those who assail life and limb. Desperadoes who infest the "Saloons," as they are called, with which every Western settlement is sure to be provided as soon as the shingled roofs are placed on the earliest upheaval of planks which can be called a dwelling, have far greater immunity and freedom than burglars or robbers.

Wherever the train stopped for water on our journey in New Mexico, western Colorado, or eastern California, the rectangular wooden box, with a veranda, open doors, windows screened by muslin curtain, perhaps a flagstaff with the Stars and Stripes flying, a large signboard, and some high-sounding name—the "Grand Alliance," "Union League," "El Dorado," "Harmonium," "Arcadia" or the like—was visible, with the usual group of booted and bearded miners and their horses hitched at the doorposts in front. Inside you would be certain to find men of the same class at a bar, behind which, known for miles around, the affable Charlie, Bill, or Bob was dispensing drinks and mixing cocktails, "slings," and other drinks in which the badness of the spirit is artfully disguised by a stimulant of a more active character and more pronounced flavor known as "bitters," and kept in subjugation by the liberal use of ice. For even in these burning regions ice is stored as the one thing needful. The rudest miner is accustomed to it; iced drinks are consumed by classes in America far below the social level of those who never taste them in [England].[19]

The American Custom of Spitting

I am bound to say I think the habit of spitting has very much diminished, but from numerous evidences, from the presence of spittoons in every room and in the passages of the hotels, and from public admonitions, such as one we saw at some of the theaters, that the audience would not spit upon the stage, I believe that it still exists. What the cause of this habit may be it is not easy to determine … I would be inclined to attribute it to the drinking of iced water, but ladies in America use the national beverage quite as freely as the men, and spitting is a masculine failing. Can it be a result of the climate? Smokers and non-smokers alike indulge in the practice so that tobacco cannot be charged with the disagreeable custom.[20]

The Naming of Saloons

A lot can be told about the feelings and mood of the outlaws of the 1880s by the names of the saloons they frequented. In old Fort Worth there were the Alamo Whisky Sample Room, the Beer Garden, the Bon Ton, the Cattle Exchange, Farmer's Saloon, the Headlight Bar, the Horse Head Saloon, the Occidental House, Our Comrades, Our Friends, the Red Light, the Stag Saloon, the Tivoli Saloon, the Trinity, the Waco Tap, and, of course, the White Elephant.

Up the trails from Texas were Dodge City Saloons: the Alamo (on Front Street, beside the Long Branch), the Alhambra (which belonged to "Dog" Kelley, the mayor), Bond and Nixon's Dance Hall, the Comique Theater, the Green Front Saloon, George M. Hoover's Saloon and liquor store, the Junction Saloon, the Lone Star Saloon, the Long Branch (which was partly operated by Luke Short before going to Fort Worth), the Occident, the Old House, the Opera House Saloon, the Parlour, the Saratoga, and many other saloons, establishments with bars, bawdy houses, and other theaters like the Varieties.

In Hays, Kansas, was the saloon with the most colorful name in the West: John Bitter and Company's Leavenworth Beer Saloon. Also in Hays were Kate Coffee's Saloon, Tommy Drum's Saloon, Cy Godard's Saloon and Dance Hall, Ed Godard's Saloon and Dance Hall, Hound Kelley's Saloon, Mose[s] Water's Saloon, Odenfeld's Saloon, Paddy Welche's Saloon and Gambling House, Pat Murphy's Saloon, and across the street from it, the Prairie Flower Dance Hall.

Up the railroad to the east in Abilene, Kansas, drovers had seen their favorite houses of amusement on Texas Street at the east-west railroad tracks that divided the town into the local residents to the north and the wild cattle-drivers' side of town to the south (a similar arrangement as in Dodge City later). The most popular saloon was the Alamo. The Bull's Head Tavern was another popular spot, and places like the Novelty Theater had a bar. The Beer Garden was a house of ill repute in the area about half a mile south of the tracks where the city fathers tried to move and isolate such establishments. Interestingly enough, this area is the same that is now being used as a reconstruction of Old Abilene for tourists.[21]

Give the Cheese a Chance!

One of Dodge City's cattle barons came into his favorite saloon and restaurant and ordered a beer with ice, a sandwich, and some fine Limburger cheese. The gentleman put his feet up on the table and leaned back for his cigar. The proprietor brought the beer and cheese first. The cowman pushed up in his chair to smell the cheese and called out, "Bring me another cheese. This one's no good. I can't smell it at all!"

The barkeep replied, "Well, take your damn feet off the table and give the cheese a chance!"[22]

Thieves, Thugs, Fakirs, and Bunko-Steerers

THOSE WHO ROBBED, BULLIED AND MURDERED, GYPPED AND SWINDLED, AND GAMBLED AND CHEATED THEIR WAY ACROSS THE WEST.

NOTICE!
To Thieves, Thugs, Fakirs and Bunko-Steerers,
Among Whom Are
J.J. Harlin, alias "Off Wheelers;" Saw Dust Charlie, Wm. Hedges,
Billy the Kid, Billy Mullin, Little Jack, The Cuter, Pock-Marked
Kid, and about Twenty Others:
If found within the Limits of this City after TEN O'CLOCK P.M., this
Night, you will be Invited to attend a GRAND NECK-TIE PARTY, The
Expense of which will be borne by
100 Substantial Citizens
Las Vegas [New Mexico], March 24th, 1882[23]

Actually, the Old West WANTED *posters were nothing like what we have seen in movies and collected in the 1950s out of cereal boxes. Very few posters bore illustrations, almost none had photographs. No wanted posters ever existed for Belle Starr, no posters for Jesse and Frank James ever bore illustrations (the James family guarded the photos of their family well), and no photos are even known to exist of Sam Bass (although some have been put forward as Bass photos, family members who saw them in the 1930s discounted them as not looking like Sam or the rest of the family).*

By the same token, the robberies often weren't quite what we have come to believe in the twentieth century. The following accounts and clippings give a good cross-section.

The Fox Guarding the Henhouse

The country I grew up in is fairly flat, but broken by deep ravines with streams and trees. The flatter land was usually kept clear for grass and cattle grazing. The gullies and groves of trees were a good place for boys to play and fish and swim in the streams or puddles. Roads crossed the flat prairies, but sooner or later had to wind down into a ravine and cross the streams, since bridges were expensive and considered unnecessary. In a ravine, shaded by trees, was a perfect place for an ambush.

There were several wagon and stagecoach robberies in the late 1870s over in the next county, in one of those hollows. The stage line ran through the southeast corner of Cooke County, and the coach was held up by a masked man in a heavy greatcoat and leather gloves. He stole passengers' watches and wallets, the mail bags, and the strongbox, on the rare occasions that the coach carried one.

Every time the stage was robbed, the sheriff would file various reports with the county, and the county clerk would process them into the county records. The sheriff never seemed to be able to catch the robber; he always seemed to know when the sheriff was on the trail. The local people laid the crimes to ex-guerrillas from Quantrill's band, who knew no other way of

$20,000 REWARD!

Office of the Clerk of Carbon County,
Rawlins, Wyoming, August 29th, 1878.

A Reward of $2,000 each will be paid by the Commissioners of Carbon county, for the arrest and conviction of the parties who murdered Deputy Sheriff Robert Widdowfield and H. H. Vinson, in Big Canyon, on Rattle Snake Creek, near Elk Mountain, in Carbon county, Wyoming, on Monday, August 19th, 1878. The party that committed the murder is supposed to consist of from eight to fifteen persons. All information in the possession of the Commissioners will be furnished on application. The following is a description of the property taken murdered men :

One dark gray mare, branded H. L. on right shoulder, and A on left hip; heavy California saddle, light gray blanket, and new bridle. One light gray mare, eight years old, branded O C on left hip, and anchor with cross on left shoulder; had California Saddle newly leathered, with hand holds on hind tree. One bay mare, branded C B on left shoulder, white spot in forehead, very heavy build, and with a great many saddle marks.

By order of the Board of County Commissioners of Carbon county, Wyoming Territory.

JAMES FRANCE, Chairman.

Attest : **J. B. ADAMS,**
County Clerk.

The $20,000 reward for killers—who later proved to be "Big-Nose" George Parrott and a man named Dutch—proved to be unnecessary. When the killers were caught, both were lynched (see pp. 127–129). Very few WANTED posters in the "outlaw period" of 1860–1890 bore drawings, and almost none bore photographs. Note the description of the stolen horses: it proved more useful than descriptions of the killers would have been. (Reprinted courtesy of the Wyoming State Museum, Cheyenne) life. Finally, two things happened on the same day that solved the mystery.

The stage came in late saying it had been robbed...and the county clerk didn't show up for work.

The clerk's office was soon searched, and many records were found missing. The trash barrel outside the window contained the empty mailbag and strongbox from the robbery the night before. The clerk's house was empty. The fox had been guarding the henhouse! No wonder the robber always knew what the sheriff was up to.[24]

Joseph Cruze's Bugle

When the War Between the States began, Joseph S. Cruze enlisted as a private in Company C of the 33rd Texas [Confederate] Cavalry, in October of 1862 at San Antonio. The army at that time, in that part of the state, fought Mexican outlaws near Eagle Pass more than Yankees. Soon after joining up, he tried out for company bugler; his only qualifications were that he called his dogs by blowing on a cow horn.

Also in the cavalry was a French Immigrant named Paganel, who as a soldier of fortune had joined the Confederacy. He taught Cruze to call on the bugle, practicing on the bugle Paganel's father had carried through the Napoleonic Wars. The bugle gave many a call to arms against the bandits who, like the frontier Indians, chose the war as a good time to attack the borders of Texas. However, the two buglers were together at the last land battle of the war, a Confederate victory, at Palmitos Ranch, May 13, 1865. Most of their service had been against outlaws: ten banditos killed near Carrizo, others tracked down from Brownsville to Laredo.

After the war, Paganel went off to fight with Maximillian in Mexico, and Cruze thought he would never again see the old man of the war-worn bugle he had learned on. Almost five years later, a Mexican man came to Cruze's ranch, and presented him with the Paganel family bugle. Troops of Benito Juarez had captured the regiment in which Paganel served, and like Maximillian and hundreds of others, Paganel had been executed by a firing squad; before he died, he had entrusted the bugle to a fellow prisoner not under sentence of death, with instructions to find Cruze in Texas and give it to him. After Joseph's death in 1923, Joe Cruze donated the bugle, that had blown charge against the Mexican banditos so many times, to the Trail Driver's Museum in San Antonio, where it rests today.[25]

Seth Bullock and the Miners

There is an amusing story about Seth Bullock and some angry miners: in the fall of 1877 some disputes about wages came up between a group of miners and the owners of the mine. The miners took up fortified residence in the mine shaft in question and refused to come out with their ore until the dispute was settled in their favor. They had taken into the mine all the food and supplies they would need, right down to firewood and a small cookstove, which they placed under the air shaft to use it as a flue.

The owners got an injunction and Sheriff Seth Bullock set out to the mine to remove the "squatters." They refused to listen to the sheriff. After several days, the county judge told Bullock to do whatever he had to, short of killing anybody, to get the miners out of the tunnel.

The sheriff took his deputies up to Hidden Treasure Gulch, posted his officers at the entrance to the mine shaft, then climbed up the hill behind the entrance, up to the air shaft opening, where smoke was pouring out. Bullock opened a large bag of assafoetida and emptied it down the air shaft. When the medicinal resins hit the top of the hot stove, the stench was too much for the miners. With tears in their eyes, they came out with their hands up and surrendered to the deputies![26]

Oklahoma legendary lawman William Matthews "Bill" Tilghman was once arrested for horse-stealing in Dodge City, Kansas, but charges were dropped:

More Horse Stealing
The Thief Captured and Committed to Jail

Last Wednesday Mr. M.A. Couch and three other gentlemen arrived in this city from Walnut Creek, forty miles north of here, in search of four horses that had been stolen from them on the day previous. They immediately applied to the County Attorney for information and assistance, stating that they had tracked the horses to this city. [County] Sheriff ["Bat"] Masterson was sent for and in company with Couch and party instituted a search for the stock, which, luckily, they succeeded in recovering. Two of the horses were found in the riverbottom southwest of the city, and the other two were found in Mr. ["Ham"] Bell's livery stable, where they had been placed the night before.

The owners of the horses were very much pleased at recovering their stock, and proposed starting immediately for home without making any search for the thief; but the Sheriff, with an eye to giving His Thiefship punishment for his wrongs, made search and discovered men whom he supposed to be guilty. Swearing out a complaint himself, he arrested Henry Martin and William Tilghman.

Henry Martin was brought before Justice Cook Wednesday and examined. There being strong evidence against him, he was bound over in the sum of $2,000, in default of which he was sent to jail. Mr. Tilghman's examination took place on Thursday before Justice Cook. It was generally supposed that he would be bound over also, but he was released by the court...[27]

The Dalton Robbery

My grandma lived just down the road from the banks in Coffeyville, Kansas, that the Daltons tried to rob two banks at once, in the daylight, the only time it had ever been tried. Most of the Daltons ended up dead because they were recognized and the word got spread that they were in the bank and [the townspeople] were handing guns out of the general store to stop them.

Grandma lived about a hundred and fifty yards down the road there in Coffeyville, and was sitting on her porch when she heard the guns go to popping down there while they were robbing the bank. Then she heard the rifles [of the townspeople] going off. This big tall, skinny, young man came running away from the banks at top speed as hard as he could run down the street, yelling, "The Daltons are robbin' all the banks and killin' all the people! The Daltons are robbin' all the banks and killin' all the people!"

As he went flying by the house Grandma called out to him, "Don't worry, honey, they'd have to run awful fast to catch up with you!"

Grandma told that over and over again and just laughed![28]

A Robbery Gone Wrong

The Daltons chose Coffeyville, Kansas, for their daring double bank robbery because it was so near the Indian nation boundary that a quick getaway could be effected. But the Daltons were raised near here, and they were immediately recognized even though they were wearing fake beards. Street construction forced them to tie up their horses behind the bank in an alley instead of out in the street.

Black-Face Charlie Bryant, named for powder burns from a misfire, had been taken prisoner and was being transported to Wichita in a baggage car with a deputy. He went for the deputy's gun and the two killed each other. Without this gang member, perhaps the best shot among the Daltons, the robbery might have gone differently.[29]

Bob Dalton's Last Words

During the Coffeyville robbery, only about fifteen guns were in use, but the percentage of lives lost was greater than the toll in any Civil War battle: eight were killed and four were wounded. Bob Dalton was shot and lay mortally wounded. Emmett was almost out of the alley as the gunfight raged, when he remembered his brother Bob at the other end of the alley.

He rode back, and reached down to help Bob up onto his saddleback.

Bob said, "Don't mind me, Emmett, I'm done for. Don't surrender, Boy! Die game!"

Emmett was hit with a double load of buckshot and went down at that moment. He survived only because everyone thought he was dead until the fighting had ended. He was not lynched, although some folks suggested it, and lived to stand trial as the only survivor of the Dalton Gang's greatest and last robbery.[30]

The Robbery of the Denver & Rio Grande

We pulled out of Salida...November 2, 1882, on old No. 7 out of Denver to Grand Junction...We old travelers that were on to the ropes always took the forward seats until we reached the top of the Divide and changed to the rear seats going down the western slope, for the [tobacco] juice [on the floor of the car] was plenty deep by that time and following gravity backed up at the lower end of the car three inches or more in depth...Leaving Grand Junction at about 3:00 A.M. on November 4...we were somewhat startled at the whistle for brakes and the sudden stopping of the train...about five miles east of Grand Junction...for an obstruction on the track.

...Two men climbed aboard the tender and ordered the engineer and fireman down from the engine, and with a few shots and many threats, compelled the express messenger and mail clerk to open the doors [of the express car]. The safe in the express car baffled them. It was firmly fastened to the floor and nothing short of dynamite would open it...the combination itself was known only to the station agents along the way so the threat of death to the messenger...availed them nothing.

After removing about twenty registered letters [which often contained cash], the robbers themselves removed the obstruction from the track and after [what had been] an hour's delay, allowed the train to proceed on its way...and that's the story of the robbery of the Denver and Rio Grande.[31]

Cherokee Bill Trading Saddles

In 1920 and 1921, and again in 1936 and 1937, I taught school at Ray, Oklahoma, on the Grand River. I boarded at the home of Tom Hathcock, an oldtimer in that community, who had moved there from Missouri in 1880 as a boy. He married a Cherokee girl, a distant relative of my own wife, and they lived on the Grand all the rest of their lives.

During the long winter evenings, we sat before the fire and just talked. He often told me experiences he had had, and narrated long stories out of the past. Uncle Tom was well-known for his truthfulness, and was very serious about everything he told

He had known Crawford Goldsby, alias Cherokee Bill, personally and told me several interesting stories about the famous outlaw.

Tom said he once had a very fine horse and a good saddle of which he was very proud. One morning he saddled his horse and started up the Grand River bottom. He had not gone far when he met up with Cherokee Bill, riding a worthless old broomtail nag on a hull of a saddle. They stopped to chat, as they knew each other well. Tom said he knew Bill was on the owl hoot [trail—hiding out and traveling by night], and knew that he was desperate, but that he did not fear Bill at first, as they were friends.

At the time, Tom thought his horse and saddle were worth about two hundred dollars together, while Bill's rig and nag weren't worth but about fifty dollars on a good day. They had not been talking long when Bill said,

"Tom, how about you trading horses and rigs with me?"

Tom instantly became alert; he knew Cherokee Bill had already decided to have his horse, and that if he didn't agree to trade, Bill would probably just kill him and take the horse anyway. So, he said:

"Oh, Bill, I don't know; what do you think?"

Bill got down and looked at Tom's horse and said, "Your rig is a little the better of mine. I only have forty dollars, but I'll give you that to even up the trade."

Tom agreed and told him "it was a trade." He said he actually nearly shed tears as he saw that dirty scalawag ride away on his fine horse and new saddle.

Tom also said that he was at Fort Gibson when the United States marshals, one of whom was Ike Rogers, passed through on the train, carrying Cherokee Bill to Fort Smith for trials. The train stopped and Cherokee Bill's younger brother got on to talk to the outlaw. When the youngster was ready to leave the train, he told Ike Rogers that he would kill him. Two or three days later, Ike came back through on the train, going home. The train stopped at Fort Gibson and Ike, for some reason, was stepping off. As he stepped to the platform of the depot, Cherokee Bill's brother shot him dead, making good his promise.[32]

The Bloody Benders as Urban Legend

When I was a boy my friends used to tell a scary story about an evil family of murderers in Kansas. People out on a lonely prairie road would hear the sound of wood being chopped and would follow that sound until they came to a house. They would ask for food and lodging for the night and the family would seat them at the head of the table, calling that the "place of honor." Behind the place of honor was a curtain that closed off the kitchen. While supper was being served, and the traveler was not suspicious, one of the family would come out from behind the curtain and kill the visitor.

The visitor would be robbed and his body thrown in the river.

The family was named the Benders.

I always thought it was just a scary story, until in the 1950s I read an article in a western magazine that said basically that the story was true.[33]

The Bloody Benders

The Benders were a family of four living just off the Osage Mission Trail. Katie, the daughter, was a member of the spiritualist movement, and nailed up posters on fence posts that read:

PROF. MISS KATIE BENDER
Can heal all sort of Diseases; can cure Blindness, Fits,
Deafness and all such diseases, also Deaf-and-Dumbness.
Residence, 14 miles East of Independence, on the road
from Independence to Osage Mission one and one-half
miles South East of Norahead Station.
Katie Bender
JUNE 18, 1872

In the following twelve months, a dozen travelers disappeared off the Osage Mission Trail, but it was the disappearance of the brother of a Kansas legislator that prompted investigation, not the missing immigrants. Colonel York traced his missing brother to the Bender's place, where he had bought supper. When the Colonel began to suspect that his brother had never left the Benders', the authorities returned to find the place deserted.

Digging in the orchard and garden, deputies found the shallow graves of the missing travelers, including Colonel York's brother. In the following weeks, hundreds of sightseers came to the Benders' ranch and store, and in the century since many fantastic stories have grown up around the Bloody Benders. Some persons even came forward years later and claimed to be the Benders, but their claims were disproven, and the Bloody Benders were never apprehended, in spite of a large reward offered. A desire for notoriety is the only explanation that can be offered for the people who came forward pretending to be the first mass murderers in Kansas, and the fate of the Bloody Benders is summed up in the Kansas State Historical Society marker that stands beside the highway near the site of the crimes: "The end of the Benders is not known. The earth seemed to swallow them, as it had their victims."[34]

Captain Pieppo's Story

Kansas folklorists and historians have commented that the story of the Bloody Benders gave rise to some of the most incredible legends and post hoc explanations ever. This is the most fantastic of the Bender legends.

In late July, 1877, a mysterious Captain Don Pieppo arrived in Topeka, claiming to have been the master of the Mexican sailing ship Annita [Anita], and bearing from Galveston, Texas, letters of introduction. He claimed that in April of 1873, on the second day out of Brazos de Santiago, Mexico, bound for Galveston, a storm struck at sunset and the crew was furiously bailing at the pumps when, about ten o'clock, they heard voices in the dark sky above the ship. A huge balloon tangled in the rigging and collapsed one of the masts, bringing onto the deck a boat-like gondola with four passengers.

An old man, an old woman, and a young woman were all killed in the collision with the mast and subsequent collapse of the mast, the rigging, and the balloon. The fourth passenger, a young man, was dying, and below decks, having been told he would not survive the night, he confessed the following tale:

His father had been a ship's carpenter and balloon-seamster in Germany, and had flown across Germany on one occasion. Moving to America, and settling near Cherryville, Kansas, the family had fallen under suspicion, he said, of harboring horse thieves and murdering passersby for their money. The sister, Katie, had found a wellspring of coal gas on their property, and the family obtained a well auger and bored an escape vent, which they capped and concealed. Their father went to Kansas City and purchased material from which to construct a balloon, and they dug out a cave in a nearby hillside in which the balloon was sewn in secret.

"Yesterday evening [!]," the boy is claimed to have said, "one of our spies came to our house from Independence, and told us that the vigilantes had held a meeting and determined to come the next evening and hang every one of us."

At two o'clock that same morning, the balloon had lifted off and drifted over the Indian Territory and Texas, on the way to Old Mexico. When they tried to lower the balloon, they learned that the valve was stuck. Puncturing the balloon to let the gas leak out a little at a time, the "Benders" began their descent. Night fell, the storm struck, and the balloon crashed into the Anita.

According to the captain, the youth died, and the bodies of the four went down with the ship when the Anita sank the following day and the crew took to its lifeboats. Being rescued, and coming ashore at Sabinto, Mexico, the captain told his story, which he claimed was published several times in Spanish in Mexican newspapers at the time. Captain Don Pieppo did not know of the Benders' legend in Kansas until he arrived in 1877.[35]

The Cold Springs Stage Robbery

Scott Davis was a messenger on the Deadwood Stage in the 1870s. He told the following story to Russell Thorp, secretary of the Wyoming Stock Growers' Association, who subsequently wrote it up for the local newspapers. WPA writer Olaf B. Kongslie, of Newcastle, Weston County, Wyoming, paraphrased it for ultimate inclusion into Subject 1355 of the Writers' Project of the Works Progress Administration:

This robbery took place on the 29th day of September, 1878, at Cold Springs. This [stage] station…was located forty miles from Deadwood and twenty miles from Jenny's Stockade at a lonely spot in the mountains, surrounded by pine trees and other timber.

The stageline from Cheyenne [Wyoming] to Deadwood [Dakota Territory] was three hundred miles. It was handled and operated by Gilmer and Salisbury and Luke Vorhees, afterwards purchased by Russell Thorp, Sr. Mr. Vorhees was general manager of this stageline, making frequent trips across the rough and rugged country in his buggy, looking after the interests of the stage company and seeing that everything was carried out in proper shape.

A treasure coach was put on the stageline in 1877 for the purpose of carrying gold and other treasures from Deadwood to Cheyenne. We frequently carried as much as three hundred thousand dollars at one time in this treasure coach across the rough and rugged mountainous country from Deadwood to

Cheyenne. At the time this treasure coach was put on the road Mr. Luke Vorhees was induced by a safe company in the East to put a burglarproof safe in his coach, guaranteed to be burglarproof for twenty-four hours. It was not supposed that a gang of robbers, running around through the mountains, could get into the safe within this guaranteed time.

The original messenger guards, who were used for guarding this treasure coach, consisted of myself [Scott Davis], Jessie Brown, Gale Hill, Boone May, Billy Sample, and Captain Smith.

On the way into Deadwood, going after the treasure, Jessie Brown, Boone May, and Billy Sample were left at Beaver Station to be in readiness to pick up the coach on its return and guard it on horseback from Jenny's Stockade to Hat Creek—Gale Hill, Captain Smith, and I were going into Deadwood to bring the treasure. As it was a daylight run and having this guaranteed safe, we thought we were safe in handling it that way. Gale Hill, Captain Smith, a man by the name of Campbell on board the coach, and I left Deadwood at the usual time in the morning. This man, Campbell…was a telegraph operator going down the line to take care of the telegraph office at Jenny's Stockade.

As we drove up to the Cold Springs Stage Station to change horses everything about the place looked alright. There was nothing to indicate there were any robbers there. As we drove up in front of the barn, Gale Hill, who was riding on the outside of the coach, got down and picked up a block of wood to block the hind wheels of the coach, as the road was on the down grade. As Hill raised up after blocking the wheels and started around to the rear of the coach to get in the barn door these robbers opened fire, without calling to anyone 'hold-up' or saying a word. They had removed the chinking from between the logs of the barn to make loopholes to shoot out. They commenced shooting down through the coach, volley after volley. One of these shots struck messenger Smith on the side of the head, rendering him unconscious. Smith fell over in the coach and we supposed he was dead. I fired a good many shots out of the coach into the barn door and into the portholes these robbers had arranged but was unsuccessful in doing any good in that position.

I told Campbell I was going to get out and get across the road where there was a large pine tree so I could get better action on these robbers. Campbell remarked that if I was going to the tree he was going with me. We both got out of the coach, but Campbell had no gun to defend himself with. I turned and backed my way across the road to the tree, shooting at anything and everything that looked like a robber. When we got halfway across the road Campbell had swerved off to the left so that he was exposed, as the coach was not between him and the tree. I called to him to get in line of the coach while I kept shooting at those portholes, thinking that perhaps I could accomplish something. Campbell went down on his knees in the middle of the road. Those robbers fired another volley, striking him and killing him instantly.

Just before I reached the tree one of the robbers showed up and exposed himself at the head of the team as I was urging the stage driver to get out of there and make a run for it. As the robber exposed himself I turned quickly and fired, wounding him badly. He threw up his hands, fell over backwards, crawled around the horses, and made his getaway back of the barn. Then the robbers who were left made up their minds that the only way they could capture me was by taking the driver down off the coach, bringing him around to the rear of the coach, and there one of the robbers placed the driver directly in front of him, crowding him towards me, knowing that in order to kill him I would have to shoot through the driver. I took in the situation at once and remembered that Mr. Vorhees told me that any time that robbers held up the coach we could rely on this guaranteed safe holding the money for twenty-four hours. I made up my mind to back myself through the pine trees, make my escape, and after getting a saddle horse down at a ranch a short way off, go down the stage road and meet Boone May, Jesse Brown, and Billy Sample, and return as quickly as possible and capture these robbers while they were in the act of blowing up the safe or trying to open it some other way.

I succeeded in getting a saddle horse, making a ride of eight miles, meeting May, Brown, and Sample on the road coming towards Cold Springs expecting to meet the coach every minute. We came back, making the ride as fast as possible and were successful in reaching Cold Springs just at the time the robbers succeeded in opening the safe. They consumed about three or four hours in getting into the safe, which was guaranteed burglarproof for twenty-four hours. We made a run on the robbers through the pine timber, wounding one of them.

Later on, the rest of the robbers were captured and all of the money except a few dollars they had used in buying a team to get out of the country was gotten back.

Malcolm Campbell, sheriff of Converse County, Wyoming, also told a story about Scott Davis:

The Deadwood Treasure Coach

Persimmons Bill was one of the outlaws that robbed the Treasure Coach out of the [Black] Hills. When popular stage driver Johnny Slaughter was shot off the Deadwood stage, the companies hired dead shots and began to kill the robbers off. "Quick-shot" Davis was one of the guards and messengers. "Stuttering" Brown was another.

Brown knew about Persimmons Bill and promised to kill him if he ever crossed his path. But soon after he started work, Brown was shot from the driver's seat just as Johnny Slaughter had been. Both murders were attributed to Persimmons Bill. He was later hanged back in Tennessee.[36]

The company that ran the stageline is reported elsewhere as Gilmer and Saulsbury. Stuttering Brown is identified as being from Salt Lake and Persimmons Bill is identified as an alias for one William F. Chambers.

*After two grim stage stories, it's appropriate to reprint this eyewitness account from the **Sidney** (Nebraska) **Telegraph** in July 1877.*

The Program of a Hold-Up of 1876

This is the way the road agents do it on the Cheyenne route to the [Black] Hills:

Captain of the gang: "Halt."

Stage Driver: "All right."

C. of G.: "How many passengers have you on board?"

S.D.: "Four."

C. of G.: "You're a liar. You've got three for you dropped the banker at Crook City. Get down off the box and throw up your hands and stand with your back to me. Passengers will alight on the opposite side of the coach and throw up hands, and keep in line with the driver."

The "captain" then issues the following orders:

"No. 1, attend to the team and see it doesn't break away. No. 2, cover the passengers and shoot the first one who turns his back from you or lets his hands down. No. 3, search the passengers from hat to toe of boots."

These orders are carried into effect with mathematical precision, and almost invariable success, the captain of the freebooters having a general supervision of the raid, acting as sort of a double guard.

C. of G.: "No. 3, have you searched that big brown-bearded fellow's shirt? I saw him put away $300 in it at Deadwood yesterday."

No. 3: "You told me so this morning, but I can't find it. The pocket is there, but nothing is in it."

No. 2: (to impatient victim who attempts to turn his head) "Keep that nose to the front or I'll blow the top of your head off. (Victim complies.)

C. of G.: "Where the h—l are those fellows' watches? I saw a gold chronometer worth $250 on that little cub to the right at Rapid City this very morning and he was more anxious to show it then than now. Look in his boots." (Boots develop nothing.)

"Search the stage and pry off the treasure box, and don't lose any time. No. 2, see that your men are covered."

The treasure box is wrenched off, the mail rifled, passengers relieved of all they could not conceal, when the following order if given by the C. of G.: "Driver, take your seat on the box."

(Driver complies.) The C. of G. delivers himself of something as follows.

C. of G.: "Passengers, these are hard times and it's every one for himself. You're here to make money and so are we. You've got valuable claims in the Hills, and we've failed. Most of us have lost all we had and there's a few of us who are professionals at that business. We've worked stages in Montana, Idaho, California, and even Mexico; it's easy business and light work— only requires a little nerve and bluster. Now, you fellows are all armed and have talked this subject of stage robbing over to the crowd, just how you would serve the d——d road agents in case they molested you. Pointed out the exact spot where you would shoot and even contemplated scalping the robbing villains. You stand there trembling in your boots, robbed, with your hands above your head, while we road agents go through you for all that's out and go back for fresh braves like you. When you get to Cheyenne tell an awful story of how you fought and shot and blustered and gave us a piece of your mind, when in fact you didn't have the spunk to draw a gun or open your mouths, and when you get home to the bosom of your families, tell them you're going to stay there, wouldn't scalp a road agent if you could and couldn't if you would. You will now take your places in the coach and proceed. Hope you will sleep comfortable. Now, let go the team."

And that's all there is to it. The robbers return to Deadwood and the victims proceed on their melancholy way. These are the facts in the case of the usual stage robbery on the Cheyenne route, which occurs about twice a week in case it is a good week.

The apparent humor of the stage robbers is also echoed in the biographies of Sam Bass and his gang, claiming many saucy remarks they are supposed to have made at the unsuccessful stage robberies they committed. If it's true the holdups on the Deadwood stage must have been, as legend says, and contemporary clippings confirm, very different from the grim events depicted by Hollywood. One somewhat amusing image that is often reported is the robber seeing a pair of boots he likes and making the victim sit on the ground and raise his foot for a sole-to-sole boot-size check.

Wyatt Earp's Close Call

The man who came closest to shooting Wyatt Earp in Kansas was himself! Sunday night [January 9, 1876] Wyatt Earp and his deputies were sitting in the Custom House Saloon, and as Wyatt leaned back in his chair, his pistol fell from his belt. [He apparently did not use a scabbard at the time; just after the War most men carried their pistols in their belt, high up. The quick-draw holster is largely a Hollywood invention.]

He had loaded six chambers instead of letting the hammer rest on an empty chamber in the cylinder. The gun hit the floor and fired upward. The bullet passed through Wyatt's long coat and ricocheted off the wall into the ceiling, creating a general stampede from the saloon, the occupants thinking someone was outside shooting at Earp through the window.[37]

Doc Holliday in Leadville

Long after the shoot-out at the O.K. Corral, "Doc" Holliday came up here to Leadville and enjoyed the hot springs over at Glenwood for his health. He died at Glenwood Springs. When he was here he was on his last leg. He had no money, but he gambled. He dealt, too, I believe, here. He got into a gunfight because a fellow loaned him a five-dollar gold piece to cover a card hand and he lost the hand.

The next day the fellow came and wanted to collect the loan and Doc couldn't pay him right then—he had no money. So the fellow said he'd kill Doc if he didn't pay up.

Doc didn't wait. He drew and fired on the threat alone and killed the man. John Morgan, the man who built the Silver Dollar Saloon, named after silver king Horace Tabor's daughter Silver Dollar, put up Doc's bail while he was awaiting trial. Doc was acquitted on the grounds of self-defense.

Because his health was so bad he went on up to Glenwood Springs to take the waters. There was a sanitarium up there and he died a year later.[38]

Three Masked Men
Show Some of the Denizens of Evanston How to Do
a Hold-Up Act Scientifically
"HOW IT FEELS TO HAVE A CANNON POINTED AT
YOU," AS RELATED BY THE PRESS REPORTER.

You may have read of, but you can never appreciate nor can pen portray, the peculiar sensation of being "held-up" by a gang of masked robbers unless you have had the practical experience attending. This the religious editor of The Press now has, and would gladly have lost the fine Waterbury watch and some sixty-five cents distributed 'round through his clothes at the time, rather than have missed this hair-raising event.

It occurred last Saturday night, near the hour of twelve, about thusly: Your reporter had just emerged from the barber shop into the thoroughfare that leads out through the resort for liquid refreshments, gambling hall, and bath room [house] of Snyder and Painter, en route homewards to his virtuous couch, when he was accosted by a "gentleman" apparently about forty feet high, with a large dark-complexioned revolver with the business end pointed "our" way, who remarked, "Hands up!!!" We complied with alacrity and without equivocation or mental reservation. After Mr. Forty-foot had scrutinized us hurriedly and sized us up as harmless and without money he turned his gun on Mr. Thomas Painter, one of the proprietors of the place, and paid particular attention to, and never took his gun off, Thomas. The second gentleman masked, probably not over thirty feet high, leveled his light-colored cannon at Mr. William Van Valkenburg, and by way of parenthesis, apparently, on the remainder of the crowd, consisting of Frank C. Whishman, better known as "Slim," George Marx, Dan Souls, and this, the most humble scribe on earth—at that particular writing.

In the meantime the third gentleman, with something disguising his mug, who has generally been termed "the little fellow," probably because he was not so promiscuous with his gun as the others, leisurely sauntered over to the faro table, rifled the drawer—$80 in gold—then to the roulette table, and in one fell swoop swiped into his bag that which he had taken out of the till—$209.75 in good old [William Jennings] Bryan silver, $20 in gold and $1.75 in small change was overlooked in the shuffle.

About this time James Mills, Jr., happened to appear at the front door and protrude his proboscis into the game; but he retired as suddenly as he came. This interruption evidently startled the three strange gentlemen and they proceeded to line up the crowd on the west side of the room, and with their "cannons" pointed in "our" direction, made good their escape through the rear as abruptly and noiselessly as they had appeared at the front entrance probably not over three minutes before—to "us" it appeared nearer the same number of hours.

Two shots were fired by the intruders after they had reached the alley, which together with the alarm given by Mills, in a few moments called forth dozens of our citizens, some who have related since "what they would have done had they only been there."

...Van Valkenburg looked as though he had just lost a jackpot.

We much prefer to look through the small end of a vinegar cask than through the large end of a gun barrel.

Frank Whishman, better known as "Slim," played a tune on the ceiling with his elongated digits that was quite musical [during the hold-up]. Although George Marx isn't as tall by seven feet, he had his hands nearly as high as "Slim's."

The [author] Press man has always regretted his smallness of stature and had hopes of growing some yet, but the hope is dissipated since the "holdup."

Our reporter has patronized the barber shops occasionally and takes a bath [at the bath house] every six months, whether he needs it or not, but hereafter it will be different...

The man that stood the least chance in town of being held up was our night watch[man]. We are informed that it was after ten Sunday morning before he was aware that a robbery had been committed...[39]

Deadwood Stages
HOW THE HIGHWAYMEN ROB THE STAGES AND PASSENGERS

At present there are four different stagelines running into Deadwood—from Bismark, Fort Smith [South Dakota], Sidney, and Cheyenne [1877]. The latter was stopped and robbed three times in succession last week by some of the most expert road agents the country ever heard of. The first night they attacked the stage between the Cheyenne River and Hat Creek. Once they made the messenger surrender the treasure box, which contained $900, they told him he ought to quit working for a company that did not carry more money than that. The second night they stopped the stage again in the same place and asked for the box. The messenger told them it was bolted to the stage. They then ordered the passengers, six in number, to get out, holding the "drop" on them with their guns, and made them all sit down on the ground while they tried to unfasten the box; but having no tools to work with gave it up for a bad job and robbed the passengers of their money and jewelry, amounting to $4,000.

While they were trying to open the box one of them found a box of cigars belonging to one of the passengers, and passed them around to the party sitting down and they all smoked together. The robbers were all masked and well-armed, and bidding the passengers goodby, told the driver to start.

On the third night they stopped it again near the same place and took the treasure box from two well-armed messengers who tried hard to protect it, but were not quick enough to keep them from getting the "drop" on them [the messengers]. The box contained $12,000 in gold dust and $2,000 in drafts and checks. The latter they handed back, saying they had no use for them.

During the excitement one of the passengers discharged his revolver accidentally and one of the road agents fired, wounding the driver in the side. As soon as [the robber] found out his mistake, he said it was the meanest thing he had ever done in his life and he was sorry. [The robbers] told the messengers to tell the company to send down a pair of gold scales, as they had some difficulty in dividing the dust with a spoon. They were five in number and all had horses. It is supposed that they are a party that left here for the Big Horn [Mountain] country [in present Wyoming], and all are well known here.[40]

A John Wesley Hardin Legend

I am related to John Wesley Hardin, and, you know, those television ads for the Time-Life book series are wrong. John Wesley never shot a man for snoring, although he did fire off a few shots and threaten to shoot the man. The man got up and left the flophouse where they were sleeping.[41]

"Little Arkansaw"

On the night of August 19, 1895, in El Paso, Texas, "Little Arkansaw" was in a saloon. John Wesley Hardin had that nickname when he was in Texas because he was known to be from Arkansas. An eleven-year-old Western Union delivery boy came in with a telegram for Hardin. Hardin took the telegram and gave the youngster a generous tip.

Then he put his hand on the boy's head and pointed to his tall glass of whiskey.

"Son," he said, "do you see that? Take my advice and don't ever touch that stuff. It'll get you into trouble every time."

The boy promised not to drink, and after he left, Hardin was shot moments later by a personal enemy named John Selman. Selman shot Hardin in the back while Hardin was shaking the dice for a throw in a gambling game. Hardin was saying:

"Four sixes to beat..." when the bullet cut him down. He was hit three times as he fell.

The boy told me this years later when he was better known as L.H. "Jack" Hubbard, president of the Texas State College for Women at Denton, Texas.[42]

Hardin's Gold in the Grave

My Great-aunt Emma was my great-grandmother's sister. She lived down around Dermott, Arkansas, and was a very aristocratic Southern lady. She was a cousin to John Wesley Hardin, and he appeared on her doorstep one day, not long before he was shot and killed in El Paso, Texas. He had attempted to pull off a bank robbery in East Texas and had been wounded. He rode on horseback, wounded, from there to Dermott, which is quite a way under those circumstances.

The Texas Rangers and the local lawmen in Texas knew him on sight, and he knew they could shoot him without asking any questions. He had come to Arkansas to hide out, having ridden through the rain and contracted pneumonia by the time he reached Dermott. Aunt Emma put John Wesley to bed and conned a local doctor out of the medicine she needed. She nursed Hardin back to health in a few weeks.

Just before he rode out, after recovering, he told her that he had stopped at the Rohr community graveyard on his way into Arkansas. He said he had gone to his own mother's grave and buried a saddlebag with both paper money and gold coins in it.

There is no marker on Hardin's mother's grave because he was so stingy with his money. Only he knew the exact location of the grave.

A few weeks later Hardin was dead in Texas.

Several members of the family had heard the story, and had searched for the gold around the unmarked grave. But around the little clapboard church is a large, deep slough, and parts of the graveyard have since sunken into it. The money has never been found.[43]

The Marlow Brothers

The Marlow Brothers were five brothers, the sons of a doctor who lived in the Chickasaw Nation. Sometime in the early 1880s they settled on a place along Wild Horse Creek. They lived in a dugout house where the east side of the town of Marlow now stands. He had his medical practice out of the dugout. After the father died, the boys were mostly working cattle or horses for a living. By the mid-1880s the town had begun to develop and by about 1887 commercial enterprises began to develop there.

One brother was a gambler, and was gambling in Graham one night with the deputy sheriff and some others. The Marlow boy won and a difficulty developed. The Marlow boy shot and killed the deputy and fled to the shack outside Graham.

One of the older brothers, a giant of a man but somewhat simple, had also come down for a visit. Although residents of the town are still divided over whether the shooting was justified or not, the sheriff rode out to the Marlow shack and had a terrible argument. The brother, Boone, decided to give up. Boone came out, along with his older brothers, and the bigger Marlow boy was confused by all this, and did not quite understand what was going on. When the sheriff went to put the manacles on Boone, even though Boone was going in peaceably, the bigger brother began to protest. They manacled the smaller brother, but when they tried to manacle the gigantic fellow he went wild. The sheriff was badly injured as the posse overpowered the giant brother and all three Marlows were taken to jail in Graham.

The remaining two brothers were still at home in Marlow, but when they heard about what had happened, they came down to Texas and ended up being arrested and put in jail. Now all five Marlows were in the jail at the same time. A mob began to form and made an attempt to break in and exact presumed justice. The sheriff decided the prisoners needed a change of venue, and a lawyer for the brothers got a court order from the judge in Weatherford to have the brothers removed to Weatherford. Instead of removing the brothers by day, the sheriff took them from the jail in the darkness of night, which made the brothers suspicious.

Two brothers were on horseback, shackled together at the wrist. The other three were in a wagon, all three shackled together. Three or four miles out of town, a vigilante mob appeared out of nowhere. The brothers had feared such a thing and grabbed the pistols from the deputies that were accompanying them, which may mean that the deputies were unaware the ambush would occur. A big gunfight ensued, with two Marlows being killed and several members of the mob being killed. The brothers struggled to get all together in the wagon, but one brother seeing that the brother to whom he was shackled was dead, took out a knife he had kept concealed and sawed his dead brother's hand off to get away. He remounted the horse he had been put on and rode away. The three in the wagon, one of whom was dying, got control of the wagon and drove away fast. As they drove toward Weatherford, the brothers in the wagon saw that their brother was dead, and getting the knife they also cut the hand off that brother and pushed the body out onto the road to lighten the wagon.

One brother, shot in the escape, made it all the way back to Marlow, and died near where the little community of Hell was located. The judge at Weatherford set free the two brothers who escaped unscathed. In an eloquent speech he said that the brothers had been denied due process and the terrible events of the ambush would not have taken place if due process had been followed.[44]

The two living Marlows went to Colorado and lived out their lives there. The story of the ambush has been the basis for many other fictional stories, most of them not nearly as interesting as the events themselves. And almost every Hollywood movie about outlaws being shackled together and cutting the hand off the dead shacklemate is based on someone's retelling of the story of the Marlow brothers.

Outlaw Hide-Out

The Devil's Den was a hide-out for outlaws, and some of them met the Landlord there. In the crevice called the Devil's Den, three dead men were found with three saddles in 1883. At Dead Man's Cave a skeleton and a rifle were found about 1905. The Outlaw Outlook was an overlook where a sentry could stand and see all the flat land around the Den. The place was used by Belle Starr, Jesse and Frank James, the Daltons, and the Youngers.[45]

The Cave at Turner Falls

At Turner Falls there is a cave about a hundred yards above the falls that Jesse James used to use as a hideout when he was crossing Indian Territory. The cave had a hidden upper entrance on the hilltop, and a large lower entrance above the river. In the east wall of the cave was a natural window about two feet across that gave a perfect view of the trail up. A lookout could keep guard, and shoot at any lawmen coming up the river. The front entrance could be defended, and if things got tough, the James boys could get out the upper, hidden entrance and get away.[46]
[See Photo on Page 2]

Belle at Devil's Den

Belle Starr had friends in Texas, where her family lived after the Civil War, and in Missouri, near Carthage, where they had once lived. She also had friends in the Indian Territory, near Eufaula. There was a very profitable business in stealing horses in Texas, driving them across Indian Territory, and selling them in Missouri, then stealing horses while you were in Missouri, driving them back across the Indian Territory, and selling them in Texas. One Missouri man had a horse stolen, the horse went to Texas, was sold, was stolen a year later and driven back to Missouri, and offered for sale there. The horse thieves just happened to offer the horse to its original owner. He just smiled and paid for the horse, and never said a word about the fact that it had been his horse.

When Belle was helping move stolen horses across Indian Territory she often stayed at a log cabin in what is now known as The Devil's Den, and then went on the next day toward her home at Younger's Bend on the Canadian River.[47]

PROCLAMATION

OF THE

GOVERNOR OF MISSOURI!

REWARDS

FOR THE ARREST OF

Express and Train Robbers.

STATE OF MISSOURI,
EXECUTIVE DEPARTMENT.

WHEREAS, It has been made known to me, as the Governor of the State of Missouri, that certain parties, whose names are to me unknown, have confederated and banded themselves together for the purpose of committing robberies and other depredations within this State; and

WHEREAS, Said parties did, on or about the Eighth day of October, 1879, stop a train near Glendale, in the county of Jackson, in said State, and, with force and violence, take, steal and carry away the money and other express matter being carried thereon; and

WHEREAS, On the fifteenth day of July, 1881, said parties and their confederates did stop a train upon the line of the Chicago, Rock Island and Pacific Railroad, near Winston, in the County of Daviess, in said State, and, with force and violence, take, steal, and carry away the money and other express matter being carried thereon; and, in perpetration of the robbery last aforesaid, the parties engaged therein did kill and murder one WILLIAM WESTFALL, the conductor of the train, together with one JOHN McCULLOCH, who was at the time in the employ of said company, then on said train; and

WHEREAS, FRANK JAMES and JESSE W. JAMES stand indicted in the Circuit Court of said Daviess County, for the murder of JOHN W. SHEETS, and the parties engaged in the robberies and murders aforesaid have fled from justice and have absconded and secreted themselves:

NOW, THEREFORE, in consideration of the premises, and in lieu of all other rewards heretofore offered for the arrest or conviction of the parties aforesaid, or either of them, by any person or corporation, I, THOMAS T. CRITTENDEN, Governor of the State of Missouri, do hereby offer a reward of five thousand dollars ($5,000.00) for the arrest and conviction of each person participating in either of the robberies or murders aforesaid, excepting the said FRANK JAMES and JESSE W. JAMES; and for the arrest and delivery of said

FRANK JAMES and JESSE W. JAMES,

and each or either of them, to the sheriff of said Daviess County, I hereby offer a reward of five thousand dollars, ($5,000.00,) and for the conviction of either of the parties last aforesaid of participation in either of the murders or robberies above mentioned, I hereby offer a further reward of five thousand dollars, ($5,000.00.)

IN TESTIMONY WHEREOF, I have hereunto set my hand and caused to be affixed the Great Seal of the State of Missouri. Done
[SEAL.]   at the City of Jefferson on this 28th day of July, A. D. 1881.

THOS. T. CRITTENDEN.

By the Governor:
MICH'L K. McGRATH, Sec'y of State.

The rewards offered by the governor of Missouri—$5,000 for members of the James gang and $10,000 for the James brothers themselves—were high by the standards of the day. The rewards for the James boys were never fully claimed: Jesse was shot, and Bob Ford said he received only a few hundred dollars; Frank turned himself in. The James gang represents the robbery style based on the guerrilla tactics of Quantrill's Raiders, but they deserve, and receive, their own chapter later in this book.

Under the Black Flag

DURING THE WAR BETWEEN THE STATES,
GUERRILLAS...IRREGULAR SOLDIERS NOT
BOUND BY MILITARY LAW...RODE FOR BOTH THE
UNION AND THE CONFEDERACY UNDER THE
BLACK FLAG OF "NO QUARTER."

Quantrill's Raiders—I

William Clarke Quantrill was a schoolteacher who turned to guerrilla warfare when anti-slavery guerrillas, called Jayhawkers, killed his brother. [Or so says the legend, which is not confirmed by research.] He organized a band of tough, crack, and often cruel Confederate cavalry that struck back at Union guerrillas or presumed pro-Union families. His band first came to Texas to rest from frontline action, according to the local folks, in 1862.

While fighting was thick and hot in Arkansas and Louisiana, Federal troops didn't reach Texas until Reconstruction. The only major battle in the War Between the States fought in Texas was a naval encounter at Aransas Pass. This made North Texas the ideal place for Quantrill's men to recuperate and rearm.

Quantrill's men quartered in Cooke, Grayson, Fanin and Lamar counties where Southern sympathizers sheltered them and the ferries over the Red River at Colbert provided them with travelers to prey upon. Sometimes pro-Union men were killed, or Confederate deserters, but for the most part the people of the Red River Valley were safe from the guerrillas by unwritten code.

Sometimes the old town of Sherman was the brunt of drunken revelry by Quantrill's men: they would ride up and down the main street firing into the air. Other times the city of Sherman would hold a dance and Quantrill's men would be invited, would charm the ladies, and behave as perfect gentlemen. One day the guerrillas would steal horses, the next they would take food to a Confederate widow and hoe her cotton for her. And if any plain old outlaws threatened the area, Quantrill's men would bluff them away or gun them down. One old timer said it was like having a vicious guard dog; they kept the robbers away but the family was scared of them, too!

One sad exception: a gang of guerrillas invited themselves to stay at a cotton plantation, as they often did, but failed to mention to their hostess that they had just killed a man for the money he got for a wagon of cotton. The deceased had been her husband, and a Confederate disabled veteran!

The widow suspected her houseguests and turned them in to the Confederate authorities. She never got her money back, and the men were never tried; they were drummed out of Quantrill's troops and were never seen in Texas again. They were the one bad apple in the bunch, some folks said. Others said the whole barrelful was rotten![48]

Quantrill's Raiders—II

My mother always told this story about Quantrill's Raiders. Mother was raised in Elm Springs, Arkansas, four miles west of where Springdale sits now. She was a member of the Methodist Church there, and the family had been members for generations, there in Washington County. Well, one night during the Civil War, during the regular church service, everybody was down on the floor praying. Great-grandpa Wasson was down on the floor praying, and he had kind of moved out into the aisle.

He was out praying up a storm when, all of a sudden, in the door walked some of Quantrill's Raiders. They came walking up the aisle, and there in their path was Great-grandpaw Wasson, facing the pulpit so he didn't see them come in, and didn't hear them over the sound of the prayer.

Just to let him know they were there—some of the members up front had seen the Raiders come in and were by now getting very quiet—one of the Raiders put the end of his rifle barrel at the base of Great-grandpa's spine and ran the barrel slowly up his spine and back down again. That stopped the praying cold.

Suddenly the men nearest the walls of the church-house stepped to the nearest coal-oil lanterns and blew them out, leaving the Raiders standing in the aisle in the darkness. In the confusion that followed, the menfolk pushed the women and children to the open windows and passed them out onto the grass before the Raiders could get a match lit.

When the church was lit again, Quantrill's men robbed the church of the money in the collection plate, and relieved the men of all the money they had in their pockets, but the children and womenfolk, by now in the woods outside, were not bothered. The Raiders left as quickly as they had come, back into the night.[49]

Quantrill's Raiders—III

When Quantrill's Raiders were in Kentucky, during the war, just before Quantrill was killed, they stopped at the house of a newly married young couple. They came in and forced the young woman to cook and serve them supper. They sat around the table and ate and thanked her when they left.

After they left she refused to wash the dishes; she broke all the dirty dishes and threw them out the kitchen window so she would never have to eat off dishes Quantrill's Raiders had eaten off of.[50]

Quantrill's Bones

In the Kansas Historical Society is a relic card that reads: "W.C. Quantrill's bones from W.W. Scott of Canal Dover, Ohio, given by F.G. Adams, 1888." A handful of bones of the Black Flag Commander were taken from their unmarked grave in a bizarre attempt to gain fame. Quantrill died in Kentucky [on June 6, 1865] after being shot by Federal troops [on May 10]. He left money for a decent burial, but the attending minister feared the grave would be disturbed and buried the guerrilla leader in an unmarked grave in Louisville.

Following the War, Caroline Clarke Quantrill, William's mother, was approached by *Iron Valley Reporter* editor, W.W. Scott, about a purported biography of her son. He traced the guerrilla's life and death and eventually found out the site of the grave. He returned to Canal Dover, the Quantrill home, and brought Mrs. Quantrill to Louisville. The grave was opened and Mrs. Quantrill identified the skull by its teeth. Scott claimed the next step would be to rebury Quantrill's bones in a marked grave in a proper zinc-lined box. Instead he offered to sell the bones to the Kansas Historical Society for the museum, thinking the hatred of Quantrill would make the item valuable.

Eventually Scott brought "samples" to Topeka and gave them to the Society [they were displayed for a while but not since], but of course, no one would buy the skull or the rest of the bones. Scott died, as did Mrs. Quantrill. The whereabouts of the skull and the rest of the bones are unknown, but three of Quantrill's bones are in the Kansas State Historical Society Museum in Topeka.[51]

Throughout the War Between the States the Confederate guerrillas and sympathizers were generally referred to as "bushwhackers," owing to their tactic of hiding in the bushes by the side of the road and whacking enemies off their horses as they rode by, or just using the "bush" as the area from which to "whack" their enemies. Union guerrillas and sympathizers were generally called "jayhawkers" because of the identification Kansas pro-Unionists had with a mythical Kansas bird of the same name. There are countless stories and legends about the two groups and most families with roots in the Middle Border have one or more stories to tell.

The Jayhawkers

My great-great-grandfather Columbas [or Columbus] "Lum" House was a soldier in the Confederate Army who was once captured by jayhawkers. They did not kill him on sight, as was sometimes done, but took him prisoner instead. He was left on his own horse [a thing seldom done because of the risk of escape] because they tried to trade him horses and no one else could ride his C.S. Army mount. His hands were tied behind his back and Lum knew he would be killed sooner or later, so he kicked his horse in the flanks and held on with his legs for dear life. The mount bolted and the jayhawkers opened fire. The horse was shot from under him and Lum was shot through the jaw. It gave a lot of blood so they left him for dead, thinking him head-shot. By the grace of God he managed to get up, get untied, and get back to his unit on foot.

While Lum was off to fight, great-great-grandma Betsy House and her sister Nearve [Minerva, also spelled Nerva] Thompson had a bad experience. One day a group of jayhawkers came to the house they shared during the war. Well, the very first thing they did was steal some of the chickens. Now, Betsy was a kind woman and talked to them nice, and asked that they only take one chicken apiece, but Nearve didn't like it one bit! She told the jayhawkers to 'Go to Hell!' This made the jayhawkers mad and they started to hang Nearve's two boys. Their father had been dead quite a while.

Betsy tried to reason with the jayhawkers; thinking very quickly she told them there was some tobacco hid under the house. She sent the two boys under the house to get it. Now, in those days folks kept bee gums wherein they'd keep bees to make honey. The gum tree trunks were hollowed out and kept by the house. Betsy said the tobacco was hid in the bee gum. The boys knew better, so they both crawled into the bee gum and out the other end into the tall grass behind the house. They stayed in the woods until the jayhawkers gave up and went away.[52]

The Hanging of Champ Ferguson

Immediately after the War Between the States, Confederate Captain Champ Ferguson, a Tennessee guerrilla similar to Quantrill, who claimed to have personally killed over a hundred Union soldiers, went back home. Troops came to his home in July of 1865, got him out of his house, took him to jail, and tried him on charges of war crimes. Now, this is after the war, and he had laid down his arms...I'm not saying he had taken an oath of allegiance...and come home to continue his civilian life.

He was convicted of murder for acts of war committed while he was under commission from the Confederacy. He was hanged in August of 1865, for war crimes identical to the acts committed by Union guerrillas, all of whom were pardoned immediately for all they had done. You think of all the Confederate ex-guerrillas, knowing of this, who decided to take to the tall grass before charges could be brought against them. I think the hanging of Champ Ferguson may have started some of the outlaws moving farther West and living outside the law.

Since many of the officials of the civil government were ex-Union men, and all the Army of Occupation in the South were, of course, Union men, some of the ex-guerrillas had no qualms at all about fighting against the lawmen.[53]

Cullen Baker

Cullen Montgomery Baker is almost unknown today; he was once the most-feared outlaw in Reconstruction-era Texas. New York newspapers printed fanciful accounts of his exploits, partly as a justification for harsh post-Civil War policies enforced on Texas by the Union Army. Cul (or Cull) was born in Tennessee in 1836, but his family came west to Texas in 1839, with the promise of open land in the new Republic. He murdered three men before the War Between the States broke out, and murdered three more serving as a conscript in the Confederate Army. To seek protection from his past crimes, he joined the Union Army in Little Rock, but was suspected of another murder and deserted. He may have ridden with Quantrill for a short time.

Baker joined a gang of indiscriminate raiders nominally fighting for the South, but actually only using their guerrilla status as a way to rob from civilians on both sides. He probably committed a dozen more murders—not combat killings— during this raider period. After the war ended, he returned to Texas and lived along the Texas-Arkansas border along the Sulphur Fork of the Red River, where he ran a ferryboat. He quarreled with a young man named Thomas Orr over the affections of a young woman, a feud that would follow him the rest of his life.

The Union Army was the law in post-Civil War Texas when all legally elected officials and officers of the law were replaced with appointees deemed loyal to the Union, and voting rights were removed from anyone not deemed loyal. The Union-appointed governor authorized search and seizure without warrant, a violation of the Constitution the Federals had fought to preserve. When local folks grew angry over the political issues, and wished for a champion, Cullen Baker was unfortunately available.

Using the pretext of real or imagined Union sympathies or abuses of authority, Baker murdered and raided in East Texas and sometimes in southwest Arkansas. He "captured" his rival Thomas Orr and hanged him until he was presumed dead. Cutting the rope to use to hang another personal enemy, Baker left Orr on the ground instead of in the air. Orr lived; when Baker found out and came gunning for him, Orr and friends evaded the guerrilla and one of his friends. Cul and his companion took a bottle of whiskey to their camp in the swampland, and, feeling safe as they usually were in the underbrush, proceeded to get drunk. Orr and his party tracked the two and attacked without warning, killing the first of the postwar (presumed) ex-Quantrill-raider outlaws.

There is no record of Baker ever killing anyone in a fair fight. He shot mostly unarmed men, women and children, many of them freedmen, or Union soldiers surprised on patrol and shot before they could bring their unwieldy, often single-shot, arms into play. (Guerrillas rode loaded and with rifles across the saddle; soldiers rode with rifles unloaded and in the scabbard, awaiting a command from an officer.)

My grandmother's family came to Arkansas in 1823 and my grandfather's family came after the war, because his grandfather was a Confederate soldier released at the Shreveport Garrison. After the War the very first ex-guerrilla to turn to crime was Cullen Baker—a real bad man, who was not admired by the locals, at least in southwestern Arkansas. But he used the techniques he had learned in a short and fairly dishonorable career with Quantrill.

My family says that it's the Cullen Baker story that the movie "The Outlaw Josey Wales" is based loosely on. Baker did ride briefly with Quantrill; how that came about was, he lived on a farm in Missouri after his parents had died. One story says the parents were killed by the redlegs, a Union guerrilla outfit. After the war he ended up in Texas, the state least hurt by the fighting. There he turned against the Union Army of Occupation, and holed up in the "Big Brushy" or the "Thicket." The country was inaccessible. Some local legends are still told about his exploits.

In those days, I guess, a man wore his suit of clothes until they just rotted off, and it happened that Cullen Baker was going to get a new suit of clothes during a brief period of prosperity. But he kept his old clothes. When a new gang member came in, wearing clothes the law could recognize, Cullen gave the new "recruit" his old suit because they were about the same build. Not long after that, the law saw this recruit in clothing they knew to be Baker's and the poor outlaw was shot for Baker.

Baker used the same tricks that the James boys would later use. He had the advantage that the local law did not know what he personally looked like. He could ride into town and take care of his business because he just looked like the local people. He had the same southern accent that everyone else had. No one would call out the alarm unless someone who had personally known him saw him and recognized him. He also used disinformation, like several people claiming to be him, so that he was sometimes reported in more than one place on the same day.[54]

Cullen Baker's Oath

Historians and Western aficionados have always believed that the outlaw bands had secret passwords (there is excellent evidence of this), secret emergency plans and contingency plans (fairly good evidence of this), and secret signs and loyalty oaths. On the latter, very little evidence exists. One item in the original pamphlet **Life of the Notorious Desperado Cullen Baker,** *printed by Thomas Orr in an attempt to recoup some of his losses during the years of the feud with Baker, is the final paragraph, reprinted here:*

> Baker had about his person...a manuscript paper which read thus:
>
> "I, of my own free will and accord, and in the presence of Almighty God, do solemnly swear or affirm that I will never reveal to anyone not a member [of] * * by any nitus, motion, sign, sintol, word or act, or in any other manner whatever, any of the secret signs, grips, passwords, or mysteries or purposes of the ** and that I am not a member of the same; or that I know any one who is a member, and that I will abide by the prescripts and edicts of ** So help me God. (Signed) C.M. Baker"[55]

Death of Cullen Baker

This man who has probably caused more excitement and committed more crimes than any [other] man of modern times has at last fallen, and country the breathes free once more.

The circumstances of his death are as follows:

About four weeks since [Baker] went to the house of his brother-in-law, Thomas Orr of Lafayette County, Arkansas, and breaking down the door, took Mr. Orr and their father-in-law, Mr. William Foster, tied their hands behind them and kept them during the night. Next morning he hung Mr. Orr until [Baker] supposed he was dead, when he cut him down to get the rope to hang another man. This [second] man was finally released by some of Baker's men. Mr. Orr recovered after Baker and his party left. Mr. Foster [was] released about 12 o'clock that day.

On the 6th of January Baker and a man named Kirby came into the settlement again and Mr. Orr, with a few friends, determined to kill him or sacrifice their lives in the attempt. They rushed on him and succeeded in killing him about 11 o'clock a.m. The man Kirby was also killed. Their bodies reached [Jefferson, Texas] yesterday evening about 6 o'clock, and large numbers of persons are congregated around the tent where the bodies lie. Baker's corpse had been fully identified by many who had known him. This ends the career of a man who has kept the whole country in terror for months, and Mr. Orr deserves and will receive the thanks of mankind for his action in riding the State [of Texas] of a man who had declared himself an enemy of his race. The above facts we get from Mr. Orr in person.—Jefferson (Texas) *Jimplecute*[56]

The Quantrill Technique

Cullen Baker may or may not have actually ridden with William Clark Quantrill, but Baker was the first outlaw to use, in the postwar years, what we have come to regard as the "Quantrill Technique." In the 1990s criminals must be aware of silent alarms, infrared sensors, and genetic fingerprinting. In the 1860s and 1870s, the outlaw could thwart efforts of the lawmen through other means. Here are the four elements of the "Quantrill Technique," used first by Quantrill in border warfare, then by Baker, then by Jesse James and others in the 1880s:

1. In the course of the crime, loudly declare a false identification. On one occasion Cul Baker even claimed to be a militia officer seeking Cullen Baker! Quantrill identified himself falsely on several occasions, and Jesse James did the same. Other outlaws would sometimes claim to be Jesse! All this to throw the victims' and officers' attention off the real outlaw.

2. Loudly declare a false charge against your victim. Quantrill and Baker used the "he killed my brother" line; frontier dwellers would often not interfere in a "family matter."

3. As you ride out, leave a false trail, either verbal or physical. Examples: "Boys, (said just loud enough to be overheard), ride on out and meet me at Murderer's Rock." Then ride out and double back the other way; "tell Sheriff Smith that if he wants me, I'll be at Hangman's Ridge waiting to kill him." Again, ride out the road toward the ridge, then double back on rock or in a stream and escape in the opposite direction.

4. Claim indignantly that your crimes were committed by someone else using your name! Cul Baker even wrote a letter to a local newspaper and offered a reward for the capture of whomever was impersonating him. While some outlaws like Jesse James did have their names "taken in vain," no one is known to have claimed to be Baker.

5. Finally, ride nonstop to a distant place to establish your alibi. This was the specialty of the Wild Bunch (Butch Cassidy et al.,) and some consider it to be a late addition to the "technique," however, the Jameses, the Youngers, and other ex-Quantrill-raiders did use this method before Butch and the Bunch.

Since most criminal investigation 1860-1880 consisted of visual identification of outlaws, circulated descriptions or posters, and written depositions sent through the U.S. mails, the verbal "smoke screen" created by the "Quantrill technique" was a better-than-even gamble for success.

Music hall singer Fannie Keenan, the stage name of Dora Hand, is said in legend to be the only woman buried in Boot Hill, Dodge City, Kansas. This is not true, as you will read in the following stories. (Courtesy of the Boot Hill Museum and Library, Dodge City, Kansas)

They Were Buried in Boot Hill

HERE ARE STORIES, CONTEMPORARY NEWSPAPER
CLIPPINGS AND PERSONAL REMINISCENCES
ABOUT THE LAST RESTING PLACE
OF MANY OUTLAWS.

The First Boot Hill

The first paupers' and itinerants' burial ground to be called
"boot hill" was in Hays, Kansas, with the first burials in 1867,
five years before the first burials in Dodge City's Boot Hill.
Thirty-seven identified and many unidentified burials there in-
creased until it was closed down in 1874. The *Dodge City Ford
County Globe* of May 14, 1878, reported, "Hays has recorded
the burial of the sixty-fourth victim of gunplay in her Boot Hill,"
proving the size of their boot hill and the fact that interments
continued there after the official date for the closing of the
frontier graveyard.[57]

Dodge City's Boot Hill

Dodge City's Boot Hill was started in 1872 as a convenience to saloon and parlor operators on Front Street. The hill was a high point for that part of Kansas, rising seventy-odd feet above Front Street to the northwest, when no part of town was out in that direction. Graves were shallow and shabby, often unmarked because the occupants were unknown. The deceased were as likely to be buffalo hunters as gunfighters, and they died from starvation, freezing, epidemic and the more notorious "lead poisoning" from a shootout on Front Street. Some gunfighters were buried there, including some victims of Wyatt Earp's pistols, but never as many as Hollywood would have us think. Roughly thirty graves were still on Boot Hill when the *Dodge City Times* announced on May 4, 1878:

TO WHOM IT MAY CONCERN

Dodge City Kansas
April 20, 1878

All parties are forbidden to make interments on the property of the Dodge City Town Company, under penalty of the law.

W.S. Tremaine
Secretary-Treasurer, Dodge City Town Company

Dodge citizens of means were buried at the military cemetery at nearby Fort Dodge before 1878, but in that year a new city cemetery was opened a few blocks northeast of Boot Hill as the town grew. The first burial there was May 25, 1878, and in 1879 the graves of Boot Hill were opened and the contents moved to a single unmarked common grave in the new Prairie Grove Cemetery. Years later, the remains were moved again, as the town grew, to Maple Grove Cemetery to a second, unmarked common grave, when they lie today.[58]

The Naming of Boot Hill

The name Boot Hill has been debated for years by Western aficionados from other states than Kansas. Three theories were put forward:

The deceased died with their boots on, a sign of violent death, rather than with their boots off, as in bed and of old age.

The victims were buried with their boots on, with rigor mortis making difficult or impossible the act of removing the boots from bodies that generally had lain on the wooden sidewalk or in the alley for hours.

Or, the graves were marked with the deceased's boots (a myth perpetuated by such grave-marking in the "restored" Boot Hill of the 1940s and '50s) because he had no money for a tombstone or the identity was unknown.

Outlaws of the 1870s and '80s often stole money and boots from the living in a robbery, or off the dead (the most common method of convicting murderers in Indian Territory 1870-80 was proving that the killer was arrested wearing the victim's boots) and in a rough town, boots on a grave might not last very long. On the other hand, the thought that rigor prevented removal of the boots is disproven, and the issue settled on the other theories by the article in the *Ford County Globe* of February 4, 1879, on the removal of the Boot Hill burials to Prairie Grove Cemetery:

> The skeletons removed from the graves on Boot Hill were found to be in a fine state of preservation, and even the rude box coffins were sound as when placed in the ground...Some were resting with their boots on, while others made more pretentions to style, having had their boots removed and placed under their heads for pillows. Only a few of them could be recognized, as all of their headboards, if there ever were any, had long since wasted away and nothing remained to denote where their bodies lay but little mounds of clay. [Boot Hill was gypsum, rock, clay and sand.][59]

The Only Eyewitness Account

According to Ms. Darlene Smith, librarian at the Boot Hill Museum Library, there has only been found one eyewitness account of a burial in Dodge City's Boot Hill, witnessed by Carl

Ludvig Hendricks, a Swedish immigrant pioneer who was in Dodge City working with a buffalo hide merchant. This is his account:

Finally we arrived in Dodge City and had our hides unloaded…It was now almost one year since I had left Dodge City, and I must say that it was a low, miserable place with its saloons, gambling houses, and low dance halls…

…I found work with a man who bought buffalo hides and shipped them to Kansas City to a large tannery…

Now I will speak again about Dodge City. The year before I worked on the railroad, which went through it, Dodge City was started. A small railroad station was built there first and then a small hotel. When I came back one year later, there was another hotel, two saloons, two miserable dance halls, also a blacksmith shop with an attached hardware store. There were some small shanties, some of them with plastering inside. The streets were only dirt roads. There were, perhaps, 200 inhabitants, but only six women. These belonged to the dance halls. There were no police, but everyone protected himself by carrying a revolver in a holster on a leather belt outside his clothes. It seemed that the revolver was the only law that was respected.

There was a small cemetery with twenty-two graves. Two persons had died of natural causes, but the other twenty had been shot to death. Some graves were only half filled-in, and wolves had desecrated some of them and pulled out, and no doubt devoured, a good many of the bodies. Most had been buried without coffins. These were the cowboys and buffalo hunters who had come to Dodge City for a "good time." They went into saloons and dance halls, got drunk, then got into fights and were shot dead with pistols.

I remember one night after I had fallen asleep, I was awakened by several pistol shots and I heard the next morning that there had been a fight that night in a dance hall and a man had been killed. That morning as I was going to work, and had to go past that dance hall, I saw a form lying outside. When I got nearer I saw it was a dead man. I had stood there a few minutes when a man came out of the house and I said to him "this man must be dead." He answered that he had been killed in a fight that night. When I went home at noon the dead man still lay there, but when I had stopped work for the day and was going home, they had fastened the body to a big pole. As two men carried it with the head and the feet hanging down, I followed them. Each man had a shovel and when they got to the cemetery they dug a grave, not over three feet deep, threw the body into it, and filled it up. When I asked if they knew who the dead man was, I was told that it was no concern of mine.[60]

Alice Chambers' Funeral

We have heard for years that the only woman buried on Boot Hill in Dodge City was Dora Hand, a fallen angel of mercy. Subsequent research showed us that only one woman was ever buried on Boot Hill, but her name was Alice Chambers, a prostitute and dance hall girl who apparently died of venereal disease. The following newspaper article was written by a citizen present at the time, moralizing and recalling the events some thirty years after they occurred:

The coffin may have been a rude pine box, the ceremony may not have conformed to any established ritual, the mourners may have been few, but the scene was always impressive and solemn—and if the castaway was a female, sobs and cries relieved the sorrow and distress...

Boot Hill, by reason of its proximity, was the handy burying ground for male and female, whether the deceased met instant death by pistol shot or in the slow process of disease contracted in an extreme indulgence of immorality. These cases were not rare—when the candle burns night and day the light soon goes out.

We remember that one of our local preachers, a Rev. Adam Holm, was asked to perform the last sad rites of a deceased female, (whose frailty in living had soon caused the light to go out) but he refused to conduct the burial service because the deceased was of immoral character...

Some one with kindly heart took charge of the service—there was a magnificence in the stifled voices of the men, and there were sermons in the sobs of the women as the coffin was silently and steadily lowered between the narrow chalk or gypsum walls of the grave and the clods of dirt as they fell upon the top of the pine coffin sent no echoing note below but these dull hollow sounds were wafted in the desert air...

...A couple of boards marked the head and foot of the earth tomb, and these were soon removed or rotted down; and all of the unknown bones were heaped together in another resting place...[when moved by the City to a new, plotted cemetery].

Excavation on Boot hill has probably removed all the bones of the unknown bodies; and there is not even a memory to gild the past, except the rude speech of reminiscence.[61]

Fannie Keenan: Angel of Mercy

Dodge City was a wild town in the 1870s; Front Street was peaceable, and a city ordinance made revelers check their guns at the saloons and dance halls north of the Plaza [at the east-west railroad tracks]. But south of the tracks, across the imaginary "deadline" drawn by city fathers, guns were permitted, law officers seldom went, and Texas trail-driving cowboys blew off steam after months on the road.

In the saloons and theaters on both sides of the deadline, the ladies of the evening plied their trade in pretty calico dresses instead of the finery associated with California dance halls. One of these fallen angels was also an angel of mercy. Her name was Fannie Keenan, and she came to Dodge in the summer of 1878 and sang at the Varieties [Saloon] and the Comique [theater]. She was one of the most popular performers ever to appear in Dodge. At the Alhambra Saloon and Gambling House, run by Dodge City Mayor "Hound Dog" Kelley, there were gunfights over Fannie's affection, and as many as six men may have been put down in Boot Hill fighting for her honor or her favors.

By night, Fannie was a singer, dancer and possibly more, but by daylight, when the Dodge City gamblers and gunmen were sleeping it off, Fannie was out doing charity work. She wore widow's weeds and sang in church choir; she grubstaked poor Texas cowboys who'd lost everything, or she'd redeem their hocked saddles; when epidemic illness struck, she nursed some of the sick. Some of the north-of-the-tracks society found out about her south-of-the-tracks work, and she lost her position in polite company. But the saloon owners, the cowboys, the soldiers [of nearby Fort Dodge], and the [buffalo] hunters loved her.

She died south of the deadline, shot by mistake in a feud between a cowboy and the colorful mayor, her old boss, "Dog" Kelley.[62]

The Death of Dora Hand

Some storytellers say that Fannie Keenan (Dora Hand) was the only woman buried in Boot Hill. This is not true; this is the story of the death and burial of Dodge City's fallen angel of mercy.

"On Friday morning, about four o'clock, [October 4, 1878] two shots were fired into a small frame building, situated south of the railroad track [and the Deadline] and back of the Western House [hotel], occupied by Miss Fannie Garretson and Miss Fannie Keenan. The building was divided into two rooms by a plastered partition, Miss Keenan occupying the back room. The first shot, after passing through the front door, struck the floor, passed through the carpet and facing of the partition and lodged in the next room. The second shot also passed through the door...through the plastered partition, and after passing through the bed clothing of the second bed, struck Fannie Keenan in the right side, under the arm, killing her instantly."

A coroner's jury was summoned, officers questioned saloon owners and patrons, and a posse was mustered by Mayor "Dog" Kelley. Wyatt Earp, Bill Tilghman and Bat Masterson were among the posse. By Saturday they brought in James Kennedy, a cowboy who had a grudge against "Dog" Kelley, half-owner of the Alhambra Saloon and Gambling House. The frame house belonged to Kelley, and he often slept there. Due to an illness, he had been sleeping at the post hospital at Fort Dodge. He had rented the house to Misses Garretson and Keenan.

She was given the largest funeral ever seen in Dodge City, and was buried in Prairie Grove Cemetery [not on Boot Hill]. Her remains were moved to Maple Grove Cemetery years later. Kennedy was tried the following spring, and acquitted, for no other reason than that he did not intend to kill Dora Hand, but Mayor Kelley![63]

*The **Fort Smith** (Arkansas)**Elevator** for March 20, 1896, with the front-page story about the execution of Crawford Goldsby, alias "Cherokee Bill" (see pp. 122–123). The **Elevator**'s masthead read:* YES, WHILE I LIVE NO RICH AND NOBLE KNAVE SHALL WALK THE WORLD IN CREDIT TO HIS GRAVE. *This colorful newspaper, whose style can be likened to today's tabloids, shed great light on the life and times of the Middle Border.*

They Were Hanged
by the Neck

MOST OF THE NARRATIVES IN THIS SECTION
WERE EXTRACTED FROM NEWSPAPERS AND CLIP-
PINGS IN FAMILY SCRAPBOOKS, BUT THE CON-
TENT OF THESE TALES IS NATURALLY AND
UNAVOIDABLY UNPLEASANT.

Hanging was the standard method of execution in the late 1800s. These short clippings from Fort Smith-area newspapers give insight into the events of the time:

HANGING OF TATUM—Yesterday the execution of Major [a name, not a rank] Tatum, for the murder of Rev. H.J. Merrill, six miles above [Van Buren, Arkansas] on the opposite side of the [Arkansas] river on Sunday morning, January 31, [1869], took place west of the penitentiary. About 2,000 people witnessed the hanging...Fifteen minutes before one o'clock Tatum appeared on the ground in a closed carriage, accompanied by Rev. John

Peyton…Driving to the foot of the steps leading to the scaffold, the parties descended from the carriage…Colonel Oliver, the sheriff, read the sentence of the court, fastened a cap over his face, tied and adjusted the rope around his neck…His neck was broken by the fall." (*Van Buren Press,* Van Buren, Arkansas, March 30, 1869.)

The black cap, usually of silk, covered the entire face, and the famed hangman's knot was not always pre-tied as seen in the Hollywood Westerns.

A CARNIVAL OF HANGING … It might have been expected that with the number of previous hangings, that the morbid appetite of the masses would have been satiated, and but few present on this occasion, but the crowd was as great [as], if not greater than, at any previous execution. Since yesterday people have been coming from all quarters and the roads thronged with comers until the town [of Fort Smith] was crowded, and very early this morning they hastened to take positions as near the gallows as possible to make sure of being present at the first move in the drama. The number present must have been between 6 and 7,000.

At seven o'clock the irons were taken off [the manacled prisoners] and the criminals made preparation for the final scene. At the request of the prisoners the black gowns were dispensed with and they were dressed neatly but plainly in the usual citizens' dress, furnished by their friends or by the jailor, Major Pierce." (*Van Buren Press,* Van Buren, Arkansas, April 25, 1876, page three.)

The criminals were William Leach, Isham Sealy, Gibson Ishtonubbee (the latter two Chickasaw Indians), Orpheus McGee (a Choctaw Indian) and Aaron Wilson (a black man). These five, all under sentence for murder in the Indian Territory, represented the approximate racial distribution of that territory, implying that there was no racial bias in sentencing. The open-air hanging in Van Buren would be replaced within the walls of old Fort Smith by an enclosed scaffold and the admitting of only forty-odd witnesses when the court was later moved to Fort Smith and came under the jurisdiction of Judge Isaac Parker. The black gowns would also disappear from custom in the 1880s and 1890s.

The act of lynching—hanging without benefit of a trial based on presumed guilt and controlled by a mob—was still common in the violence of postwar Arkansas, as evidenced by this clipping:

HORRIBLE LYNCHING AFFAIR—Delos Heffron, who brutally murdered D.F. Halstead at Salem [in northeast Arkansas] about ten days ago, was lynched Sunday morning the 29th ult. [Most recent, i.e. of June.] About 1 o'clock that morning a band of thirty masked men suddenly made their appearance at the jail [in Salem] and demanded the keys of the sheriff, having previously overpowered the guard of seven men. The sheriff declared he would die before he would give up the keys. The mob seized him, but could not find the keys. They then broke down three walls with sledge [hammers] and came to Heffron's cell. He broke up a chair and prepared to defend himself. The mob threw fireballs into the cell, and by their light fired twenty-five shots at Heffron, disabling him, then seized him, took him to the railroad bridge and hung him. None of the mob were recognized. Heffron was a saloon keeper, a desperate man and the terror of the town. He is the seventeenth man hung by regulators in that section of the State in the past three years..." (*Fort Smith Weekly New Era* of July 16, 1873.)

Vigilante mobs were often "not recognized" by their neighbors, often faced down valiant sheriffs, and broke down building walls to terrorize and execute wrongdoers in a desperate attempt to end lawlessness through a lawless system that caused criminals to leave the country for safer climes.

Origin of the Lynch Law
It Began in Virginia and Was Neither Violent Nor Mob-like

[The] Lynch law had its origins in Virginia, according to the conclusions of a gentlemen who has been investigating the early history of that state. It was not mob law, as it is now understood.

It was orderly, methodical and fair in its processes and was strongly opposed to violence or mob rule. Its distinctive feature was simply that the decrees and findings were executed sternly and swiftly upon the spot of their delivery.

Charles Lynch, whose name is associated with the summary proceedings now known as acts of "lynch law," was a Revolutionary soldier, and after the War ended took up his residence in Pittsylvania County. The region in which he lived became at one period infested by bands of Tories and outlaws, whose depredations upon the defenseless people extended from the lower parts of North Carolina and Virginia to the passes of the Blue Ridge [Mountains] and the headwaters of the James and other mountain streams. Deserters from both [American and British] armies added strength and semblance of organization to their operations. Wherever they appeared the terror stricken inhabitants were plundered, harassed and mercilessly subjected to every variety of insult and outrage. A remedy was needed for this insufferable state of things, a remedy that would at once strike such terror to those miscreants as would relieve a community already suffering from the effects of hostile invasion [by British troops]. Colonel Lynch was the man to take the lead in such an emergency. He succeeded in organizing a body of patriotic citizens, men of known character and standing.

Having laid his plans before them and securing their approval, he at once proceeded to put them into execution. At the head of his followers, he promptly got on the track of the unsuspecting enemy, captured many, and caused the others to flee from the country. When any of these outlaws fell into his hands, they were not taken at once to a tree and hanged or tied to a stake and shot, as is now done under the perverted system of the present day. This was not according to the Code of Colonel Lynch and his followers.

So far from such a lawless procedure, a jury was selected from Lynch's [military] men, over which he presided as judge. The captives were tried separately, the accused allowed to make his own defense and to show cause, if he could, why he should not be punished. If [he was] found guilty, the punishment was inflicted on the spot. The general impression has been that in all cases of "lynch law" the penalty was death; this is a mistake. A writer who knew Colonel Lynch well was assured by him that he never willingly condemned a criminal to capital punishment; that prisoners were frequently let off with a severe flogging and then liberated on condition that they would leave the country. (*New York Herald*)[64]

Changes in the Execution Procedure

"...The witnesses will be limited to about forty [inside the new walls immediately surrounding the scaffold]. None other than members of the press, the clergy, physicians, attorneys and court attendants will be admitted—and only a limited number of these. A guard will be placed on the [stone outer] walls surrounding the Garrison [of old Fort Smith], and will have positive orders to shoot any person or persons who may attempt to enter the gates or scale the walls or steps..." (*Fort Smith Weekly Elevator,* Fort Smith, Arkansas, September 9, 1881.)

The guards on the outer garrison walls were clearly there to prevent anyone entering the yard, not escaping from it, as the wording of the article above shows. Escape from within was prevented by the presence of marshals and the jailer.

The **Fort Smith Elevator** *(a daily) and the* **Fort Smith Weekly Elevator** *both covered the trials and hangings and had very specific style elements ranging from the spelling "jailor" instead of "jailer" to the way internal headlines accentuated the text.*

Many stories of the hangings have come down to this era in the folklore of families, either orally, as scrapbook clippings, or both. These are the most fascinating and repugnant narratives, and may be only for the stout of heart.

Hangman's Tree in Montana

A few rods south of Helena and just west of the present overland stage road where it crosses the Dry Gulch and directly in the gulch there stands a venerable pine whose massive lower branches of weird fantastic growth extend twenty feet or more from the gnarled and moss-covered trunk. Years since it lost its foliage and now it is gradually yielding to decay, and ere long a clod of vegetable mold will alone remain to mark the site of the famous Hangman's Tree. Could the old pine speak what tales it could tell; but perhaps 'tis best that speech is not given and that with the life of the old tree should pass the recollection of those early days when forbearance having ceased to be a virtue, a short shrift and hempen cord became necessary to rid the country of the desperadoes that infested it, and thus secure long-needed protection to life and property for honest citizens ....

Now [1875] law and order reign throughout the Territory and justice is attainable and administered through regular channels and it is to be hoped that never again will circumstances call for or justify the formation of such an organization as was that of the vigilantes of Montana.

In 1862, 1863, and 1864 Virginia City and Bannock were the headquarters of Henry Plummer's cruel band of highwaymen and cut-throats. Plummer secured an appointment as sheriff and then made his cutthroat lieutenants his deputies. For a time this arrangement worked admirably for the toughs, as they could rob and murder with impunity. After they had killed over a hundred and twenty citizens [mostly miners, killed for the gold dust they were carrying] and plundered stages, express shipments, and private [this word is illegible in the clipping; presumably "shipments"] until no one felt safe or dared to leave with, or send, money out of the country—and anyone who dared to demur to this order of things or suggest that the robbers were other than honest and perfect gentlemen did so at the imminent peril of his life—it occurred to a few resolute men that it was time for a change, and quietly conferring with each other, an organization was soon affected, including several hundred of the best men in Virginia, Bannock, and Helena.

Laying their plans cautiously but well and executing them promptly, they meted out merited justice to twenty-nine of the ruffians, including Plummer and all the members of his band, all of whom were made to "dance upon nothing at the end of a rope." Five of them were hanged at one time from the crossbeam in an unfinished storeroom adjoining the building in which your correspondent writes this communication. These executions ended the scene of terror, and since then peace and quiet has been the rule in Montana. The dying speeches of some of the desperadoes were peculiarly characteristic and worthy of note. Erastus Yager, generally known as "Red," said to his captors, "You have treated me like a gentleman, and I know I am going to die; I am going to be hanged; it's pretty rough but I merited this years ago." And with the rope around his neck his last words were, "Goodby, boys. God bless you! You are on a good undertaking."

Henry Plummer begged hard for his life, asked to be chained down, offered to leave the country forever, and declared he was too wicked to die. Another, John Wagner, said, "Cut off my arms and legs and let me go; you know I could do nothing then." Jack Gallagher's "I hope that forked lightning will strike every strangling son of a b—h of you." Ben Helm, looking at the muscular contortions of Gallagher [as he was hanging] said, "Kick away, old fellow, I'll be in hell with you in a minute .... Every man for his principles...Let her rip!" George Shears, when arrested said, "I knew I should have to go up sometime, but I thought I could run another season." When told to mount the ladder which served for the time being as a scaffold, he made use of the following language: "Gentleman, I am not used to this business, never have been hung before. Shall I jump off or slide off?" Being directed what to do, he said, "All right; goodby," and leaped into eternity. From the confessions of the felons it is conclusively shown that the vigilantes acted with such discrimination that not an innocent man suffered at their hands.[65]

PRISONERS EN ROUTE TO FT. SMITH.

Prisoners en route to Ft. Smith, one of seven engravings on page 396 of **Harper's Weekly** for May 15, 1875. This is the first reprinting in this century of this engraving, which shows white deputy marshals under "Hanging Judge" Isaac Parker, of the Western District of Arkansas, who was seated only five days before this illustration was published. In fact, at the time the illustrator was working, Judge Caldwell of the Eastern District was sitting for the resigned and disgraced Judge Story, awaiting Parker's arrival.

The Hanging Judge

ALTHOUGH THE NAME HAS BEEN CAPRICIOUSLY
APPENDED TO MORE THAN ONE JURIST, THERE
WAS REALLY ONLY ONE "HANGING
JUDGE"...AND FORT SMITH WAS HIS HOME.

*Postwar politics and incredible gerrymandering made the
United States Federal Court for the Western District of Arkansas and the Indian Territory, headquartered at Van Buren
(fifteen miles east of old Fort Smith) a court with an unwieldy
task; desperation made it corrupt. The court was moved to the
garrison of an old Indian-wars fort, right on the Arkansas-In-
dian Nation line, at a bend in the Arkansas River, off Garrison
Street, the main street of the frontier town of Fort Smith,
Arkansas. To that court was sent by the President of the United
States Judge Isaac Parker, who proved incorruptible enough to
win praise from the opposite political party and men who would
have been opposing him had they met on the field of battle.*

The *"white man's" idea of justice included the quaint notion that "white men" entering the Indian nations should not be judged by Indian courts, but allowed to commit their crimes, hide out, menace the Indian population, and only be dragged back to Fort Smith for trial under white man's laws. As you might suspect, Indians who committed crimes in the United States were summarily tried by the prevailing laws. The obvious inequity escaped the legal thinkers of the day. Often, for crimes committed against white men, other white men and even Indians would turn themselves in to Judge Parker's court rather than face the whippings and shooting Indian courts dealt out.*

If the Indian courts had been given complete authority within their own nations, the Caucasian criminal element might have quieted down quite a bit. As it was, criminals from all over the United States fled to Indian Territory where Indian courts could not touch them, and the U.S. courts couldn't catch them, at least not easily. And, of course, there was also a considerable criminal element among the people of the Territory as well, and all criminals, black, white or red, were brought to Fort Smith if the crime they had committed was against a white person.

The judge they all faced at Fort Smith was a remarkable man, even though many, especially the condemned, accused him of excessive cruelty.

*Judge Isaac C. Parker was a Republican, and J.H. Sparks the editor of the Fort Smith **Weekly Herald,** was a Democrat; yet he offered this high praise of Judge Parker:*

Under the administration of the Honorable I.C. Parker, the new judge of the [Western] District, the irregularities, abuses, and speculations which so abounded when little [Judge William] Storey [sic; Story] was on the bench, are being regulated, rectified and stopped. [Parker] came here a stranger just before the commencement of the term, and has so conducted [him]self both as a citizen and judge as to fully sustain the enviable reputation he had attained in his own state—Missouri—and with the confidence and regard of every substantial citizen, regardless of political proclivities—a distinction awarded to few since the days of Reconstruction (but few deserved it!—Editor, Herald).

In fact, Judge Parker is pursuing the commendable policy of reform, and of substantial reduction of expenditures..."[66]

When Isaac Charles Parker came to Fort Smith as the Judge of the United States District Court of the Western District of Arkansas, which included the Indian nations and the Indian Territory, on May 2, 1875, he wasted no time in starting a session of his court. Here is the heart of the eloquent and quite lengthy charge to the grand jury, May term, 1875.

[Speaking of the U.S. statute that extended into the Indian country the laws of the United States:] "This statute gives to the court jurisdiction possessed by none other; it therefore throws upon you and upon me, and upon every officer of the court, the responsibility of seeing to it that all the laws for the protection of the country and its people to be enforced, that the good shall be protected from the bad, and that with the aid of the Indians, through their local laws, and by their co-operation with, and assistance to, the officers of this court, life, liberty and property shall be as safe as it is possible, under the circumstances surrounding that country, to make them.

"While no one in that country should be harassed or oppressed, yet everyone who has violated the law should be made to feel its power, and every law for the protection of the people should be executed in good faith, having in view all the time the purpose of the law, to-wit: to protect the people.

"I trust the citizens of the Indian Territory will cheerfully and freely co-operate with, and aid, the officers of this court in arresting and bringing to punishment all offenders against the laws and treaties of the United States."[67]

The Fatal Trap Was Sprung

After reading many Western novels and seeing many Hollywood "Westerns," Americans have the idea that hanging was a quick and merciful death, over in a painless instant, and somehow glamorous or romantic. Anyone holding that opinion is invited to read this account, by an eyewitness reporter for the **Fort Smith Weekly Elevator,** *of the hanging of five condemned* *men at Judge Parker's court in 1881. This is the most accurate and powerful account of which these editors are aware, even though it holds elements of the modern "tabloid" news magazines in its writing style:*

We visited the jail early, and remained until all was over, that the readers of the Elevator might not miss the least detail of the execution.

THE LAST NIGHT, the condemned all retired Thursday evening at the regulation hour—8 o'clock. They were granted permission by Jailer Ayers to be up and about when they pleased. The Indian boys went to sleep early, Brown, Padgett and McGowen did not get to sleep until about 11 o'clock. All awoke early and were up at 6 o'clock yesterday morning. They [ate] a hearty breakfast and smoked a cigar afterward.

THE CONFESSION: A rumor had reached our reporter about 8 o'clock in the morning that the Manley brothers had confessed to the killing for which they were to hang—they having heretofore protested their innocence. In company with Rev. Jeffet we visited them and they acknowledged to us that they had committed the crime, but refused to give any particulars of the killing further than had been given [in court].

At 9:45 a detachment of the Frontier Guards marched into the enclosure in charge of Capt. P.T. Devany, and a portion were detailed to guard the walls [of the old fort] while the balance acted as escort to the Marshal's posse who had [charge of] conducting the prisoners to the gallows.

THE START: at 9:50 Jailer Ayers entered the box in front of cell No. 2 and called for Brown, Padgett and McGowen, who responded promptly, and after a hurried handshaking among the condemned and their fellow prisoners, they entered the box [a kind of heavily clad iron double-door system.] All of them looked deadly pale and glanced nervously about them. They held up their hands, Padgett first, then Brown and McGowen, and were handcuffed by the jailer. The trio were then passed [out of the box] one at a time into the hallway, extending across in front of the cells. Two deputy marshals took charge of each man as he was passed out [of the box.] They stood some minutes in the open court, while the jailer went to notify the Manley boys that their time had come.

The brothers were found busily engaged in religious devotions, at the rear door of the large cell, with Rev. W. Lewis, the rear guard of the prison. They were unconscious of the flight of time until tapped on the shoulder by Mr. Ayers. They turned quickly, and shaking hands with the guard and interpreter, passed to the front of the cell, bidding farewell to all as they walked down the great cell for the last time. They entered the box and presented their wrists for the handcuffs in a mechanical sort of way. After being ironed they were passed out [of the box] as the others, two deputies escorting them.

While waiting in the court[yard] for the brothers, the guards and attaches of the jail crowded around Padgett, Brown and McGowen and bid them good bye. At 9:55 the line of march was taken up for the enclosure [in the yard of the old fort] in which the scaffold stood waiting its victims...

When about one-third of the way [to the gallows], BROWN FAINTED DEAD AWAY.

A halt was made, and a copious supply of ice water poured on his head revived him. He arose to his feet remarking, "I have been very sick for some time and am feeling very weak."

Padgett and McGowen glanced anxiously about them during the halt and evinced signs of weakness themselves. The march was resumed and the enclosure was reached without further stoppage or delay.

As the party entered the open gates of the enclosure, each of the murderers glanced up at the ugly-looking framework from which they were to leap into eternity.

The scaffold stood eight feet above the ground. A stairway of twelve steps [making the landing the thirteenth step], three-feet-six-inches in width, led up to a platform 14x15 feet. The trap was twelve feet long by three wide, and so arranged as to give way in the center when sprung, each half being on hinges. The cross beam overhead is seven feet two inches above the platform, and is of heavy timber. The ropes were so arranged as to give about six feet [of] drop. A deep trench had been dug directly under the trap, so as to prevent the feet of the condemned men from striking the ground. Every attention was given and great care taken to prevent any botch work...

THE MANLEY BROTHERS had nothing to say, save that they acknowledged they had committed the deed for which they were about to die.

Padgett, McGowen and Brown called several [observers] by name, bidding them good bye; they shook hands with each other and said farewell.

THE BLACK CAPS [which completely covered the head] were placed on them at 10:30 and the noose adjusted and the scaffold cleared [of other personnel]. Padgett did not want the cap on. McGowen's last words while waiting the fearful drop, issued from under the cap in a clear voice, and addressed to his companions, "As we drop out of this world together, let us hope we may meet in the next." They stood in silence a moment waiting, with abated breath, the last second. Each drew in a long breath as the FATAL TRAP WAS SPRUNG.

The drop fell at 10:32. The dull thud with which they fell will echo in the ears of many a man who witnessed the sickening scene. The necks of Padgett, McGowen and Amos Manley were broken. The brothers died a terrible death. For a few moments, they continued to draw themselves up and down in a fearful manner, the chest heaved and both of them writhed in inexpressible agony. The blood gushed in torrents from the mouth of the younger and soaking through the black cap trickled down in a sickening stream over the white shirt bosom, dying it blood red [sic], while its wearer swung to and fro, striking against the form of his brother whose struggles were almost equally as agonizing as his own. Their pulse at 10:33 was as follows: Amos Manley 60, Abler 120, Brown 72, McGowen 108, Padgett 96. The pulse of Amos ceased to beat in 12 minutes, Abler's in 12 1/2, Brown's in 6, McGowen's in 5, and Padgett's in 7.

Abler Manley died the hardest death. He was 15 1/2 minutes dying. McGowen was pronounced lifeless at 10:47 after hanging 15 minutes. Amos Manley ceased to live after 14 1/2 minutes, and Brown in 13 1/2; Padgett was dead in 13 minutes.

After hanging 22 minutes, the bodies were cut down and Padgett's was taken out into the yard and placed in a wagon which was in waiting for it, and was driven off by his step-father. The others were taken [to be] buried on the reserve hack of the National Cemetery.

The group of curious lookers-on dispersed. The Frontiers marched back to their Armory, and in ten minutes afterward no one would have known there had been a hanging within miles of the place.

Marshal Dell deserves great credit for the efficient management he showed in conducting the affair and the considerate manner in which he treated the condemned. The clothes given them and the coffins furnished were better than those generally given criminals. There was not the slightest hitch about anything and many are the compliments passed on him for the feeling he evinced on the occasion...[68]

A Leap for Life

Charlie Thomas killed a man in the Indian Territory [in 1877] and turned himself in, claiming self-defense. He was brought before Judge Parker and found guilty of murder. As the Judge was reading the usual formula in passing sentence, the prisoner, who was not shackled, gathered himself up and sprang like a panther straight at the judge. At first it looked like he was attacking the judge, but later it was learned he was leaping for the only open and unguarded window, behind the Judge's chair on the west side of the courtroom, leading out only four hundred yards to the Poteau River, wherein he might swim to freedom.

He bounded up onto the bench [the judge's desk] and was about to vault on over and out the window when his foot caught a railing behind the bench. As the momentarily stunned bailiffs sprang into action Judge Parker caught the prisoner by the shirt collar and pulled him back down.

He struggled, but the Judge ordered him released and left unshackled until he finished reading the sentence, at which time the man was carried directly to the jail.[69]

The Hangman

The most colorful and misunderstood character in Judge Parker's court was the executioner George Maledon. The world at large first learned of Maledon in S.W. Harman's book **Hell on the Border,** *printed by the Elevator publishing company that had printed so many of the stories in its newspaper. Harman had* *been the foreman of the jury that convicted Cherokee Bill, and in addition to publishing his book also toured with Maledon. Persistent false stories have developed about Maledon being ghoulish, but contemporary accounts show this to be "urban legend."*

The **Fort Smith Elevator** *of December 30, 1898, reported on the tour as follows:*

> Soon after the close of the old court's jurisdiction over the Indian Territory in the autumn of 1896, Mr. Harman made arrangements and secured the services of George Maledon, "the Prince of Hangmen," who, as an officer of the court, had been the instrument by whom many of the condemned felons had suffered death, as provided by law, and made a tour of the country, stopping mainly at the smaller towns, and, in a tent, exhibited Maledon, the ropes he had used...and a large quantity of photographs of notorious outlaws.
>
> "...people of all classes flocked to the show ground, crowded about the lecturer and filled the tent, viewing the gruesome relics and listening to the old hangman's recital of soul-stirring events..."[70]

The Executioner's Craft

He hanged eighty-eight men who were convicted under Parker and was so thorough in his arrangements that he never made a failure. He prepared "dummies"—wooden logs the same length [as the height] of the men to be hung—oiled the ropes, dropped the dummies down through the trap and allowed the ropes to stretch so they [the victims] would not turn around. When the drop fell each victim would be in the same position as when [he had been] on the platform, feet about twelve inches from the ground. He made an art of execution. I only witnessed one execution—that was the execution of six Indians in January of 1890.

In private life Maledon was very unassuming, very quiet, and mingled with few people. I did not find him repulsive in appearance as was claimed by many.[71]

In fact, George Maledon did not hang all eighty-eight men hanged during Parker's term on the bench. But he did execute the majority of the sentences. On one execution he begged off because the criminal was an ex-Union soldier, like Maledon, and Parker granted his request. Maledon reused his ropes, one rope being used to hang twenty-seven men.

The hanging referred to in the above narrative was that of Harris Austin, John Billee, Jimmon Burris, Sam Goin, Jefferson Jones, and Thomas Willis on January 16, 1890, all convicted murderers.

There are many remarks attributed to George Maledon. After his career ended, he gave lectures and showed off hanging ropes used in his trade as a moral example to turn young people away from crime. Many of the purported interviews with him or alleged transcripts of his talks present him as a ghoul, gloating over his victims. Local people in Fort Smith say that this was not his nature. One printed comment from his term as executioner is generally accepted as being authentic:

He said he has hanged few truthful men, for nearly all he has ever hanged persisted in declarations of innocence, even with their last breath. Just before he left Fort Smith, an old lady, who visited the prison, and was escorted through it by him, asked him if he ever had any qualms of conscience or feared the spirits of the departed. He replied:

"No, I have never hanged a man who came back to have the job done over. The ghosts of men hanged at Fort Smith never hanged around the old gibbet."

While he has often expressed regrets that it became necessary to execute a human being he has always felt that he only performed his duty as an officer of the law.[72]

The Only "Escape" from Parker's Gallows

There was one perfectly planned "escape" from the gallows at [Judge Isaac] Parker's court, but it wasn't quite what you'd expect. A man named Frank Butler had already been convicted of murder, of which he was very likely guilty anyway, and, since

Parker kept court in session long hours to keep up with the case load, Butler was being brought out for a night sentencing.

He was being kept in the stinking, raucous basement jail under the courtroom itself, and two deputy marshals were escorting him, planning to go across a short stretch of grass, up ten steps to the porch, and into the courtroom hall. As Butler stepped out of the basement, and up two steps, he flung out his arms on both sides and knocked the two marshals to the grass. George Maledon turned and quickly locked the heavy door behind them, then stepped out onto the grass and drew his pistol. With a single shot, he downed the running prisoner, and the marshals placed a stone at the spot where Butler fell dead. It was found to be seventy-five yards from the spot where Maledon stood to fire.

But there's more to the story: the dead prisoner's mother and father were waiting outside the walls of the old fort to receive the body! That was the plan. There was at that time no appeal from Parker's court, and the family didn't want to see their son hang. Knowing Maledon's incredible aim, the "escape" was not from death, but from the gallows only.[73]

The Execution of Cherokee Bill

Further insight can be gained into the condemned man's life on the 1880s equivalent of "Death Row" by reading of Cherokee Bill's last days:

> Up to last Thursday [March 12, 1896], Crawford Goldsby, alias Cherokee Bill had made no preparations to meet his doom, but spent much of his time each day in playing poker with other prisoners, manipulating the cards through the gratings of his cell door.
>
> When the news was received from Washington that the President would not [intercede in the case], Bill was removed from his cell on the west side to one near the door on the east side, and was then cut off from communication with his fellow prisoners, none of them being allowed to come in ten feet of his cell without special permission [from the jailor].
>
> He played his last game of poker on Friday last with Charley Smith and Henry Starr, just before he changed cells.

[HIS LAST HOURS] The usual noise and hubbub that is always heard within the big iron cage that surrounds the cells was noticeably lacking this morning. Cherokee Bill's fellow-prisoners, many of them under sentence of death, seemed to be impressed with the solemnity of the occasion, and an air of subdued quiet pervaded the jail. Many of the men who are already standing within the shadow of the gallows gathered in a group near the cell occupied by the condemned man and conversed in low tones. To his most intimate associates since his confinement, Cherokee distributed his small effects. Henry Starr, George Pierce and others were remembered.

By 10:30 the corridor in front of the Cherokee's cell was crowded with newspaper representatives, deputy marshals and other privileged individuals, all taking note of every passing incident. Occasionally the condemned man would throw aside the curtain which concealed the interior of his cell and make his appearance at the grated door in order to give some instructions or to make some request of the officer who stood guard...

From the time he killed [a jailer named] Keating [in an escape attempt] up to the day of his execution he has been kept shackled and confined in his cell, and for a long time no one was allowed to see him, not even his mother. He kept a blanket hung up over the door of his cell, and when visitors called at the jail to see the noted outlaw he would exact a fee from each of them before he would show himself, and by these means he got in considerable money.[74]

Big-Nose George Parrott (sometimes confused with Flat-Nosed George, who rode with Butch Cassidy) suffered terribly from two lynchings, although he was not the only outlaw hanged twice. Beyond that, his corpse suffered a most bizarre fate (see pp. 129–130.) (Courtesy of the Wyoming State Museum, Cheyenne)

Dead Outlaws on Display

IF AN OUTLAW CUT THE HEAD OFF HIS VICTIM
HE WAS A GHOUL...IF A BOUNTY HUNTER CUT
THE HEAD OFF AN OUTLAW TO CLAIM THE
REWARD...

*Two bizarre things accompanied most hangings or violent rob-
beries during the latter part of the Nineteenth Century: the
criminal-turned-victim was often photographed after death,
and grisly "trophies" of the criminals were often displayed in a
sideshow atmosphere under the guise of educating the public of
the evils of whiskey, of crime itself, of leading a "dissipated" life,
and so forth.*

*When Patrick Coughlan (or Coughlin) was executed for
the murders of Constables Stagg and Dawes, at Evanston,
Wyoming, in August 1895, the* **Wyoming Press** *of December 19,
1896, reported the following conversation:*

(Sheriff) "Do you have anything to say?"

(Coughlan) "Nothing, except my request that I don't have my picture taken [after my death]."

Sometimes the photos of criminals killed at crime scenes may have been necessary to identify the criminals or to claim the reward, but photos taken after hangings were only "mementos" for the legal participants.

The taking of body parts from criminals was also sometimes used as a method of identification or for purposes of collecting a reward, and was not illegal in the Nineteenth Century. One example was told by Wyoming Sheriff Malcolm Campbell:

Campbell told that in 1878 a guard on the Carbon County stagecoach killed a South Pass murderer for whom he knew there was a reward offered; he cut off the dead criminal's head and carried it in a gunny sack to Rawlings, as evidence. The reward was not paid for five months, and Campbell expressed the belief that the reward was only paid to allow the authorities to dispose of the "disagreeable evidence."

But body parts were taken for other reasons as well, reasons that would be as illegal today as they are objectionable. Country doctors announced plans to "study the criminal mind" through phrenology, brain size and shape, etc., and showmen exhibited (always for a fee!) heads, hands, ears, brains, and other things under the guise of education and moralization.

Elmer McCurdy

A lot of people think I'm kidding them, but this actually happened: at an amusement park in California, they were filming an episode of [the television program] "The Six-Million-Dollar Man," [in 1976] and the hero was chasing some bad guys through a horror-ride with fiberglass corpses and everything. One corpse was hanging by its neck like an old-time Western outlaw, and during the filming, the corpse was damaged...knocked over, or something...and there were human arm bones inside the arm of the figure. It wasn't a fake, it was a real human corpse, that turned out to be from a carnival back at the turn of the century. The corpse was finally identified, and it was a train robber from Oklahoma.

He [Elmer McCurdy] robbed the wrong train back in 1911, and missed the gold shipment he was trying for. All he got was money from passengers...he had thought it was a freight train...and he went out and got drunk, he was so disappointed. The law caught up with him and he was killed in the shoot-out. No one claimed the body, and the undertaker put the body on exhibit...for educational purposes, you know...to recoup his expenses. Somebody there in Oklahoma knew a good thing when they saw it, so they came up and pretended to be the bereaved relatives, claimed the body and promptly put it on the carnival circuit for years and years. I guess the carnival went broke and sold out.

Anyway, the corpse had carnival tickets in its mouth, and they [Los Angeles County coroner Thomas T. Noguchi and his staff] figured out who it was with the help of the historical society in Oklahoma, and a few years later the body was returned to Guthrie, Oklahoma, by train, met by a black horse-drawn hearse and buried in the pioneer cemetery [in 1977], making him the last old-time outlaw to be buried![75]

Big-Nose George Parrott

My great-great-uncle was George Parrott, lawmen of the time called him "Big Nose" George. He went into the Black Hills [of South Dakota] at the time of the gold rush there, in 1879. From a hideout in the Powder River Country he stole horses, then began to plan a payroll train robbery on the Union Pacific Line just east of Carbon, Wyoming. He may have been in on some of the robberies of the Deadwood treasure coach, but that was never proven.

To rob the payroll train, Uncle George and several other men...including one who was later caught, named "Dutch"...pulled the spikes out of the ties on the "outside" rail of the tracks at a downhill curve. Then they wired the rail so that when the train was coming they could pull the rail over just an inch, and ditch the engine and coal-car on its side. Jesse James did this once, and it crushed the engineer and almost killed the fireman. The day the rail was wired, a section foreman came along inspecting the rails. He saw the wire, understood what it meant, and went on as though he had seen nothing amiss. Then he ran his handcar on to Carbon and flagged the train. Uncle George had kept his men from shooting the foreman, but they knew their plan was foiled when the train didn't come through.

The gang took to the mountain, Elk Mountain in the Medicine Bow Range, and a deputy sheriff named Widdowfield and a Union Pacific railroad detective named [Tip] Vincent came out of Rawlins looking for them. The officers walked into a trap on the slopes of Elk Mountain and were both killed. Their bodies weren't even found for weeks. [Robert] Widdowfield and Vincent were both well-known and respected in the Carbon area, and the local folks were in a lynching mood.

A month or two later "Dutch" was captured, and when he was being transferred from Laramie to Rawlins, the train stopped in Carbon, where a masked mob came on board and carried "Dutch" off. He was lynched from a telegraph pole, because there weren't any trees of hanging size at Carbon.

Two years later, the sheriff at Rawlins, whose deputy had been killed, tracked Uncle George all across Wyoming, South Dakota [Dakotah Territory] and Montana. He caught up to him in Miles City, Montana. By horseback and train, south through eastern Wyoming, the sheriff brought Uncle George back to Cheyenne, then to Laramie, and on toward Rawlins through Carbon. Remembering what had happened to "Dutch," he had the keys to the manacles in the hands of another officer in another car of the train, and Uncle George manacled to the iron frame of the train seat. Sure enough, at Carbon, a mob boarded and demanded the keys. Not finding them on the sheriff, someone got the axe from the wood-car and the seat was broken up. Uncle George was dragged off the train and strung up from the overhead gate-bar of a horse pen. Given some time to talk, after he had been hoisted once, Uncle George confessed to the killings of the two Rawlins lawmen. The crowd was stringing him up again, but local officials broke it up, and turned the prisoner back to the sheriff.

In September of 1880, Uncle George was found guilty of participating in, or even masterminding, the murders on Elk Mountain, and was sentenced to hang...again. He tried to escape, and in the attempt nearly killed the jailer. His escape was prevented, and the mob that gathered took matters into their own hands. They dragged him out to the railroad tracks and ran a rope over another telegraph pole. He was hoisted up to die, but he was a large man, and the rope gave way. Another rope was secured and he was dragged up again; this time he had gotten his hands free from the lightweight rope and he grabbed the pole. He begged to be shot, but the mob wasn't listening. Finally, he lost his grip and swung away from the pole. A local doctor had been persuaded to come along and declare the body dead. When they lowered Uncle George, the doctor said he was still alive. The mob raised him one last time, and left him there until morning. No one from our family went to Wyoming to claim the body. It was turned over to the doctor who had declared him still alive the night before. Many years later, we learned that the body had been used in a kind of medical research.

Uncle George was the only outlaw ever hanged more than once.[76]

The Skeleton in a Barrel

I was living in Rawlins, Wyoming, in 1951, when a strange final chapter developed in the story of the outlaw "Big-Nosed" George. The local dime store was digging a new basement, and they uncovered a tightly sealed whiskey barrel. Inside there was a large skeleton, with its skullcap missing. At first, no one could figure out who it was. Then someone put it all together.

When Big-Nosed George was hanged, nobody claimed the body, and it was given to a local doctor, John Osborne, who announced that he would use the corpse in medical research. He sawed the top off the skull, to "study the criminal mind." His assistant later described the skull in a newspaper interview as "thick-boned, with only one thin place. This indicated a very small mentality. The sutures were grown together and the grey matter could not expand. This led to his life of crime." All this and more came out in the papers in 1951.

Dr. Osborne also removed the skin from part of the corpse [some say it was the chest, others that it was the thighs] and, incredibly, had a pair of shoes made from the skin! Later, Dr. Osborne went on to be governor of Wyoming, then a congressman. This brought the outlaw's story into prominence in about 1896, and some people remembered having read the story when the barrel was opened in 1951. They went to the office of Dr. Lillian Heath, Osborne's assistant, still living in Rawlins, who had kept the skullcap and was using it as a doorstop. When placed on the skull, the top piece fit perfectly, and everyone knew who the skeleton was.[77]

ROBBERY OF FURTEE'S STORE.

THE ENGINEER INTERVIEWED.

MUNCIE SIDING—BRIGANDS COMPEL THE STORE-KEEPER TO FLAG THE TRAIN.

SECTION MEN FORCED TO OBSTRUCT THE TRACK.   THE CONDUCTOR UNDER FIRE.

KANSAS BRIGANDS—ROBBERY OF A RAILROAD TRAIN AT MUNCIE SIDING.—From Sketches by L. T. Stanley.—[See Page 14.]

Kansas Brigands—Robbery of a Railroad Train at Muncie Siding, from sketches by L.T. Stanley. This illustration, from page 13 of Harper's Weekly *for January 2, 1875, has been reprinted once before, about two inches in height, in a book about Jesse James. This is the first legible reprinting of this illustration in this century. The detail of the sketches, based on interviews with victims, acts almost as a photographic series would in depicting the "Jesse James style" of train robbing.*

KANSAS BRIGANDS.

On the 8th ult. an express train on the Kansas Pacific Railroad was stopped and robbed by five masked robbers at a small station called Muncie, in Kansas, a few miles west of Kansas City. About half past three in the afternoon Mr. John Purtee, who owns the village store, saw five men on horseback coming up the track from the direction of Kansas City, each carrying a rifle or carbine. Hitching their horses, they entered the store, masked, silenced Mr. Purtee by threats of shooting, emptied his till, and demanded all the fire-arms in the place. They compelled the section men at work there to block the road, and ordered Mr. Purtee to flag the train. While waiting for its arrival they captured a young farmer, who was riding a rather good mare, and ordered him to dismount. The mare they kept, and taking the sorriest horse of their own, proceeded to shoot it, firing some eight or ten shots into it before it fell down. A wagon containing women and children was also captured, altogether twenty-five persons being guarded by five bold and desperate men.

The train came up a little before four o'clock, and was brought to a stop by the flag. One of the brigands boarded the engine, and compelled the engineer to uncouple the engine and express car from the passenger coaches, and run up the line to where it was blocked. Two of the ruffians then captured the express messenger, and by threatening him with instant death persuaded him to unlock the treasure chest, from which they took $25,000 in greenbacks, $4000 in gold-dust, and some valuable papers. While this was going on some lively firing took place at the conductor, Mr. Brinkenhoff, who was making his way back to flag a freight train following in the rear of the express. He was brought to uninjured, but upon learning that his errand was one of mercy, the brigands allowed him to proceed. When their work was finished they made off. One of the perpetrators of this daring outrage, of which we give several illustrations on page 13, was captured the day afterward in Kansas City, and the money and jewelry found on him identified.

*This article, "Kansas Brigands," accompanied the **Harper's Weekly** illustration seen on page 131. At the time, the robbery had not yet been attributed to the James gang. The "brigands" allowed conductor Brinkenhoff to stop the freight train and prevent a collision, and they merely blocked the track rather than damage the rails as they were said to do in other robberies.*

Jesse and Frank

THE MOST FAMOUS, MOST-LOVED, MOST FEARED
OF THE OUTLAWS: THE OLD LEGENDS, THE OLD
FACTS ...THE NEW LEGENDS, THE NEW FACTS!

The Boldest Robbery Yet!
An Express Train on the Cairo and Fulton R.R. Plundered!
Mail, Express Cars and Passengers Robbed.

The daring and coolness which characterized the robbery of the Hot Springs stage, about a week since, was completely eclipsed on Saturday last by the ROBBERY OF THE EXPRESS TRAIN, from St. Louis on the Arkansas branch of the Iron Mountain Railroad. The express train, which left St. Louis at 9:50 Saturday morning, was due at GAD'S HILL about 4 o'clock the same afternoon, which station it reached within a few minutes of time. Gad's Hill is only a signal station, and comprises not more than half-a-dozen wooden shanties. As the train approached, it was "flagged" and stopped for the purpose of taking on passengers. As soon as it came to a standstill, the switches, both in front and rear of the train, were opened and guarded, so that if the engineer moved it in either direction, the train would inevitable run off the track. To the conductor's cry of "all aboard," FIVE MASKED MEN appeared, and while one, the leader, stood guard on the platform, the others took possession of the train, and immediately proceeded to "go through" the passengers and the mail and express packages. For the following "subsequent proceedings" we are chiefly indebted to Mr. W.N. Wilson, the express messenger on the train. And here let us remark that WILSON'S PLUCK AND SELF-POSSESSION, his coolness and general conduct won not only the favor of all the passengers and employees, but credit from the robbers themselves. As stated, as soon as the train had stopped, four of the bandits jumped aboard, while the leader kept guard and issued instructions. They were all armed with a brace of large revolvers each, and the leader and two others carried double-barrelled shotguns also. They directed their attentions to the mail and express coach. In the compartment assigned to the former they secured the agent, and then, without a moment's unnecessary delay, but deliberately enough, commenced the RANSACKING OF THE MAIL BAGS, and directing their special attention to packages containing registered letters. And their search was not in vain, for here they made the largest haul of the day. With joy the knaves discovered a registered package containing two thousand dollars in currency, forwarded by the Second National Bank of St. Louis, and addressed to the Clark County Bank at Arkadelphia [Arkansas].

[A portion of the clipping is missing, having broken away at a fold.]

RIFLING OF THE EXPRESS CAR. The result of the search was the securing by the bandits of $1108.80...

[The name of persons on the train and amounts they lost in the robbery followed.]

That they are the same party that robbed the Hot Springs stage there is scarcely any doubt. They talked and acted similarly, jocularly mentioned that occurrence two or three times, and one of the horses in their possession was recognized as the one stolen from the stage team.[78]

The Widow and the Banker: A New Theory

The best-known story about the James boys, and you may have heard it, is the one about Jesse and Frank and the widow—

the story of the widow and the banker. This story has presented them as the American Robin Hoods, and the author of *Jesse James Was His Name,* the only fully documented book about them, spent a lot of time trying to track down this story, and never did. I've been working on it, too, and I think it actually did occur, and it occurred after the Gad's Hill robbery, in Missouri in 1875, I think, in January.

The James Brothers stopped at a widow's house for food, and while she was preparing it, she was crying. She had two little children, and they were crying, too. When asked why she was crying, she said she was a young widow, and the mortgage was due on the farm and she couldn't pay it. They supposedly said, "We don't like bankers, either, and what we'll do is, we'll leave enough money here for you to pay off that mortgage. But you be sure to have the banker burn the mortgage."

So they leave, and the banker comes. And to his astonishment, the lady has the money in gold, and he burns the mortgage papers. Then as he leaves, of course, these masked men hold him up and steal all his money.

Well, that story is not unique with the Jameses. I've seen it told about other outlaws. I just recently found out that this story is told about Dick Turpin, the English highwayman, except that it wasn't a widow, it was the innkeeper of Dick's favorite inn, and the banker was the king's tax collector. Now, Jesse James had a very strong sense of humor, and Frank James had studied Shakespeare extensively, and could recite many passages from Shakespeare's works. In *Henry IV, Part 1,* Acts I and II, they go and rob some pilgrims at Gad's Hill. Frank would have known that, and would have chosen the platform at Gad's Hill, Missouri, as a joke. There was no other reason in the world for stopping a train there, except as a joke to anyone learned enough to get it. There wasn't a station there or anything.

Jesse gave one of the conductors a piece of paper, and told him to go on to the next station where there was a telegraph, and to send the story to the *St. Louis Dispatch.* He had written the entire article himself, leaving blank the amount of money taken, to be filled in by the express company. The *Dispatch* printed it word for word, including the headline, as it had been written by Jesse.

I believe that the episode with the widow was also known to Frank, and possibly Jesse, from folklore, and that the story about them instead of Dick Turpin was already being circulated. It would be just like Jesse to see an opportunity, when actually stopping over at a widow's home, to make the folklore become truth. He would have used some of the money from Gad's Hill as part of the extended joke. In one letter to a newspaper the Jameses had signed their names as Dick Turpin and other outlaws from history.

The Jameses were also constantly trying to win public approval, tipping conductors on trains they robbed, saying, "Have a drink on Jesse James," returning money when a woman identified herself as a Confederate widow, or taking money from a working man, and then taking his hand into theirs and examining the callouses, and returning the money saying, "We don't rob honest working men."

They constantly played up to the common people of this part of Missouri to improve their public image. Making the legend of the widow become the truth would have been an opportunity too good to miss. I think it really did happen, both as the origin of and the result of the folktale.[79]

In the opinion of the editors, this "public relations campaign" may have been the reason so many common people did support the James Brothers, and part of the reason Frank James was acquitted not once but twice of any crimes. As Mr. Perry points out in another story, the James Boys were never convicted of a crime.

The Widow and the Banker—II
The urban-legend quality of "The Widow and the Banker" makes it the most-often-heard Jesse James narrative. Here is one version handed down in a Missouri family:

My grandfather, Max Brown, is no longer living, but when I was a boy he told me this story about his grandfather, also named Max Brown. My great-great-grandfather lived in Independence, Missouri, near the James Brothers family farm [in nearby Centerville, now known as Kearney]. In those days, the James boys weren't considered bad men; the local folks looked on them as heroes because they fought against the banks and the railroads [who were accused of stealing from the poor].

Great-great-grandfather Brown had quite a bit of money, but wouldn't keep it in a bank because he didn't trust banks. But he wasn't at all afraid of the Jameses. He kept his money in a trunk at the foot of his bed, and they knew it. He told them that if they ever needed money, they should just come into the house and get it. Sometimes the James boys would come in while my great-great-grandparents were asleep. They would just wake up the next morning and some of the money would be gone, and a few nights later the money would be back.

One time a banker was about to foreclose on a Confederate widow who didn't have enough money to pay the mortgage. The James boys heard about it and came by the house the day the banker was scheduled to go out to the widow's house and issue the foreclosure order. They took enough gold to pay off the widow's note and rode out to the house place. They gave the widow the money and told her to be sure to watch the banker burn the foreclosure order and the note [loan document] from the bank. Then they rode off and hid in the brush.

When the banker arrived, the widow gave him the full amount due. The banker kept asking where she got the money, the widow refused to tell the banker anything, and demanded that he burn the order and the note right then. He had no choice but to do so. When the papers were just ashes in the fireplace, she ordered the banker off her property.

On his way back to Independence, the banker was stopped by masked men, and robbed of all the gold he had just collected. The next night, that gold was back in my great-great-grandfather's trunk![80]

Frank Is Jailed in Laramie

Frank and Jesse James spent some time up here in Wyoming to get far away from the places where they were known and wanted, and even got blamed for a train robbery that they didn't do! [Sam Bass' gang was guilty.] You always hear that Frank and Jesse were never caught, but actually Frank was. Frank was drunk one night in Laramie and was arrested and put in the jail for the night. No one up here recognized him and it wasn't until he had been let go and been gone for several hours that the other prisoners in the jail told the sheriff who Frank was!

The James boys had a ranch up here near Kaycee that they used to get away from the heat. They'd rob a bank and then ride for hours and get miles and miles away and establish an alibi for themselves because no one would guess they could have traveled that far so quickly.[81]

Frank at Sanger Brothers

George D. Hendricks, Texas folklorist, related this to the editors; he heard it from Dr. Morgan Young:

When I was a boy your dad told me this story about Frank James. Frank James was selling shoes and boots for Sanger Brothers in Dallas after he reformed and tried to go straight. While my grandfather was a debt collector, Frank was in the shoe department at about the same time. Morgan [Young] told me this story and it's the only time I remember hearing it, but I can believe it!

One day, here comes this bully...he wants to buy a pair of boots.

The bully saunters up to Frank James; Frank was a very calm and peaceful man, paying attention to his own business.

The bully yells, "I want to buy me a pair of boots! Show me all the boots you got!"

Frank shows him every boot in the whole place.

"Oh, them ain't no good," says the tough character. He stands up and says, "I'll have you know that I am Bill Duggings and I'm the roughest and the toughest, and full of fleas, and I ain't been curry-combed below the knees! Now, just who in the Hell are you?"

Frank just looks up at him and says very calmly, "Well, I'd like to sell you a pair of boots, and if you must know, my name is Frank James."

The bully swallows and says, "I'll take that there last pair!" He pays up and runs out without his change.[82]

Jesse's Gun

Almost everybody claims to have a Jesse James gun. One story about one of the many guns Jesse James is said to have used goes like this: Jesse was riding alone and came to a farmhouse where he knew the family to be sympathetic. He was being pursued at the time and the family hid him in the loft. The lady of the house was an old Negro woman and he gave her a pistol that he did not want to have on him if he should be caught. It must have had some identifying marks. The lady stuck the gun, an old .44 cap-and-ball, into a bucket of lard and smoothed the lard over so the pistol was not visible.

When the danger was past, Jesse left without the gun. The lady kept it in the lard and kept that bucket of lard for years and years. When the lady was in her nineties, before she died, she brought the gun out, perfectly preserved from the grease, and gave it to her family. She told them to save it because Mr. Jesse would be back to get it someday.

I don't know if it's true, but it sure makes a good story![83]

Jesse's Coffin

The first coffin used to bury Jesse James was bought at the very old and established coffin-making firm of Meierhoffer, Fleeman, Smith and Seidenfaden, in Saint Joseph. They sold the James family the coffin that eventually disintegrated in the grave. The James family bought it under the assumption that it was solid metal. The lid was solid metal, with a one-inch-thick glass window over the face of the deceased, but the body of the coffin was wood clad in metal.

I am amazed that you find people who think of the James boys as folk heroes. The James gang killed eyewitnesses to keep from ever being prosecuted, and everyone up around Saint Joseph was pleased when Jesse was dead.

After Jesse was shot, the funeral home and coffin-maker disavowed the James money, saying they had refused to take any tainted money.[84]

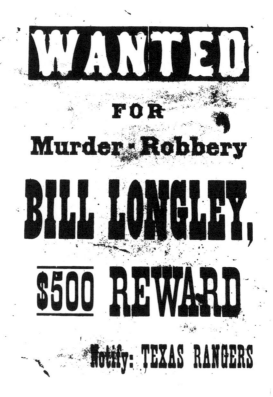

This authentic WANTED *poster, printed on the thinnest newsprint available, shows why so few such posters survive. They were never intended to last, since rewards changed and most criminals were eventually apprehended. In this case no description or specific instructions were needed: everyone in Texas knew or knew of Bill Longley, and it was understood that the nearest ranger could act as the law in his apprehension.*

Villains, Vigilantes, and Villa!

POSTWAR BACKLASH AND OUTLAW DESPERA-
TION IN THE 1870s DEPRESSION BROUGHT
VIGILANTISM TO AMERICA ALONG WITH OTHER
OFTEN UNWANTED GUESTS.

Campbell Captures the Cannibal

One of the most heinous villains in the history of the West seems to have been Alferd Packer, the "Man-Eater." His captor, Wyoming Sheriff Malcolm Campbell, must be, as Packer's nemesis, one of the greatest heroes.

The Packer story begins in Colorado.

A party of twenty-one gold prospectors from Provo, Utah, many of them fresh and tender-footed "pilgrims" from the East, agreed to join a former Union soldier named Alferd Packer on a prospecting trip to the Colorado gold fields in the fall of 1873.

Packer was to be the guide and his expenses paid by the remaining prospectors. Packer claimed to be an expert mountaineer, but led the party of greenhorns into Colorado in the winter. By January they were out of food and were rescued by friendly Ute Indians under chief Youray [Ouray]. Most of the men stayed with the hospitable Utes, but Packer convinced five to go on with him, claiming they would be the first to see "color"—traces of gold— in the spring thaw.

Shannon Wilson Bell, James Humphreys, Frank Miller, George Noon, and Israel Swan were the suckers. They trekked high in the mountains near Lake City, got lost, and camped at an overhang now called Dead Man's Gulch. Trapped in a blizzard, there they sat, slowly starving to death in the winter of 1874.

Later, Packer hiked out alone. He seemed to have some money—more than before—and suspicion fell on him immediately. He blamed the blizzard, saying three men starved, then Bell went snow-crazy and killed George Noon and was eating the dead man's leg when Packer returned from a noble hunting trip. Packer claimed he killed Bell in self-defense—and admitted eating the meat.

Others from Ouray's camp pressured the Indian Agent into an investigation. Two unsuccessful attempts to find the bodies had passed when the bodies were finally found [by John A. Randolph, a sketch artist for *Harper's Weekly,* in August of 1874, after which his grisly sketch of the skeletal and decomposed remains appeared in *Harper's*]. Packer was accused of murder, tried twice under different laws, and found guilty. He escaped, or bribed his way out with money taken from the bodies, and was free for nine years in spite of a $5,000 reward offered for his capture...

Wyoming Sheriff Malcolm Campbell told the story from his viewpoint:

I will always remember Packer, the man-eater...twenty-one prospectors had banded together to go from Salt Lake into Hinsdale County, Colorado, where a big gold rush was on. The party hoped to get through the passes before the snows closed them, but they came to the western foothills of the Rockies and the Indians told them the trails were impassable, so they went into winter quarters.

Packer and five others went on alone. In April, after the spring melt had begun, the sixteen others went on too and came to the Indian Agency of General Adams, and found Packer drinking and gambling. He had been penniless the fall before and the party's suspicion was aroused. A man named John Cabazon [also spelled Cabezon], nicknamed "Frenchy," accused Packer of robbery-murder—no one knew about the cannibalism yet— and the Agent sent a party with Packer and the General's chief clerk to record the findings of the expedition. At camp one night Packer tried to escape and was dragged back to the Agency where he confessed that the men had camped, starving, and one of the party had gone insane from hunger and killed the other four while Packer was away looking for the trail out. Packer said he was obliged to shoot the crazed man in self-defense.

Packer led the search party to the starvation campsite that June [other sources say Packer did not lead the searchers to the bodies]. Four bodies were there, lying in a row, and the fifth was nearby with signs of having been clubbed, not shot. Packer confessed he had cut meat from the bodies and eaten it and carried a large amount with him as he left camp, but he still said he had only killed one man, and that in self-defense. He said he had thrown away the uneaten meat when he came into sight of the Indian Agency.

He said the meat cut from a man's breast was the sweetest he had ever eaten, that he had lived off it for two months, and that he had become very fond of it.

Packer escaped the log jail where he was awaiting trial and was not seen again until 1883 when I was called in to stop a fight at Fort Fetterman [in Wyoming]. I took one "John Swartz" prisoner, locked him in the old government jail, and he was released the next day when an intimidated waiter refused to press a charge against him. A few weeks later John "Frenchy" Cabazon was freighting [by covered wagon] in the area near Fetterman and stayed the night at the road ranch of John Brown on LaPrele Creek. There he recognized Swartz as Packer, although Packer did not get a good look at Cabazon. Cabazon came to me and we obtained a letter of orders to arrest Packer/Swartz at once.

My brother, Dan, who had followed me West and worked as a freighter, was sometimes my deputy and I appointed him to accompany me to Crazy Horse's cabin on Wagon Hound Creek, where Swartz had relocated. We drove up in a buckboard and saw Swartz, whom I recognized, out and about the yard, unarmed. Seizing this as our best chance, we wheeled the wagon into the haystack and jumped out covering Swartz.

While I was handcuffing him he said this was the first time in twenty years he had been out without his gun and we would never have taken him had he been armed. I read the telegram from Albany County Sheriff Louis Miller, checked the telegram's identification signs—the forefinger of the left hand off at the second joint and the little finger of the same hand off at the first joint, the missing two upper front teeth (now replaced by artificial teeth)—and we fixed dinner and fed the horses before the ride back. Packer sat beside me while I drove the buggy and Dan kept the Winchester ready.

That was Friday. The next Monday we took the stage to Laramie City, spending the night at Point of Rocks in Downey Park. I catnapped beside Packer as he slept.

The snow stopped us once or twice and Packer and a lady passenger stood aside while the driver and I shoveled the way clear. At Rock Creek we spent the night in a hotel in an upstairs room with two beds. I didn't sleep at all, but the man-eater seemed to sleep well. The next day we took the train from Rock Creek to Laramie, where the sheriff met us, and, to Packer's disgust, there was a huge crown of gawkers.

Sheriff Miller and I took him to Cheyenne the following day where another crowd was gathered. We turned him over to Clair Smith, sheriff of Hinsdale County, Colorado.[85]

Malcolm Campbell never received any reward for arresting Packer, and never gave the rather routine assignment any more thought. He was rather surprised to become famous for the act. He was present when Packer signed his second confession, which still probably did not reflect the truth of the bizarre incident.

Packer was sentenced to hang, but a loophole in the law caused him to be sentenced to forty years in prison. He was paroled by the governor of Colorado in 1901 as the result of a publicity campaign to increase the circulation of a Denver newspaper. After living a while in Sheridan, Wyoming, he died and was buried in Littleton, Colorado—the only convicted cannibal in the United States up to that time.

Alf Bolen's Foster Parents

My great-great-grandfather was Calvin Cloud, and he and my great-great-grandmother took in and raised Alf Bolen [sometimes spelled Bolin], the man from whom Murderers' Rock got its name and reputation. [Murderers' Rock is also called just plain Murder Rock by some of the locals, and it is a large promontory that stands above the old Springfield road that led southward from Springfield, Missouri, through Ozark and into Forsyth, then south into the wilds of north Arkansas.] From that rock Alf and his gang sighted, stalked, waylaid, and murdered more than two dozen travelers. Alf was an orphan from New Orleans, and the Clouds took him in and raised him like a son at their home near the old settlement of Ponce De Leon, called Poncy, in Stone County, Missouri.

Alf left the Clouds as a young man and ended up riding with Sam Hildebrand, the southeast Missouri guerrilla leader. But he wasn't loyal to the Confederacy, he just stayed long enough to learn some of Hildebrand's tactics, then he came back into Stone County—this is before Taney County was split up. He and his band of outlaws had been robbing and killing civilians on both sides of the conflict, and the Union Army made a special sortie to capture or kill him in 1862. Two companies of soldiers left at the same time from Reeds Spring, and the other from Galena, and caught the Bolen gang in a pincer-like maneuver. There was a pitched battle, and most of the gang were killed.

Three men and two horses, with only one gun amongst them, got away. Alf was one that got away. He and his two fellows went up the James River to where Great-great-grandfather Cloud lived and they rode onto the family farm wearing their hoods. Great-great-grandpa came out at the sound of hooves and one of the hooded riders demanded in a loud voice that they be given three fresh horses and all the guns and shells on the farm. Great-great-grandpa walked off the porch and recognized the voice of Alf.

"Why, Alf," he said, "don't you know you can have anything on this farm that you need?"

Seeing that he had been recognized, Alf took the one rifle and shot great-great-grandpa dead on the stoop. Great-great-grandma came out and Alf shot at her, but missed and she fell to the floor. Thinking the neighbors would have heard the shots the three men rode away on their two tired horses. Alf continued to terrorize the Forsyth area for two more years before he was killed.

After Alf's death, Great-great-grandma Cloud was called over to Ozark to identify Alf's severed head. She rode through a snowstorm to reach the Union outpost at Ozark and identify the head of the man she had loved and raised as a boy. She was the only living soul not wanted by the law who could identify Alf, and she was proud to do it.[86]

Hampton Holt's Story

When I was a boy Hampton Holt told me he was about fourteen or fifteen years old and was helping drive a freight wagon along the Springfield-Galena-Berryville road. There was a Civil War skirmish at Galena one day. Hampton crawled back under the loading dock where the wagon was parked to keep from being hit by a bullet. He said the smoke from the black powder guns was so thick that he couldn't see his hand in front of his face.

I figured out years later, after Hampton was dead, that the confrontation he had witnessed was when the Federal troops came in 1862 to stop the guerrilla activity after the murder of the

Federal paymaster at the Slick Rock Crossing on the James River. This was the same action that wiped out most of Alf Bolen's first gang.

The legend is that, even though the paymaster and all his men were killed, they succeeded in hiding the gold coin somewhere near the Slick Rock Crossing.

The Federal troops at Berryville were earning between fifteen and eighteen dollars a month, and there were five hundred Federal troops in Berryville at the time. So, it was a considerable amount of gold the bushwhackers were after. And it's still there today.[87]

Alf and Uncle Billy Smith

Alf Bolen has always been credited with the killing of "Uncle" Billy Smith, an old man who lived alone at Pinetop in Taney County, near the Arkansas state line. When Smith's body was found, it was missing its ears, which were lying in the cabin. There were signs that Bolen and his men had come looking for money, tortured and beat the old man to death, and when no money was found, they threw Smith's body into a nearby gully and stayed in the cabin until the food was gone before moving on.[88]

The Death of Alf Bolen

The Union Army put out a reward of $1,000 for the capture or killing of Alf Bolen, and the troops rode the countryside constantly in search of Bolen and other bushwhackers and robbers. Company B of the First Iowa Cavalry was occupying Ozark, and they took a prisoner named Richards, who lived with his family near Highlandville, and was an acquaintance of Bolen's. Richards was told that any charges against him would be dropped if he could help kill or capture Bolen. He agreed to try in return for a pardon from the military court.

It was January of 1863, and an Iowa private dressed in civilian clothes went with Mrs. Richards back to the cabin, and the young son went to Alf Bolen's hideout with a message. Alf came to the Richards' place and was told of Richards' capture.

While he was kneeling at the fireplace for warmth, and drinking a cup of coffee, the Iowa private stepped out of hiding and clubbed Bolen unconscious. Daring not to risk Bolen reviving—Bolen was a powerful man—the soldier struck again and again until he was sure the murderer was dead. The body was taken outside and its head removed with an axe. The body was left in the deep snow and the three—the soldier, the woman, and her son—walked through the snow back to Ozark.

After the head was identified, Richards was freed and went with his family and a small troop of Federal soldiers back to his cabin where the body was buried in an unmarked grave.

Back in the 1970s, some flatlanders who had moved to Forsyth thought it would be a good idea to have a tourist festival and call it "Alf Bolen Days." A few quiet phone calls from the local folks explained the real nature of the man and the flatlanders quickly dropped the idea.[89]

The Hogs Ate It

Even though it is strictly against military regulations, the Union Army at Ozark put Alf Bolen's head on display on a high pole for several days. A high winter wind blew it down, pole and all, one night, and…apparently…the hogs ate it.[90]

Belle at Marble Cave

My grandfather, Truman Powell, took Belle Starr through Marble Cave [now known as Marvel Cave] in south-western Missouri in about 1886. When tours of the cave were first being given to the public to recoup some of the losses from never having found any precious minerals in the cave, a woman came to Truman and said she wanted to tour the cave. Back then you entered the cave on wooden ladders and the tour was by lantern-light. She said she was looking for her brother. She had heard reports that the Baldknobbers, a vigilante organization, had thrown a bushwhacker, an ex-Confederate, into the cave to die.

Truman said that the miners had never seen any bones down in the cave, but she insisted, saying she might see or recognize a button or some other relic that might be found. He led her in and around the Big Room, now called the Cathedral Room, and back out. She found nothing. After she left, one of the men there said anxiously,

"Don't you know who that was?"

Truman said no.

"Why, that was Belle Starr," said the other man.[91]

The Founding of the Baldknobbers

*One of America's most colorful and controversial vigilante organizations came into the American consciousness when Harold Bell Wright wrote his novel **The Shepherd of the Hills**. The story presents the latter-day Baldknobbers, who were first organized as a law enforcement group, then ordered to disband, then reorganized clandestinely as a sometimes law-breaking gang.*

Many Ozark natives still take sides quietly with their ancestors who were Baldknobbers or who were anti-Baldknobbers, and prefer not to discuss their family folklore. One prominent Ozark lawyer, a direct descendant of the man who wrote the group's constitution (which was then memorized and burned), would like to show how the early-day Baldknobbers were honest and respectable men. Here is his account:

My grandfather, Alonzo S. Prather, was born in Mount Vernon, Indiana, the son of Hiram Prather, who was an officer in the U.S. Army in the war with Mexico. Alonzo S. was graduated from a now-defunct college in Southwestern Indiana, and he and his five brothers and father all volunteered for service in the Union Army the day Fort Sumter fell. He became a second lieutenant, fought at Shiloh, was wounded in the battle of Chickamauga, took part in the Battle of Atlanta and marched with Sherman to the sea, and remained with Sherman to the end of the rebellion...

He was appointed receiver of lands for Arkansas, and lived in Harrison...[later] he was made or appointed prosecuting attorney of Madison County, Arkansas, and lived at Huntsville. He was appointed Superintendent of Education for all the counties of northwest Arkansas. He went over that wild country setting up rural schools in people's homes. While in Huntsville he was selected as one of the commission that established the Arkansas Agricultural and Industrial College [later the University of Arkansas] and his name is on the cornerstone of the original building. It must be understood, of course, that he was one of the so-called carpetbaggers by the rebels...

From Arkansas the family moved by covered wagon to Kansas...The family moved from Kansas to Taney County, Missouri, and had a farm on what is now known as the Long Beach Road. He was a neighbor of the Nat Kinney family. [One of the thirteen original founders of the Baldknobbers.] In Taney County he practiced law and dealt in land. He was a Mason and one of the leaders of the Grand Army of the Republic [Union veteran's organization]....He was elected several terms to represent Taney County in the Missouri House of Representatives.

During the time that the Taney County Courthouse was destroyed by fire, he was able to obtain the enactment of an appropriation of five thousand dollars from the state of Missouri to aid in replacing the courthouse.

Alonzo was one of the original thirteen men who organized the vigilante committee officially designated in the records as the Committee for Law and Order, later dubbed "the Baldknobbers" by their bushwhacker [Southern sympathizer] foes. Mark Twain, writing of the West in one of his books, stated that the West could not have been settled without its vigilantes. There is an official badge of the group still in existence in Taney County, in the possession of Mrs. Maude Nagel...It is a red silk ribbon with black lettering which reads "Citizens for Law and Order. Stand Up for Taney County."

I shall not go into the Baldknobber story except to say that most modern writers have followed the line of Harold Bell Wright in his book *The Shepherd of the Hills* and painted the vigilantes as bad men. Wright was not writing history, but a novel—a love story—and he added the character of Wash Gibbs [a villain] for "color." Allow me to say that all this [true history of the Baldknobbers] happened shortly after the Rebellion. The

Ozark Mountains area was filled with ex-bushwhackers and thieves, and no civil law existed...the men who organized the vigilantes, most of them, had recently returned from that war [serving the Union Army]. They were accustomed to order and discipline. Many had returned home to learn from their families of the dreadful treatment all had received from the bushwhackers...[92]

The Committee was in existence from January 1885 until May 1886. Captain Kinney called the members together for a meeting on the courthouse lawn at Forsyth, about five hundred men. Alonzo wrote the articles of dissolution. Governor Marmaduke had sent the adjutant general, Jamison, to Forsyth, where he met with Captain Kinney and other members and suggested that they disband.
And so they did.

Bill Miles and the Baldknobbers

My father used to tell us about a bad man that originated up in Taney County, Missouri, during the Baldknobber days...his name was Bill Miles. This Miles got in an altercation with one of the Baldknobbers and killed one of them. Nat Kinney was the captain of the Baldknobbers, and Miles swore they could not get justice in Taney County, and got a change of venue up to Springfield.

Nat Kinney had lived in Springfield and run a saloon there, and had fallen in an open construction pit on the sidewalk (it may have been a cellar) and had sued the city of Springfield. The Miles thought that might help their case! They lost the case, but the Baldknobbers were out to get the Miles boys.

So Miles, or so my father said, was at the Fourth of July picnic and at the spring for a drink of water...maybe he was trying to get a drink for an older lady. The Taney County sheriff and one of his deputies converged on him, and he knew they aimed to kill him. Miles pulled his gun first and killed them both. He fled to Texas, and then to Colorado and killed a trail boss out there. Somebody who knew him, dad said, saw old Bill working on a ranch in Oklahoma and said his hair was snow white.

The folks there on the ranch in the bunkhouse said they heard a horse coming up on the mountain one night, and Bill ran and got a Winchester and put a shell in the barrel and got behind the door.

The old boy that came in was one of the crew. The Bible says "the guilty flee when no man pursueth." Anyway that was the last my dad ever heard of old Bill Miles.

He had started out to be a Western bad man. He had at least four killings to his credit. But he just ended up a white-haired old man who was always on edge.[93]

Shelton and the Baldknobbers

My dad used to tell about the hanging of three of the Baldknobbers. A special fence was built around the scaffold to keep the huge crowd that gathered to witness the hanging from interfering. They cut a hole out of the jailhouse through the wall straight into the enclosure so the condemned men would not have to pass through the crowd of supporters and detractors and start a riot.

One poor condemned, his neck didn't break when he dropped down through the trap, and they went down to get him, and he begged them not to hang him again. He was bleeding out the nose, and they said they had to, it was the law, and he said, "Well, for God's sake, get it over with!"

They hanged him the second time and that time it "took," and that was more or less the end of the Baldknobbers.

The reason my dad talked about the Baldknobbers so much was that one of my cousins "creased" one of them with a bullet. He had had a run-in with one of the "captains" of a division of Baldknobbers, a former Union officer. His name was Shelton, my cousin was, and in an argument the "captain" grabbed an old saber off the wall and charged him, and he ran for his life. When they ran past the chop block, and the axe was there, he swooped it up and chased the "captain" back to the house. He cut his coat in the back and he (the cousin) ran into the house. A few minutes later, my dad said, after the Baldknobbers had left, he thought my cousin heard a cowbell out in the cornfield, but he was suspicious and told his wife, "That's not our cow."

He loaded his gun up and found out where the movement was out in the field of corn, and what row the bell was in, and fired out that way.

The bell went silent, but it sounded like a whole herd of cows running away through the corn. After a minute or two the "bell cow" got up and ran away, with the bell clattering, so my cousin figured he'd creased the Baldknobber.

Well, that cousin went out to the Black Hills after that, to get away from the feuds, and I'm not too sure he didn't end up an outlaw himself.

I heard about a bank robbery in Utah where the robbers did everything wrong. The man that held the horses was waiting in the wrong place, they left so fast that they left the money they had gathered up on the counter, each one thinking the other one had it, and they all three ended up shot. One of them was named George Shelton, and that was my cousin's name, so maybe that's where he met his end.[94]

At "The Shepherd of the Hills"

My family, the Garrisons, were Christian County Baldknobbers, descended from a Revolutionary War hero. When the controversy got heavy, my family went to Arkansas for a few years. The Baldknobbers in Harold Bell Wright's novel were composite characters, but some of the names suggest real people. The villain in the novel *The Shepherd of the Hills* is Washington "Wash" Gibbs, and there was a real Baldknobber named Wash Middleton. Glen Braden, the young actor who played Wash Gibbs in our outdoor drama last year is the great-grandson of Sam Snapp, a man who was murdered by Wash Middleton.

One of our actresses who plays Sammy Lane, the heroine of the novel, is Mindy Stewart. When the Baldknobbers dragged the Taylor Brothers out of the Forsyth jail and hanged them as their first vigilante act, the Taylor brothers were in jail charged with the killing of Mindy's great-grandparents.

We have in the cast of our play several descendants from people on both sides of the vigilante war. Most of the participants in the conflict were just swept up in it, without much choice, forced to take one side or the other.[95]

Kid Wade and the Vigilantes

Kid Wade, the famous Nebraska outlaw was a relative of mine. I can't recall exactly how we're related...he's a cousin...but the Historical Society traced the family and worked it out for me. The kid was hanged when he was just out of his teens. He was controversial, and was at the top of the wanted list put out by the Nebraska vigilantes. When "Doc" Middleton was arrested...I think that was 1882...he escaped and left the country. A year later he was arrested on a farm in Iowa. My folks lived at Le Mars, Iowa, at the time. He was tried and convicted of horse-stealing, and spent a year in the state prison at Anamosa.

After he was let out, he went up around Carnes, Iowa, and got in trouble for some large-scale horse theft up around Sioux City. He escaped again and was tracked by the vigilantes to the farm at Lemars. There were four of the Holt County vigilantes, and they caught him by trickery in January 1884. He was taken back to Nebraska by way of Boyd County. They went from Carnes to Long Pine to Morrison's Crossing to Bassett.

While he was being held secretly in Long Pine by the vigilantes in February, he was questioned closely and his statements seriously implicated a number of prominent county residents as being part of the trail along which stolen horses were moved. The vigilantes apparently realized that the Kid could never stand trial in open court and give out these statements that would damage the reputations of local citizens who might or might not have been guilty.

One Long Pine resident named Carlton Pettijohn, Sr. claimed that everyone on the jury would be as guilty as the Kid. Anyway, he was convicted by a vigilante court, but by nightfall another party of vigilantes, said to have been led by Captain

O'Neill, came and got the Kid. It was Carlton Pettijohn, Jr. that gave me some of the details of the story. He's still living. Old Mr. Pettijohn was the first settler in the Long Pine area, and my wife's family was the second family of settlers there in that two-county area.

Anyway, that same night the vigilantes took the Kid away, saying that the vigilante court had enough evidence to take him to trial at the Holt County seat. But instead, they went fifteen miles the other way, to Morrison's Crossing. Now, they actually turned the Kid over to the county sheriff, named Herschheiser, and his deputies, but that may have just been to clear the vigilantes of what came next. Another group of masked men took the Kid away from the sheriff that night after the sheriff, two deputies, and the Kid had stopped for the night back at Martin's Hotel in Bassett.

There were about a dozen masked men with their revolvers drawn, maybe the vigilantes, and maybe local citizens who would have been implicated in any court trial.

They took the Kid and left. The next morning he was found hanged from a railroad whistling post on the east edge of Bassett. The body was frozen. Now, I've also heard it told that when the passenger train came in that morning the body was found atop two cords of wood, having been hanged and already cut down.

I guess the biggest part of the Kid's horse stealing had been to take a party up across the border to the Indian reservations and steal a large number of unbranded Indian ponies. Then they would come back from Dakota Territory and move the horses east at safe places each night, selling the horses as wild ponies as they traveled east. And he paid the price for it!

Another branch of my family that had homesteaded at Valentine, a cousin, was on that passenger train that morning. Long Pine was as far as the rail line went west. He was just coming west then and he saw this Kid Wade that had been hung, and he almost got on the train and went back home to Iowa![96]

Villa and the Doughboys

Pancho Villa and his men were consummate experts at fighting, fleeing, and seeking sanctuary in the northern Mexican desert. It was a common occurrence that federales pursuing Villa's men would encamp in the center of an arroyo or canyon for the night, and the villistas would be encamped only a few hundred meters above them in a cave in the canyon wall, watching with amusement and overhearing the frustrated federales' conversations. When Pershing pursued Villa after the Columbus raid this same event transpired.

Pershing and his men sat around a fire in a wide arroyo seco, and Villa himself stood at the mouth of an overhang, listening from above them when the gringo soldiers began to sing camp songs in the twilight as they were eating their beans.

After a while he turned to his men under the ledge, removed his cigarro, and said, *"¿Se hadó el buey con tapadero?"* [translating] "The ox got drunk with blinders on? What a ridiculous song! These gringos are ridiculous!"

He walked away from the ledge.

It wasn't until years later, when one of Villa's men told the story, that someone figured out and explained what the gringos were singing...

"It's a long way to Tipperary..."[97]

Villa's Raid

While we lived at Mesilla [New Mexico] we went to El Paso to see a friend, Judge R.L. Nichols. [My wife] Polly's [previously] broken ankle was giving her unending suffering and we wanted to find a good bone specialist for her...While Polly was in the hospital at El Paso, Pancho Villa raided Columbus, New Mexico, a small town across the border from old Mexico.

It was before dawn of March 16, 1916, that Villa attacked Camp Furlong and the one-cow town of Columbus, protected by the Thirteenth Cavalry. The attack was well-planned and some of the Villa men were recognized as having been in the town a few days before to scout out the defenses. The soldiers and civilians all ran out in their nightclothes, firing what guns they could get to. Downtown, the Villa men raided stores and shot businessmen [who lived above their shops and came down to protect their interests].

When dawn came the Villa men retreated because they became easy targets for the rifles and machine guns of the soldiers. It had been a brutal massacre of civilians and some loss of life to the cavalry. One woman, a Mrs. Hall, was a victim of the terrible raid. She saw her husband killed and then his body pulled out on the doorstep and beaten beyond recognition. Mrs. Hall ran out into a field and tore strips off her clothing to bind a bullet wound to her hip. She was found the next morning and brought to El Paso to have the bullet removed. She was placed in the room with Polly and told the story to her and to me.[98]

Isham Dart (often called Isom Dart), the "gentleman rustler" of Colorado and Wyoming, was one of the best-known black outlaws. (Courtesy of the Wyoming State Museum, Cheyenne)

Red and Yellow, Black and White

THE SUNDAY SCHOOL SONG ABOUT JESUS' LOVE SUMS UP THE RACIAL MIX IN THE WEST: ALL RACES OF THE EARTH JOINED IN THIS IN- CREDIBLE ADVENTURE, WHEREIN WOMEN PLAYED PROMINENT ROLES ON BOTH SIDES OF THE LAW.

Isham Dart—I

According to the stories circulating in Wyoming in the 1930s, Isham Dart's "place" was at Brown's Park, a clearing in the forest in Colorado. Isham [or Isom] had a place at the head of Beaver Creek that consisted of a log cabin, a stable, and a pole corral. The cabin was furnished with a small cookstove, a bunk filled with hay on which a bedroll could be spread, and a table and chairs. The legend, or rumor, is that Tom Horn lived for a while with Matthew Rash, another rustler, and later shot him from ambush. Isham Dart is supposed to have gone south for a year to escape Horn, but after returning, was shot again, supposedly by Tom Horn.[99]

Isham Dart—II

Isham Dart was the "gentleman bandit." He never used his gun unless he had to, and was never known to shoot anyone, only threaten them if they didn't cooperate, which they did. He had been born a slave, and fought as a camp aide in the Civil War. He was known as Ned Huddleston until the "Tip" Gault gang, of which he was a member, was killed off while he was out of the camp. He took the name Isham Dart and a new identity, going straight until suspicion was off him.

He was an excellent horseman, horse breaker, and horse thief. He was shot by Tom Horn, the former Indian interpreter, who had been hired as a regulator by the Wyoming stockmen.[100]

Bass Reeves Rode for Parker

Indian Territory had a large population of black Indians, freed slaves of the Five Civilized Tribes who were adopted into the tribes as full members after the War, and a considerable population of other blacks who came to the Indian nations and Oklahoma Territory because there was land available to rent, sharecrop, or homestead. Many famous black law enforcement officers served the Indian nations and the United State Courts in the Twin Territories representing the approximately 16% of the population of that race.

Bass Reeves, a black deputy United States marshal for Judge Parker's court, was one of the most interesting officers. None of the black officers ever rose to the office of marshal, they were always deputies, but the deputies did most of the hard work of capturing the outlaws wanted by the court. Bass had an incredible memory; he couldn't read or write, so he would take his subpoenas...a whole stack of them...to a fellow officer who would read them out loud. Bass would memorize every detail of every subpoena hearing it only once.

He went up against some of the roughest characters: one time his hat brim was shot off, his reins were shot out of his hands, and the legend has it that on one occasion his belt buckle was even shot off by a shot from the side! Yet out of his nineteen years of service, he himself was never shot.

Bass had a fast horse, a sorrel, and two different times an outlaw would get away from him because of that horse. One time Bass apprehended an outlaw, and the outlaw talked him into a bet that his horse could outrun Bass'. Bass took him up on the bet, with his pride in his own horse, and the two took off on a race. The outlaw pulled ahead by the time they'd reached the tree they'd agreed to race to, and the outlaw looked back. There sat Bass on his horse tearing up the subpoena! The other time, the guy's horse was just faster than Bass', and Bass never caught up to him.[101]

Bass Reeves and Yah-Kee

Bass Reeves' most unusual adventure came when he captured an Indian named Yah-Kee. He took the Indian back to camp where the other outlaws were being held on a long "round-up" of wanted men. Yah-Kee had a medicine bag made out of gopher skin, that had his charming things in it: beads, animal hair, dried herb dust and all, in the bag. Bass had him handcufffed with the other guys at the camp fire, and the Indian kept looking over at him, smiling. Bass began to feel real sick. He kept getting weaker...so he went over to Yah-Kee and snatched his medicine bag away from him and started to throw it into the river.

Yah-Kee begged and pleaded with Bass not to throw the bag into the river, he swore he'd be his slave for life if only he wouldn't throw the medicine bag into the river. But Bass didn't listen; he threw it in. As soon as the gopher bag was gone, Bass began to feel better...but Yah-Kee took sick, and fell over and died during the night.

Another of Bass Reeves' adventures is more humorous:

Bass had dressed up like a tramp, and walked twenty-six miles from the camp where the prisoners were chained, all the way to the house of two outlaws for whom he had a subpoena.

He told the outlaws' mother that he was himself wanted by the marshals. He talked her into the proposition of working with her sons, as part of their gang to protect each other. So, the sons came around later that evening, and agreed to the whole thing. Their mother made a big meal for them all and they went to bed. That night, while the brothers were asleep, Bass handcuffed them together, and woke them up and made them walk back to his camp, twenty-six miles. Their mother followed Bass about the first six miles, cussin' him loud and long for having slept under her roof and eaten at her table!

He was something else! After statehood, Bass stopped working as a deputy marshal...most of the black officers did...and he became a police officer in Muskogee, and worked there until he retired. But while he was deputy marshal, he was amazing. He also used to preach to his prisoners at night, he had a sort of "captive" audience and he'd preach around the campfire and quote scripture to them, trying to get them to mend their ways.[102]

Zeke Miller and the Handcar

Another famous black deputy U.S. marshal for Judge Parker was Zeke Miller:

Zeke Miller, in his eighteen or nineteen years of service to the United States Court, never fired a shot! He had a large posse that worked with him, and he planned the arrests and directed the captures, but he let his posse do all the shooting.

One time, Zeke went after some men who were miles away down by a railroad track where no one could sneak up on them. Zeke went to the station master and borrowed a handcar. He went down, came up behind the outlaws, arrested them and brought them back on the handcar. But the younger one of the two outlaws, when he went to prison, Zeke wrote letters to him, and talked to him about reforming his ways. And Zeke's letters and the experience of being a prisoner made the kid reform.

Zeke liked kids, and had six or seven kids, and ran a grocery store when he wasn't rounding up criminals. His wife and kids would work the store while he was out doing his deputy marshal's duties. One time he was out looking for three guys he had warrants for, and he was out for days, and couldn't find them. He came back home all despondent because he couldn't find them. His wife was all excited because three strangers had come by the house that day, and she had fed them. He asked her to describe them and it turned out they were the ones he had been looking for! And she had fed them: he's out there on the range looking for them, and they're eating at his house.

Zeke was a marshal for a long time, and never shot anyone.[103]

Other black officers worked for the Nations:

Jake Lewis and Cherokee Bill

Jake Lewis was a black deputy sheriff in the Cherokee Nation. Lewis was at a dance one night where Crawford Goldsby, known as "Cherokee Bill," got into a fight and was about to kill another man. Lewis "buffaloed" Bill [hitting him upside of his head with the barrel of his pistol], knocked him unconscious, stopping the fight.

The next day, Lewis went out to his barn to get his horse, and when he walked in Cherokee Bill jumped up out of the hay manger where he had been hiding all night. He shot and wounded Lewis, and after that, having shot a peace officer, Cherokee Bill went off and joined the Cook gang.[104]

Mary Fields and the Freight Wagon

Getting away from Oklahoma, [the teller changes subjects] the most colorful black woman in the West, to me, was Mary Fields. She lived in the Cascades. She was as tall as I am; she was six-foot-three, a big woman. But in her sixties she was riding for the Pony Express! She was a mail carrier, and when she was in her seventies, she ran a laundry, and she used to work for the Ursuline nuns, hauling freight for the Ursuline convent in the Cascades, in Montana. She was fighting off robbers who tried to stop her freight wagon, and she outran outlaws when she was riding for the Pony Express. Nobody wanted to mess with Mary Fields![105]

Angel of Mercy—II

I believe Calamity Jane died in 1903...or 1904...but she had done an awful lot of good for the people of Deadwood [South Dakota] and whatever Calamity Jane wanted she would just go into a saloon and fire off a shot and everyone would stop and listen to whatever she had to say.

She was a good teamster, a very honest person, a crack shot with a rifle, and the one everyone wanted to have around if there was Indian trouble.

My mother used to say that Poker Alice and Calamity would come by the store and say, "Now, Anna"—that was my mother's name—"such-and-such a family out here is destitute. They've got a bunch of kids; they don't have enough to eat or clothes to wear. I want this sent out to them and this," and she'd pile up an order and she'd pay for it all and tell Mother not to tell them where it had come from.

Now, Hogle's Bar in Crawford, Nebraska, had one room for the ladies. A lot of people today don't realize that a lot of the ladies out West used to smoke and drink. They'd go around to the side door by the Hotel and they had a nice room fixed up just for ladies, so ladies could go in there and have their drink in peace and quiet and didn't have to go out front.

Now the girls that worked there, the saloon girls, they were out front waiting on the men.[106]

The Hanging of Cattle Kate—I

A DOUBLE LYNCHING...the man weakened but the woman cursed to the last.

A man and a woman were lynched near historic Independence Rock on the Sweetwater River in Carbon County [Wyoming] Sunday night [July 21, 1889]. They were postmaster James Averill and a virago who had been living with him as his wife for some months. Their offense was cattle stealing, and they

Wyoming's Cattle Kate, shown in her most famous photograph, was the alias of Ella Watson, who was hanged by vigilantes as a rustler. Her hanging helped trigger the Johnson County War between large-ranch stockmen and small-outfit cowboys who rustled on the side. (Courtesy Wyoming State Museum, Cheyenne)

operated on a large scale recruiting quite a bunch of young steers from the range of that section.

News of the double hanging was brought to Rawlins by a special courier and telegraphed to Foreman George D. Henderson of the 76 outfit, who happened to be in the capital. Mr. Henderson's firm has its own ranch in that country and has been systematically robbed by rustlers for years.

Averill and the woman [Cattle Kate] were fearless maverickers. The female was the equal of any man on the range. Of robust physique she was a daredevil in the saddle, handy with a six-shooter and adept with the lariat and branding iron. Where she came from none seems to know, but that she was a holy terror all agreed. She rode straddle, always had a vicious bronco for a mount, and seemed never to tire of dashing across the range.

The thieving pair were ordered to leave the country several times, but paid no attention to the warnings, sending the message that they could take care of themselves, that mavericks were common property and that they would continue to appropriate unmarked cattle.

Lately it has been rumored that the woman and Averill were engaged in a regular roundup of mavericks and would gather several hundred for shipment this fall. The ugly story was partially verified by the stealthy visit of a cowboy to their place Saturday. He reported that their corral held no less than fifty head of newly branded steers, mostly yearlings, with a few nearly full grown.

The statement of the spy circulated rapidly and thoroughly incensed the ranch men, who resolved to abate the menace to their herds. Word passed along the river and early in the night from ten to twenty men, made desperate by steady loss, gathered at a designated rendezvous and quietly galloped to the Averill ranch. A few hundred yards from the cabin they dismounted and approached cautiously. This movement was well advised for Averill had murdered two men and would not hesitate to shoot, while the woman was always full of fight.

Within the little habitation sat the thieving pair, before a rude fireplace. The room was clouded with cigarette smoke. A whiskey bottle with two glasses was on the deal table, and firearms were scattered around the interior so as to be within easy reach.

The leader of the regulators stationed a man with a Winchester at each window and led a rush into the door. The sound of "hands up!" sounded above the crash of glass as the rifles were leveled at the strangely assorted pair of thieves. There was a struggle, but the lawless partners were quickly over-powered and their hands bound.

Averill, always feared because he was a murderous coward, showed himself a cur. He begged and whined, and protested innocence, even saying that the woman did all the stealing. The female was made of sterner stuff. She exhausted a blasphemous vocabulary upon the visitors, who essayed to stop the vile flow by gagging her, but found the task too great. After applying every imaginable opprobrious epithet to the lynchers, she cursed everything and everybody, challenging the Deity to cheat her enemies by striking her dead if He dared. When preparations for the short trip to the scaffold were made, she called for her own horse and vaulted to its back from the ground.

Ropes were hung from the limb of a big cottonwood tree on the south bank of the Sweetwater. Nooses were adjusted to the necks of Averill and his wife and their horses led from under them. The woman died with curses on her foul lips...

This is the first hanging of a woman in Wyoming.[107]

The Hanging of Cattle Kate—II

When the Pathfinder Reservoir was drawn down recently two dead trees were exposed...just trunks...and old-timers pointed them out as the trees where Cattle Kate and Averill were hanged. Cattle Kate wasn't a rustler; she was a prostitute. People didn't like her as a result. She didn't steal cattle, but she may have taken stolen cattle in payment for her services. She was not guilty of rustling. A trail drive might be coming through and calves born in the wrong season would be slowing down the cattle going to be sold, so the drovers would sell off these calves for some extra cash. She had acquired about thirty head of cattle...one way or another...but not by rustling.

There was a sandbar down by the river here [in Casper, Wyoming] where all the local prostitutes, soiled doves, had their cribs. Dozens of small houses, all painted white, were their homes and places of business. When the sandbar area was put under urban renewal one of the cribs was saved and put up at Fort Caspar [a reconstructed fort museum].[108]

This photo of the famous "hole-in-the-wall" cabin at Buffalo Creek, near Casper, Wyoming, was retouched sometime in the last century to reproduce "better." This cabin sat on the ranch land at the mouth of the V-shaped, cliff-lined alcove that hid the only passable trail up and over the Red Wall for miles in either direction. This cabin has been reconstructed and moved to Trail Town, a museum-style attraction near Cody. (Originally published for Wheeler & Skinner, Casper, Wyoming; reprinted courtesy of the Wyoming State Museum, Cheyenne)

The Hole-in-the-Wall

AN AREA OF WYOMING GAVE ITS NAME TO THE
BUTCH CASSIDY HIDE-OUT AND GANG, AND TO A
WHOLE CLASS OF LEGENDS AS THE BORDER
PUSHED WESTWARD.

Finis McDowell's Story

In June 1899 after the closing of my school year at the
Baptist College at Clarksburg, Missouri, and at the age of
eighteen…plans were made to join my mother, brother Bill, and
sister Lizzie, who were in Wyoming, eighty miles from the
nearest station on the Burlington Railroad…from Sheridan we
spent two days on the trip by wagon to Mayoworth on the
Powder River. As we jogged along in the wagon it was a great
thrill to see the beautiful Big Horn Mountains at least seventy-
five miles away, and they appeared so close it looked like you
could reach out and touch them.

Mayoworth boasted a United States Post Office and one
store…Soon after arriving on the Powder River I landed a job on

a cattle ranch and received about $35 per month, mostly helping put up hay. This seemed like a gold mine after working in Missouri for fifty cents a day.

For several months I carried the United States mail on the pony route from Mayoworth to Barnum and return, about twenty miles one way. The mail bag was tied to the saddle and a fresh horse waited at each end of the route.

It was about then that Butch Cassidy and his men were getting famous for train robbing. Everyone knew everyone else and everyone local knew where the Hole-in-the-Wall ranch was, but Butch and his boys were good to the local people and they never feared any loss [of cattle or horses] from them. Everyone would just nod as they rode by other folks on horseback and no one asked who was who or anything. It was all peaceful and no one had any trouble if they didn't make it themselves.

...if you were a traveler and stopped at an unattended home you were welcome to enter and make yourself at home, but the code of the West demanded you leave the place as clean as you found it. Such memories are deep-seated in the hearts of the men and women who, by their willingness, made the best of all the resources the country afforded.[109]

Butch Cassidy Didn't Know Dynamite

Now Butch Cassidy was well-known, not only by the local people who lived near him, but also by the lawmen and railroad men. He had done so many robberies and was so well-known that when he stopped the Union Pacific train the messenger—the agent who cares for the safe, the money, and the mail in the express car—recognized Cassidy by his voice, although he knew him as "Curry," one of Butch's aliases.

They stopped the train and Butch called out to the messenger, locked in the express car. "All we want is the money. We won't give you any more trouble and you can be on your way."

And the messenger inside said words to the effect, "No, I'm sorry, I can't do that."

And Butch said, "Well, we've got dynamite. We're just going to have to blow up the car." They blew up the car, but they didn't know how much dynamite to use and they used way too much...way too much...and the car was blown completely apart and the money was scattered all over the place. They didn't get to pick up the money because they heard the whistle of another train right behind the one they had stopped and they suspected...and this was true...that it would have a passenger car full of sheriff's men and a boxcar full of horses and deputies.

Also, while they were in South America they took a liking to one young man and gave him the money for a trip up here [to Wyoming] to one of the ranches near Kaycee [and the Hole-in-the-Wall]. The young man used a code like "Mr. Bean sent me," and the ranchers knew that meant he was sent by Butch. They took the boy in and gave him a job.[110]

The Curry Gang

*John Clay, Jr., wrote in the Denver Live Stock Report of 1899, and was quoted by the **Diamondville** (Wyoming Territory) **News** of Wednesday, July 12, 1899:*

> ...I see that the Curry [Butch Cassidy] crowd is supposed to have robbed the Union Pacific train at Wilcox, Wyoming, some weeks ago...these boys in the old days thought nothing of staying with you [on your road ranch] all night, then starting out in the morning and branding a few of your big calves for profit...

Brown's Park

Although he had aliases—George LeRoy Parker, George Curry, Butch Cassidy—he was already a known outlaw and accused rustler well-recognized outside Wyoming. But the Butch Cassidy gang's reputation in Wyoming was excellent, as shown in this interview by a Works Progress Administration Writers' Project writer Henry Alexander, a Union Pacific machinist, at his home in Evanston, Wyoming, March 16, 1936, (WPA Subject 13156 of the Wyoming State Historical Research and Publications Division, Cheyenne).

All were familiar with a band of desperate outlaws whose hide-out was located on Henry's Fork. It was...called Brown's Park.

Among the outlaws, there was Butch Cassidy, Elsie Leigh, Tom McCarty, Mat Warner, and Bill Wall. They drifted in and out of the Lone Tree district, using the "Hole-in-the-Wall" as a refuge and hide-out. They were not typical criminals because the loot gathered from their crimes was given to the poor...

One might be riding through the country and one of these men would appear on a horse which was all tired out. If he asked for your horse you didn't argue, but gave it to him immediately, and in return got a tired but better horse out of the bargain, for they never owned anything but the best horses. Usually after two or three days you would receive a check for one or two hundred dollars [by mail].

They stole cattle from the rich men, sold them, and gave the proceeds to less fortunate individuals.

On the one hand "Butch Cassidy" was an outlaw pursued by the lawmen and hated by big cattlemen; on the other hand he was admired and protected by neighbors and small ranchers—many of whom may have been rustlers themselves— who also received generous gifts from him. To understand Butch Cassidy and the Hole-in-the-Wall gang you have to see the "bigger picture" of land, cattle, big ranchers, and small outfits. The descendants of families on both sides still live side-by-side today and most old animosities have faded, but there is still a "touchiness" about the subject, especially the Johnson County War, and to some extent, about Butch and the boys.

The Hanging of Tom Wagner

C.P. "Dub" Meek, a settler in Weston County, Wyoming, told W.P.A. writer Olaf B. Kongslie, of Newscastle, in 1936 (WPA Subject 1355, Wyoming State Historical Research and Publications Division, Cheyenne) about Custer County sheriff Billy Wood and his account of the hanging of a rancher named Tom Wagner.

Tom Wagner lived on a ranch about twenty-five miles west of Upton [Wyoming], then [known as] Merino. He owned a great deal of land and about 1,100 head of horses. No one could deny that he was honest and had come by his property squarely. The cattlemen hated him, however, because he used so much range for his stock.

Meek relates that Sheriff Wood claimed Wagner was hanged by members of the stock association, an organization of large cattle ranch owners, to break up his outfit and return the land to open grazing. No one was ever charged with the hanging.

Horsemen and sheepmen whose herds took up grazing land coveted by large cattlemen, anyone who fenced the range impeding the movement of cattle to and from grazing land and water, and anyone who branded as their own the as-yet-unbranded calves born during the winter when stockmen let the cattle roam freely…all these were seen as enemies to members of the stock association. On the other side, small ranchers and individual cowboys were determined to start their own herds and settle land for themselves. The Casper, Wyoming, *Natrona County Tribune* of May 4, 1892, described the situation thus:

…it was found that stock would live the year around in this country on the native grasses…each man keeping track by some peculiar mark burned upon the animal and called a brand.

…during the branding round-up [each spring] there would once in a while be a [newly born] calf that would be missed and this was called a maverick…nearly all [cattle] companies paid a premium to the cowboys for [finding and] branding these mavericks, besides keeping the boys under wages for the entire year. But soon came hard winters and the stock died in large numbers causing stockmen to discharge nearly all of their cowboys in the fall, who began upon good land to start their own ranches…

The Johnson County War

At this point, let us shift to what Wyoming Sheriff Malcolm Campbell had to say:

Many cowboys were laid off seasonally and ran out of money from drinking and gambling before the spring roundup caused their rehire. With cattle running loose—only identified by brand—on the open range, rustling was a natural temptation. Meanwhile large ranch owners, some of them Englishmen, fenced in and controlled far larger parcels of land than shown on the plat maps. Small ranchers and settlers fought large ranchers over water rights and fence lines that didn't agree with county records.

Mavericks, calves whose mothers had died of exposure, been stolen, or who simply were not yet branded, were supposed to be rounded up in proportion to the number of head in a herd. But some drovers rounded up so many calves off the open range that their cows would have had to give birth twenty-five times a year to account for that number of young beeves. Large cattlemen retaliated by holding pre-roundup roundups all winter, paying out-of-work cowboys to find and brand any calf, regardless of the cow's brand.

During the terrible winter of 1886-87 [the "Long Winter" in the *Little House on the Prairie* books] cattle losses were up to as much as eighty percent. Now exact counts were made of frozen cattle corpses and the true magnitude of the rustling problem was seen. Both sides armed for an unavoidable conflict.

The Johnson County War was about to happen, in the spring of 1892.[111]

The cattlemen of the southern portion of Wyoming believed their only recourse to stopping the rustling and mavericking that was taking place and to prevent the mavericking that would take place at a rival northern Wyoming stockmen's association scheduled roundup a month earlier than theirs was to take action themselves. They hired stock detectives who spent long weeks among suspected rustlers under the guise of ordinary cowboys. The detectives turned in a list of sixty men for whom they claimed to have incontrovertible evidence of rustling—names on a much longer list were reported to be innocent or to have no clear evidence against them. The southern stockmen knew that court trials in the northern portion would not convict those accused by the detectives so they hired Texas gunmen to come and join them in a vigilante raid of epic proportions into the north. One of their first stops was at the cabin of two alleged rustlers, Nick Ray and Nate Champion. A siege resulted in the shooting of both men and the burning of the cabin. Afterward, besiegers found, and chose to preserve, a diary kept by Champion of his last hours:

The Diary of Nate Champion

Me and Nick were getting breakfast when the attack took place. Two men here with us, Bill Jones and another man. The old man went after water and did not come back. His friend went to see what was the matter and he did not come back. Nick started out and I told him to look out, that I thought there was someone at the stable and [that] would not let him come back. [Later he wrote:]

Nick is shot, but not dead yet. He is awful sick. I must go and wait on him.

It is now about two hours since the first shot. Nick is still alive. They are still shooting and are all around the house.

Boys, there is bullets coming in like hail. Them fellows is in such shape I can't get at them. They are shooting from the stable and river and back of the house.

Nick is dead. He died about nine o'clock. I see a smoke down at the stable. I think they have fired it. I don't think they intend to let me get away this time.

It is now about noon. There is someone at the stable yet. They are throwing a rope at the door and dragging it back. I guess it is to draw me out. I wish that duck would go farther so I can get a shot at him.

Boys, I don't know what they have done with them two fellows that stayed here last night.

Boys, I feel pretty lonesome just now. I wish there was someone here with me so we could watch all sides at once. They may fool around until i get a good shot before they leave.

It is about 3 o'clock now. There was a man in a buckboard and one on horseback just passed. They [the stockmen's regulators] fired on them as they went by. I don't know if they killed them or not. I seen lots of men come out on horses on the other side of the river and take after them.

I shot at a man in the stable just now. Don't know if I got him or not. I must go look out again.

It don't look as if there is much show of my getting away. I see twelve or fifteen men. One looks like [the name was scratched out, but whether by Champion or the regulators is unknown]. I don't know whether it is or not. I hope they did not catch them fellows that run over the bridge toward Smith's [the rider and buggy driver].

They are shooting at the house now. If I had a pair of [field] glasses I believe I would know some of those men. They are coming back. I've got to look out.

Well, they have just got through shelling the house again like hail. I heard them splitting wood. I guess they are going to fire the house tonight. I think I will make a break when night comes, if alive.

Shooting again. I think they will fire the house this time.

It's not night yet. The house is all fired. Goodbye, boys, if I never see you again.

Nathan D. Champion

The forty-five regulators, led by Major Frank E. Wolcott, a very respected citizen of southern Wyoming, killed Champion, but the two men captured at daylight were sent away unharmed and eventually spirited out of the state to prevent them from testifying against the regulators. The man in the buggy got away and spread the alarm, resulting in the raising of a huge counter-vigilante army that trapped the regulators and would have caused a huge bloodbath had the United States Army not intervened, in Hollywood style, the "cavalry" riding in in the nick of time. The casualties were amazingly low in the short-lived Johnson County War, but the emotions ran very high.

Although the reading of Champion's diary is somber and sobering, Malcolm Campbell, a Wyoming county sheriff, pointed out:

Champion knew from the very beginning what was happening. In all that he wrote he never once protested his innocence nor questioned his fate. He did not ask who these attackers were or why they were attacking his cabin, as he would have done had he been innocent.[112]

The Vegetable Garden Story

A pioneer lady in Utah, Mrs. Minnie Rasmussen, looked out her cabin window one day and saw men in her garden stealing vegetables. She ran outside and ran the men out of her garden with a broom. They laughed, but left quickly on horseback, running ahead of her as she swatted at them.

About a month later, she awoke one morning to find that someone had left a huge packing crate on her front porch. On it there was a note that said, "From Butch Cassidy and the Wild Bunch. We appreciate the groceries from your garden."

Inside the crate, packed in straw, was a full set of fine china.[113]

The Fate of Cassidy and Sundance

The Wyoming Territory was such a sparsely inhabited place that everybody knew everybody else, and recognized all their neighbors on sight. Butch Cassidy and the Sundance Kid were well-known to their neighbors, and paid good money for horses and supplies, and the ranchers protected them by keeping them informed if anyone from "outside" came looking for them.

When they came back from South America, everyone knew who they were, and did not report them to the authorities. They didn't die down in South America. They ranched up near Kaycee up until near the time of their deaths.

Lonnabaugh [the Sundance Kid] died and is buried here in Casper [Wyoming] in a grave that's unmarked now. It used to have a wooden headmarker painted red, but that's long gone. Parker [Butch Cassidy] moved finally to Lander, Wyoming, and lived out his life in a hotel there. He died and was buried there, and his grave was marked with the name George Leroy Parker, although that's not his real name, either.[114]

Butch Cassidy and His Loot

Our country has been settled for a relatively short while, so we don't have many legends. Those we have are apt to be about outlaws, most especially, about Butch Cassidy and his followers.

The Brown's Park area, just south of the Wyoming border, is located in both Colorado and Utah. This fact, together with its natural isolation, made it an appealing hideout for outlaws, among them Butch Cassidy and his gang. I was told this story some twenty years ago by someone who had heard it firsthand from one of its supposed participants, a filling station owner in the village of Baggs, a little north and east of Brown's Park:

The many friends and even some of the family of Butch Cassidy know very well that he did not die in a shootout in South America. He returned briefly to his old haunts to take care of unfinished business. The Baggs gentleman remembered Cassidy saying he had stashed a good portion of his take somewhere in the neighborhood, so he was half expecting the long, shiny black car that pulled up to his filling station one summer day.

The gentleman in the back seat had his hat pulled down to shadow his face but [the station owner] was pretty sure he recognized the outlaw. When the driver of the car had finished filling the tank, and pulled the machine out to disappear down the road in a cloud of dust, the station proprietor closed up shop and followed at a safe distance, naturally not wishing to be seen.

The limousine turned up a rough track into a nearby canyon and the gentleman hid in his automobile behind some brush until, after some time, the black car came jouncing past on its way out. When it seemed safe, the filling station operator drove out of his hiding place and up the canyon, following the car tracks in the dust.

Sure enough, there under a half-hidden rocky overhang was a deep, freshly dug hole.[115]

The End of the Outlaw Era

THE LAST BANK ROBBERY IN THE UNITED STATES
WHERE HORSES WERE USED IN A BUNGLED
GETAWAY HAPPENS TO ALSO BE THE LAST EF-
FORT OF THE LAST OF THE GREAT ROBBERS:
HENRY STARR.

*Different storytellers and outlaw biographers identify a dif-
ferent date for the "end of the outlaw era." Some experts name
a hanging incident in a barn just after the turn of the twentieth
century, others specify the date of someone's death (Frank
James, Cole Younger, Emmett Dalton), and still others identify
the date of enactment of a law or the coming of statehood to
some wild territory. The collectors of this anthology believe that
the outlaw era that began just after the Civil War ended in the
Middle Border area, with the last bank robbery ever attempted
in which horses were used for the getaway. The last horseback*

*robbery in America was also the last attempt at crime by Belle
Starr's clan, and it is appropriate that this collection should begin
with Belle and end with Henry Starr, Belle's nephew.*

*Henry Starr was the son of Hop Starr. Hop was the brother
of Sam Starr, Belle's second husband. Sam and Hop were sons
of Tom Starr, a powerful leader in the Cherokee politics of the
day. Many relatives of Tom Starr were wealthy and respected
citizens of the Cherokee Nation, one was even a judge. Other
members of the Starr family turned their bitterness (over feuds
within the Cherokee Nation, and over the declining power and
respectability of the Nation) into a life of crime.*

Henry Starr and Frank Cheney

Henry Starr made his outlaw headquarters at the home of
Frank Cheney, outside Wagoner, in the Indian Nation. Cheney
was a Texan, and along with Starr, five more men made a gang
of seven. Although there was plenty of train traffic at Wagoner
Switch, the gang robbed the train at Pryor Creek station because
Wagoner was well-guarded.

The railroad offered a $1,200 reward, and the Pryor Creek
stationmaster and crew offered another $1,000, presumably put
up by local owners or businessmen.

Starr was seen in Wagoner before the Pryor Creek robbery,
and years later as he planned to re-enter bank robbing as a
business, but he stayed out of town most of the time. The
Wagoner area was always his headquarters, though, especially at
Cheney's until Henry was captured.[116]

Starr and the Wagoner Banks

*After serving time in prison in Colorado, Henry Starr came
back to Indian Territory and lived here through statehood.
When he was unable to earn a living that satisfied him honestly,
he decided to go back to a life of crime. He liked the idea of
robbing two banks at once, because this doubled the take for a
single risk, and because he already enjoyed a certain notoriety
for having been the only person to ever succeed in robbing two
banks at once, back in Stroud.*

In Wagoner, Oklahoma, a town Starr was very familiar with, there were two banks opposite each other on the northeast and southwest corners of the intersection of Main and Cherokee. The owners of the banks, First National and the American Bank, heard that Henry Starr was coming to town, and Sheriff Clay Flowers hired riflemen to sit in the top floor windows of the buildings on the remaining two corners and upstairs in the Cobb Building.

When Starr came to town, he saw the riflemen posted above the intersection and knew that he was expected, and that he could not succeed. After that, he turned his attention to Arkansas, where he had robbed a bank in Bentonville once before, and finally settled on Harrison, Arkansas, where he was killed.[117]

Starr and the People's Bank

On Friday, February 18, 1921, Henry Starr and two accomplices entered the People's Bank on the corner of the square in the little Ozark town of Harrison, Arkansas, intent on robbing the bank. While Starr and his men held guns on the cashiers, one customer walked calmly behind them into the vault. The man was W.J. Myers, the retired president of the bank, who just happened to be in for a morning visit with his former employees.

Starr and his men did not see Myers enter the vault, where he calmly took the loaded Winchester he himself had set in a corner years before, stepped outside the vault and shot Starr. As Starr fell, he told his men to flee. Hit in the spinal cord and kidneys, Starr was not likely to live long. As the getaway car sped off, Myers shot out a tire. They fled to the southeast and burned the car near Crooked Creek bridge on Willow Street, headed toward Bellefonte, when they had ruined the wheel so badly they could not drive on.

The accomplices stole horses as a heavy snowstorm began, making this the last horseback bank robbery in the Middle Border area. While they fled, Starr was taken to the upper floor of the jail just off the square, where he suffered and died at 1:45 P.M. the following Tuesday, the 22nd. Before he died, Starr gave cashier Cleve Coffman the pistol he had used, saying "he deserved it as he certainly looked down it enough."

Starr's body was embalmed at Cline's Mortuary and Furniture Store, where it lay in state upstairs and was briefly displayed in the front window, the last of the outlaws to be on display. I saw it there myself, on my way to my father's office. When Starr's mother, Mrs. Mary Gordon, sister, Mrs. Ewing, and his wife and sons came to claim the body, they chastised the funeral home for putting the body on display and were disturbed by it being on public view for about a day and a half.[118]

W.J. Myers' Story

My grandfather was W.J. Myers, who shot Henry Starr. When the robbers came in, my grandfather, who was retired from the bank, happened to be at the bank visiting and happened to be at the vault. He had put that rifle in the vault himself. As they started to scoop up the money from the teller's cages, and like that, he stepped out and fired. I still have the rifle.

For years and years after that, at different times, the family would get death threats from Starr's henchmen. Starr stole a lot of money in Arkansas, Missouri, and Oklahoma, and took the money back to his part of Oklahoma, and always paid well anyone who helped him or sold him anything. He was sort of a hero among some of the folks in Oklahoma. He had a lot of friends.[119]

Dr. Ross Fowler's Story

My father was also a doctor, and his office was upstairs over the People's Bank on the southwest corner of the Harrison square. The jail was just behind the bank, across the alley to the south. There was no hospital and no clinic in town yet then, so Starr was kept in the jail after he was shot and arrested, and my father just picked up his medical bag and walked down the stairs and a few steps to the jail to attend Starr several times a day.

It was obvious that Starr was critically injured, his spinal column was damaged or severed by the rifle bullet, and his condition deteriorated rapidly. He lapsed into a coma the last

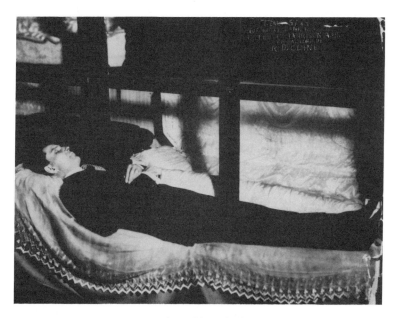

Henry Starr, Notorious Bank Robber, killed at Harrison, Ark. Embalmed by R.D. Cline, reads this photograph of Starr's body lying in state at Cline's Mortuary and Furniture Store in Harrison. This is the first time this photo has appeared in an outlaw book. (Courtesy of the Boone County Photo Archives of the North Arkansas Regional Library, negative no. 71675-1. Reprinted by permission.)

few hours of his life. He died at 1:25 P.M. on Tuesday after the robbery on the previous Friday, February 18, 1921. Without the antibiotics we have now, there was no hope for his survival. His mother came to see him on Monday, but my father had begun to administer laudanum because he was in such severe pain. His mother did speak to him before he died.[120]

Henry Starr's Pistol

I remember well the day the bank was robbed. The bank was on the southwest corner of the square, with the door on the west side where the get-away car was parked. Henry Starr said he robbed from the rich and gave to the poor. The last thing he told his men during the robbery in Harrison was, "They've got me, but do no shooting! Just get gone!" All he would have had to say was to shoot, and his men might have killed everyone in the bank, but Henry Starr didn't believe in killing.

Before he died, Starr gave his pistol to Cleve Coffman, the bank cashier, with Miss Ruth Wilson notarizing the paper deed. Mr. Coffman was working with me at the time, and sold the gun and paper to a man from Missouri for $75.

The pistol ended up in the large collection of guns in the Ralph Foster Museum at the College of the Ozarks in Point Lookout, Missouri, just thirty-five miles from Harrison. No other book about Henry Starr mentions this fact.[121]

Starr's Body on Display

I was a young lady in grade school when Henry Starr was shot. When he died, he was embalmed down at R.D. Cline's, on the square. The body was up on the top floor for a while, and when the bell rang for lunchtime, my friends and I all ran down the steps of the old three-story brick school, three blocks down to the square, and upstairs at Cline's.

We stood there for the whole lunch period, in a circle around the coffin, staring down at the body, then we could hear the bell ring back at the school, and we ran all the way back for our fourth period class.[122]

Family Folklore and Descendants' Tales

ALONG THE MIDDLE BORDER IT IS COMMON FOR FOLKS TO CLAIM TO BE DESCENDED FROM A FAMOUS OUTLAW OR LAWMAN. MOST OF THE STORIES ARE FABRICATIONS. BUT MANY TIMES THEY ARE TRUE. HERE IS AN EXAMPLE OF THE DOUBTFUL DESCENDANT AND OTHER TALES OF TRUE FAMILY TREES.

Lee Sanders' Story

My grandfather Lee Sanders always told this story, and believed it, but the rest of the family did not seem to. Grandpa Lee said that Frank James spent some time hiding out in the town of Mountain Grove [Missouri], under the name Frank Nevels. This was before the pardon, so there was still a stigma attached to the James name. The house he lived in was torn down not too long ago. Grandpa Lee's mother's maiden name was Nevels, and

Tom Slaughter, while hiding out in Dallas, Texas, circa 1919. Slaughter was a colorful Arkansas outlaw. This photo was provided from the private collection of Charles E. Avery, a collateral descendant of Slaughter's and author of many articles on outlaws, westerners, and Confederates.

he always thought that she was the daughter of Frank Nevels...Frank James. He also thought that there had been a family Bible that showed the real relationships and names, but that Bible had been given to a museum!

If it is true, that would make Frank James my great-great-grandfather.[123]

Tom Slaughter

One warm summer day in 1912 my grandfather, R.T. Jordan, and grandmother were visiting a Mrs. Williams, a relative, on the outskirts of Longstraw, a logging town in northern Louisiana. Tom Slaughter, another distant relative of Mrs. Williams who was staying with her, rode up on a lathered-up horse. He spoke for a moment with Mrs. Williams and gave her some money. Then, announcing he was going to flag the train and return to Arkansas, he asked to borrow one of grandfather's horses for the ride to the railroad tracks. Grandfather agreed, and Slaughter gave him a pistol to show his gratitude before riding off. Moments after Tom left, a posse rode up, saying Slaughter had robbed the bank in Longstraw!

Because of that incident, told to me by my grandfather, I learned of Slaughter's career from one of his close relatives: Tom Slaughter was born in Dallas, Texas, in 1894. His father died while Tom was very young, and the boy was sent to live with relatives in Pope County, Arkansas, and became associated with that state. He stole a heifer, was caught, and sent to reform school. Released a year later, he went to Oklahoma and joined a gang of train and bank robbers. He would often leave a robbery on horseback to elude the police in automobiles; after he had lost the law, he would switch to an automobile for a long-distance escape. Escaping from jail became his incredible skill.

He escaped from the Dallas County jail while awaiting transfer, re-arrested twice, he escaped twice again. Jailed in Nowata, Oklahoma, in 1917, he escaped by holding up the jailer; recaptured and placed in the Bartlesville jail, he escaped again. His next arrest was in Joplin, Missouri, followed by another escape. Two bank robberies and one killing later, he was arrested in West Point, Kentucky, for a bank job in Cave City...and likewise escaped.

Slaughter pulled off a string of successful robberies in Texas: in August 1919 he took $27,000 from the Citizens National Bank in Petty...in July 1920, $23,000 from the Athens National Bank in Athens...and $4,358 from the Guaranty State Bank in Graham in October 1920. Somewhere in north Texas he buried some of this loot, and it has never been found.

Next the gang, having picked up some other recruited men, hit the First State Bank of Alluwe, Oklahoma, and planned their most daring robbery of all: three banks at once. Two banks at Sedan, Kansas, and one at Cedarville, were the target; once again horses were to be used for the getaway. But Tom's incredible luck was running out. He went into a clothing store in Sedan and bought a new suit. He paid with money still in its paper bank wrapper from the recent job in Oklahoma. The clerk became suspicious and notified the authorities. Tom was approached by two officers as he walked down the streets of Sedan. Realizing he'd been recognized, Tom tried to draw the revolver stuck in the waistband of his new trousers, but the hammer caught on his suspenders when he tried to pull it out. The Kansas officials took Tom in, and later a posse caught up to Kid Green and Frank McGivness. It was October 29.

Green and Slaughter were returned to Arkansas to stand trial for the killing of Brown at Hot Springs. As the trial began, the Texas Bankers' Association sent word that pals of Tom's from his Texas days were planning to break him out. The trial judge made a peculiar request of the governor of Arkansas, and the 5th Machine Gun Corps of Pine Bluff came to guard the courthouse during the trial. A sensation was created when near the end of the trial, jailers testified they had found knives and saws in Slaughter's and Green's cells, and one bar in the cell sawed almost in two. Finally, on November 18, 1920, both received a sentence of life imprisonment.

Tom was incarcerated in one of Arkansas' prison farms, and, true to his old nature, received ten lashes with the whip for trying to escape on April 16, 1920. Unreformed, Tom had a gun smuggled into him, and killed a guard trying to escape again. Trapped inside the prison bathhouse, he ran out of ammo and never made it outside the fences. For this crime he was tried again, and sentenced to die in the new electric chair.

While on Death Row, Tom managed to get sent to the prison hospital where, on December 9, armed with another pistol he had had smuggled in to him, he captured a prison nurse, and freed six other convicts. The nurse was forced to wake the guards on three corners of the prison wall, and the convicts disarmed them. The guards were taken hostage, along with a number of prison trusties. Ironically, one of the trusty prisoners was Rufus Rawlings, serving time for participating in the Harrison bank robbery with Henry Starr.

The warden and his family were placed in a cell, and the warden's car stolen for the escape. They got to the town of Benton, where they battled with police and one convict was wounded. The convicts abandoned the car and continued on foot. They camped out for the night, as Slaughter had done so often before.

During the night, one of the inmates, James Howard, stole to where Tom lay wrapped in a slicker, and shot him twice through the head and once through the heart...for the reward he would receive.[124]

Calamity Jane and Poker Alice

My father was a retired cavalry man; he retired first sergeant in 1903, but he was in Fort Robinson, Nebraska, when General MacArthur, Sr., was the post commander and Walter Reed was the doctor. My mother's folks had come in to Fort Robinson and helped build the old post in 1864. Her father couldn't pull his cartridges out—he had busted his teeth out—so the Union Army discharged him and he came out West. Now, Mother, she worked for a store back in the early days and at Fort Robinson there were a lot of houses of prostitution. In back of the store were about a hundred and thirty cribs [small houses where one lady lived alone and worked].

There were a lot of troops in there, all kinds. But my mother knew Calamity Jane and Poker Alice Tubbs, and these girls used to work there. When they came to the store to buy supplies they didn't come around to the front door like society ladies, they came to the back. There was a button at the back door of the store and they'd push the button and it would ring a bell. It was one of mother's jobs to go to the back door and wait on these girls.

Mother lived to be ninety-one and she remembered the Battle of Wounded Knee. She was working at this store in the 1890s as a teenager. Back then the Army was sent West to guard the mining operations that provided the financially strapped Union with gold after the Civil War, and it also gave the Army posts to place all the officers that had been promoted during the War and would not normally have a career in peacetime. Most of the settlers that came into this area were suttlers, who provided supplies to the posts or retired Army men who knew the Army routine and worked freighting, haying, and so forth. Some of the early settlers ran the hog ranches, the houses of drinking, gambling, and prostitution that provided the soldiers with social pleasures off-post. Many of the women who came West were wives of suttlers, but others were dancehall girls, barkeeps, and prostitutes.

Poker Alice told mother that she shouldn't acknowledge them [her and Martha "Calamity Jane" Cannary] on the street. She said they would just wink at mother when they saw her on the street and she could wink back. So that's how they said 'hello' on the street, just by winking.[125]

Angel of Mercy—III

Calamity Jane really did have a heart of gold. Sometimes she'd find out about a family that was down on its luck, and she'd just walk into a saloon, fire her gun into the ceiling, and say, 'Look, boys, I want all your money.' The boys would all pitch in and give her all the money out of their pockets because they knew she was going to put it to some good use.

One time she was arrested for pickpocketing, and she was taken before the judge. He said, 'Did you do it, Calamity Jane?'

and she said, "Damn right I did it. He was drunk, and didn't need any more money, and I needed it to pay the medical bill of an old man who's down on his luck.' The judge said, 'That's fine, case dismissed,' and Jane took the money to the doctor and paid the old man's bill.[126]

The Pony Express

Yes, it was one of my ancestors who started, or helped start I should say, the Pony Express. When the Waddells came to this country they settled on a Spanish land grant. The king of France lost all his possessions east of the Mississippi at the close of the French and Indian War, which was won by the British. To avoid losing his lands west of the Mississippi he gave Louisiana, which then consisted of all the land west of, and drained by, the Mississippi, to his cousin the king of Spain in 1763 at the Treaty of San Ildefonso. The Waddell family comes from Scotland and the first Waddell mentioned in this country was Andrew Waddell, who in 1648 was noted to have a wife and a son on the tax records.

Later my namesake, James Waddell, was a Confederate officer, commanding a ship in the Bering Strait sinking Union shipping, and learned that the war was over many months after the Surrender at Appomattox. He sailed all the way to England and surrendered to the British rather than give up to the Union Navy.

Benjamin Waddell is the ancestor that founded the Pony Express in 1861. Three men had already established a company known as the Overland Express, a huge cartage and freightage business; the men were Waddell, Russell, and Majors. It was Russell who had the idea of the Pony Express to carry the mail swiftly instead of the Overland Express which was anything but fast.

The riders were to be orphans, without living family, and light young men, weighing only 120 pounds. That made for speed and diminished the grief if one of the young riders was lost. The job did prove very dangerous and several riders were lost, but in the legendary eighteen months the Pony Express existed they never, ever lost the mail. The letters sometimes arrived stained with the rider's blood, but the horses always ran their route and reached the next station even without their riders.

Wild Bill Hickok was never a rider for the Pony Express; he was too tall and heavy. Bill Cody rode for the Express, and he and Wild Bill were friends. Wild Bill's first big scrape was killing the McCanles "gang" who were a threat to one of the stage stations.

The largest station was the Hollenberg Station at Hanover in northern Kansas. The riders rode in relays, stopping for fresh horses that were saddled and waiting at an appointed time, so that the rider went more or less nonstop until he passed the mailbag to another rested rider on a fresh horse.

One time Cody was carrying cash; he hid the cash inside his blanket under the saddle and filled the mailbag with newspapers. Sure enough he was stopped and he handed the saddlebag over to a robber and rode on before the robber could count his "prize." William F. Cody rode on into Sacramento with the cash safely in his blanket.[127]

The Widow Villa

In the summer of 1971 we were traveling through Mexico on a vacation in a Dodge Ram camper. On an overnight stay in Chihuahua, Chihuahua, we went to the home of Pancho Villa for a tour. Inside the typical Mexican house-compound [shaped like a hollow square doughnut, with the house around the outside and the courtyard in the middle] we were met by a polite middle-aged lady who spoke perfect English. She told us that for three dollars we could tour the home...and for five dollars the Widow Villa would lead us on the tour. We did not actually shout out loud at the time, but it was hard not to. The Widow Villa? We had no idea she was still alive!

We quickly pulled out fifteen dollars and the three of us...only one who spoke Spanish...walked slowly around the home with the wonderful little lady who had been Villa's wife, Luz Corral de Villa. We did a little math in our heads to figure she was seventy-eight at the time, having married Francisco...she swore he never allowed anyone to call him Pancho…in 1909 when she was thirteen.

We admired photos of Villa, his personal effects, and finally the automobile in which he was riding when he was assassinated in 1923. It was parked in the courtyard with a roof protecting it. She spoke of him as if he had been there that morning and would be back later, not as if he had been riddled with bullets forty-eight years before. When we politely asked the question that has bothered many Americans, why did Francisco Villa enter the United States in 1912 and fight at Columbus, New Mexico, she didn't seem offended. She must have been asked before. She answered "por faltarse la revolución," because he felt a lack of revolution. Was he just yearning for the "good old days," when a semi-outlaw had become a hero general? Or was it that material he had ordered from stores in Columbus (to avoid arousing suspicion in Mexico) was overdue, or somehow withheld after he had paid for it? Instead of answering the question, we just had a new question.

La viuda de Villa died not long afterwards and we were glad that, even though it was tacky and touristy, we had asked for her autograph. She smiled and gave it graciously, the same way she did everything.[128]

This previously unpublished photo of James Robert "Bob" Hutchins, the youngest deputy to serve Judge Isaac Parker's court and the last to die (on April 29, 1951), was sold at an auction of his belongings in 1989. It is now in a private collection.

They Speak for Themselves

IN THE END, HISTORY ALONE CAN JUDGE THE
LAWMEN AND OUTLAWS OF THE MIDDLE BOR-
DER, BUT SOMETIMES THEY SPOKE FOR THEM-
SELVES IN LETTERS, MEMENTOES,
AND DIARY ACCOUNTS.

The Hutch that Hutch Built

[An antique collector and dealer speaks as she shows a handmade piece of furniture:] This hutch was handmade from packing crates by the [deputy] United States marshal named "Hutch," [James Robert "Bob"] Hutchins, who rode for Judge Parker over at Fort Smith. There was an auction of his belongings and this piece was the only item I bought...my mother bought the hand-tinted photo in the gilded frame of him and his [second] wife...the hutch was just absolutely stuffed with his papers and documents and wanted posters, and a museum paid fourteen hundred dollars for the contents of the hutch.

I love the way he put this piece of furniture together, making good use of material that someone else might have thrown away. He was a very thoughtful and methodical person. See the writing here in India ink [she shows the interior of a drawer]; that's the address label to a store in Ardmore [Oklahoma].

This drawer was just as he had left it when he died [in 1951] and there was a lot of wanted posters in here. You know, he was the one who shot and killed Belle Starr's [fourth] husband Bill [better known as Jim] July. That was when he became famous as a lawman.

There was one poster in this drawer that intrigued me. It was a wanted poster for a woman outlaw [Lou Bowers]. You don't really think of women as being outlaws, but this one was.[129]

Wild Bill's Denial

One day during the summer of 1875, while walking along one of the principal streets of Cheyenne with a friend, there appeared sauntering leisurely along towards us from the opposite direction, a tall, straight and rather heavily built individual in ordinary citizen's clothes, sans revolvers and knives, sans buckskin leggins and spurs, and sans everything that would betoken the real character of the man, save that he wore a broad-brimmed sombrero hat, and a profusion of light brown hair hanging down over his broad shoulders. A nearer view betrayed the fact that he also wore a carefully cultivated mustache of a still lighter shade, which curled up saucily at each corner of his somewhat sinister mouth, while on his chin grew a small hirsute tuft of the same shade, and barring the two latter appendages he might have been taken for a Quaker minister. When within a few feet of us, he hesitated a moment, as if undecided, then stepping to one side suddenly stopped, at the same time doffing his sombrero and addressing me in good, respectable Anglo-Saxon vernacular substantially as follows:

"Madame, I hope you will pardon my seeming boldness, but knowing that you have recently returned from the Black Hills, I take the liberty of asking a few questions in regard to that country, as I expect to go there myself soon. My name is Hickok."

I bowed low in acknowledgement of the supposed honor but I must confess that his next announcement somewhat startled me.

"I am sometimes called Wild Bill," he continued, "and you have no doubt heard of me, although," he added, "I suppose you have heard nothing good of me."

"Yes," I replied candidly, "I have often heard of Wild Bill, and his reputation, to say the least, is not at all creditable to him. But," I hastened to add, "perhaps he is not so black as he has been painted."

"Well, as to that," he replied, "I suppose I am called a red-handed murderer, which I deny. That I have killed men I admit, but never unless in absolute self-defense, or in the performance of an official duty. I never, in all my life, took any mean advantage of an enemy. Yet understand," he added, with a dangerous gleam in his eyes, "I never allowed a man to get the drop on me. But perhaps I may yet die with my boots on," he said, his face softening a little. Ah, was this a premonition of the tragic fate that awaited him?

After making a few queries relative to the Black Hills, which were politely answered, Wild Bill, with a gracious bow that would have done credit to a Chesterfield, passed on down the street out of sight, and I never saw or heard more of him until one day in August 1876 when the excited cry of "Wild Bill is shot!" was carried along the main street of Deadwood.[130]

Henry Starr's Complaint

The last of the old-time outlaws, bank robber Henry Starr of Oklahoma, made several touching remarks about his life near its end, but the reports are all secondhand and copyrighted by the various old-time lawmen or their heirs. Henry Starr wrote this about himself:

I was born near Fort Gibson, Indian Territory, on December 2, 1875, and am of Scotch-Irish-Indian ancestry. My father, George [Hop] Starr, was a half-blood Cherokee Indian; my mother, Mary Scott, is one-quarter Cherokee...

...[speaking of the jail at Fort Smith, Arkansas] The odor of a large, poorly-kept jail is worse than the odor in the animal section of a circus, and this particular jail was the worst ever. I was assigned to a cell, the bedclothes reeking with filth and covered with lice...

A lot of people will be curious to know about certain things, so I'll ask and answer. What is your politics? Haven't any. Your religion? Same. Do you think you have led a correct life? No, but it's as good as some others that are holding office. Don't you think society is going to the dogs? No, I don't; it was never away from them. Don't you feel that it's a great crime to take other people's money? Yes, I know it's wrong, but I am only a small thief; the lawyers take it all away from me, and still I go to the penitentiary. The big thieves never go to the pen, and besides, they keep what they steal. For that reason I feel much abused.[131]

Billy the Kid is Buried

The body [of William Bonney] was neatly and properly dressed and buried in the military cemetery at Fort Sumner, July 15, 1881. His exact age, on the day of his death was 21 years, 7 months, and 21 days.

I said that the body was buried in the cemetery at Fort Sumner; I wish to add that it is there to-day intact. Skull, fingers, toes, bones, and every hair of the head that was buried with the body on that 15th day of July, doctors, newspaper editors, and paragraphers to the contrary notwithstanding. Some presuming swindlers have claimed to have the Kid's skull on exhibition, or one of his fingers, or some other portion of his body, and one medical gentleman has persuaded credulous idiots that he has all the bones strung upon wires. It is possible that there is a skeleton on exhibition somewhere in the States, or even in this Territory, which was procured somewhere down the Rio Pecos. We have them, lots of them in this section. The banks of the Pecos are dotted from Fort Sumner to the Rio Grande with unmarked graves, and the skeletons are of all sizes, ages, and complexions.

Any showman of ghastly curiosities can resurrect one or all of them, and place them on exhibition as the remains of Dick Turpin, Jack Shepherd, Cartouche, or the Kid, with no one to say him nay; so they don't ask the people of the Rio Pecos to believe it.

Again I say that the Kid's body lies undisturbed in the grave and I speak of what I know.[132]

Bill Longley's Farewell

William P. "Bill" Longley, the Texas outlaw, wrote these last words to his sister before he was hanged:

...Don't be sad, be holy. I am lively yet and expect to be as long as I live. It is no use to be sad, and then I cannot be sad when I know that I am soon to be released from all trouble. For well I know that I will be better off. Hanging is my favorite way of dieing [sic] if I have to die. I would rather die that way than any other way on earth, that is except a natural death...

Wm. P. Longley[133]

Alferd Packer's Confession

I, Alferd Packer, desire to make a true and voluntary state-ment in regard to the occurrences in Southern Colorado during the winter of 1873-1874. I wish to make it to General Adams because I have made one [statement] once before about the same matter.

When we [a party of six miners] left Ouray's camp we had about seven days' food for one man, we traveled two or three days and it came a storm. We came to a mountain, crossed a gulch and came onto another mountain, found the snow so deep, had to follow the mountain on the top and on about the fourth day we had only a pint of flour left. We followed the mountain, until we came to the main range. [I] Do not remember how many days we were traveling then—I think, about ten days—living on rosebuds and pine gum and some of the men were crying and praying. Then we came over the main range.

We camped twice on a stream which runs into a big lake, the second time just above the lake. The next morning we crossed the lake, cut holes into the ice to catch fish, there were no fish so we tried to catch snails. The ice was thin, some broke through. We crossed the lake and went into a grove of timber, all the men were crying and one of them was crazy.

[Israel] Swan asked me to go up and find out if I could see something from the mountains. I took a gun, went up the hill, found a big rose bush with buds sticking through the snow, but could see nothing but snow all around. I was a kind of guide for them, but I did not know the mountain from that side. When I came back to camp after being gone nearly all day I found the red-headed man [Wilson Bell] who acted crazy in the morning sitting near the fire roasting a piece of meat which he had cut out of the leg of the German butcher [Frank Miller]. The latter's body was lying the furthest off from the fire, down the stream, his skull was crushed in with the hatchet.

The other three men were lying near the fire, they were cut in the forehead with the hatchet; some had two, some three cuts. I came within a rod of the fire. When the man saw me, he got up with his hatchet towards me when I shot him sideways through the belly. He fell on his face, the hatchet fell forward. I grabbed it and hit him in the top of the head. I camped that night at the fire, [and] sat up all night.

The next morning I followed my tracks up the mountain but I could not make it, the snow was too deep, and I came back. I went sideways into a piece of pine timber, [and] set up two sticks and covered it with pine boughs and made a shelter about three feet high; this was my camp until I came out. I went back to the fire, covered the men up and fetched to the camp the piece of meat that was near the fire. I made a new fire near my camp and cooked the piece of meat and ate it. I tried to get away every day but could not, so I lived off the flesh of these men, the bigger part of the sixty days I was out.

Then the snow began to have a crust and I started out up the creek to a place where a big slide of yellowish clay [slumgullion] seemed to come down the mountain; there I started up and got my feet wet, and having only a piece of blanket around them, I froze my feet under the toes. I camped before I reached the top, making a fire and staying all night; the next day I made the top of the hill and a little over. I built a fire on top of a log and on two logs close together I camped. I cooked some of the flesh and carried it with me for food. I carried only one blanket. There was seventy dollars amongst the men. I fetched it out with me and one gun. The red-headed man, Bell, had a fifty-dollar bill in his pocket. All the others together had only twenty dollars. I had twenty dollars myself. If there was any more money in the outfit I did not know of it and it remained there.

At the last camp, just before I reached the agency, I ate my last pieces of meat. This meat I cooked at the camp before I started out and put it in a bag and carried the bag with me. [I] Could not eat but a little at a time. When I went out with the party from the agency to search for the bodies we came to the mountains overlooking the stream, but I did not want to take them farther. I did not want to go back to the camp. If I had staid [sic] in that vicinity longer I would have taken you [General Adams] right to the place but "they" [unexplained] advised me to go away.

When I was at the Sheriff's cabin in Saguache I was passed a key made out of a penknife blade, with which I could unlock the [leg-] irons. I went to the Arkansas [River] and worked all summer for John Gill, eighteen miles below Pueblo; then I rented Gilbert's ranch, still farther down the river, put in a crop of corn, sold it to John Gill and went to Arizona.

Alferd Packer
State of Colorado
County of Arapahoe

I, Alferd Packer, of my own free will, voluntarily do swear that the above statement is true, the whole truth and nothing but the truth.[134]

Rufus Buck's Poem

After the execution of Rufus Buck, hanged alongside his four teen-aged "gang" members on July 1, 1896, the following poem was found in his cell, written on the back of a photograph of his mother, dated the day of the hanging:

My Dream, 1896

I dreamt I was in heaven,
Among the angels fair,
I'd near [ne'er] seen none so handsome,
That twine in golden hair;
They looked so neat, and sang so sweet,
And play'd the golden harp,
I was about to pick an angel out,
And take her to my heart;
But the moment I began to plea[d],
I thought of you, my love,
There was none I'd seen so beautifull,
On earth, or Heaven above.
Good-by my dear wife and mother.

1 Day of July	also my sisters,
to the year of	Rufus Buck
1896	Yours truely

H
o
l
y
Father   Son and
G
h
o
s
t

Virtue and Resurrection
Remember me, Rock of Ages[135]

Calamity Jane Explains Her Name

More than one person called herself Calamity Jane in the Old West. Here is how Martha Jane Cannary said she got her name, although the story is not borne out by military reports:

...I returned to Fort Sanders, Wyoming, [and] remained there until the spring of 1872, when we were ordered out to the Muscle Shell or Nursey Pursey [Nez Perce] Indian outbreak. In that war Generals Custer, Miles, Terry, and Crook were all engaged. This campaign lasted until the fall of 1873.

It was during this campaign that I was christened Calamity Jane. It was on Goose Creek, Wyoming, where the town of Sheridan is now [1876] located. Capt. Egan was in command of the post. We were ordered out to quell an uprising of the Indians, and were out for several days, [and] had numerous skirmishes during which six of the soldiers were killed and several severely wounded. When on returning to the Post, we were ambushed about a mile and a half from our destination. When fired upon Capt. Egan was shot. I was riding in advance and on hearing the firing turned in my saddle and saw the Captain reeling in his saddle as though about to fall. I turned my horse and galloped back with all haste to his side and got there in time to catch him as he was falling. I lifted him onto my horse in front of me and succeeded in getting him safely to the Fort. Capt. Egan on recovering, laughingly said: "I name you Calamity Jane, the heroine of the plains." I have borne that name up to the present time.[136]

Belle Starr Speaks for Herself

In volume 11, Number 16, of the **Fort Smith Weekly Elevator** *for February 15, 1889, there appeared in column three an article entitled "Belle Starr: A Few Leaves from the Life of a Notorious Woman." It said, among other things, "In many lengthy sketches published since her death, we have not read a single correct story..." But this article, too, got many facts wrong. The article, however, included a sketch Belle had written about herself and given to the* **Elevator** *two years before:*

After a more adventurous life than generally falls to the lot of woman I settled permanently in the Indian Territory, selecting a place of picturesque beauty on the Canadian River. There, far from society, I hoped to pass the remainder of my life in peace and quietude.

So long had I been estranged from the society of women (whom I thoroughly detest) that I thought I would find it irksome to be in their midst.

So I selected a place that but few have ever had the gratification of gossiping around. For a short time I lived very happily in the society of my little girl and husband, a Cherokee Indian, a son of the noted Tom Starr. But it soon became noised around that I was a woman of some notoriety from Texas and from that time on my home and my actions have been severely criticized.

My home became famous as an outlaw's rancho long before I was visited by any of the boys who were friends of mine. Indeed, I never corresponded with any of my old associates and was desirous my whereabouts should be unknown to them. Through rumor they learned of it. Jesse James first came in and remained several weeks. He was unknown to my husband and he [Sam Starr] never knew till long afterwards that our home had been honored by Jesse's presence. I introduced Jesse as one Mr. Williams from Texas. But few outlaws have visited my home, notwithstanding so much has been said. The best people in the country are friends of mine.

I have considerable ignorance to cope with, consequently my trouble originates mostly in that quarter. Surrounded by a low class of shoddy derelicts who have made the Indian country their home to evade paying tax on their hogs and who I will not permit to hunt on my premises, I am the constant theme of their slanderous tongues.

In all the world there is no woman more persecuted than I.

*Although biographer Glenn Shirley quotes a portion of this article on page 147 on his **Belle Starr and Her Times**, this is the first book to include the complete sketch Belle wrote about herself.*

Notes

The following collection notes may help to give a more complete interpretation to the narratives by describing some aspects of the tellers, when known, and the ways the stories came to us over the last thirty years.

- *Collected from …* indicates that we collected the narrative in person; *Collected by …* indicates that another storyteller collected the narrative originally, and passed it along to us.
- *Provided by …* means that the story was first told to us orally or in fragmentary form, then followed up by a photocopy, a handwritten transcription, or other method; especially true of clippings in family scrapbooks.
- *Extracted from …* refers to excerpts from longer printed sources, especially newspapers, all of which are uncopyrighted or upon which copyrights have expired, or for which the copyrights are retained by the families in question.

The Works Progress Administration's Writers' Project produced thousands of pages of interviews and retellings, and these works are the property of the state archives in which they are deposited, having been donated thereto by the federal government, but the works are uncopyrighted and un-copyrightable, and are considered in the public domain.

The editors have heard outlaw tales all their lives, and many of these stories were collected before such an anthology was envisioned. For these stories there will be no attribution possible.

Not all stories have notes, being attributed within the text.

1. Collected prior to January 1, 1991.

2. Extracted from the Works Progress Administration Writers' Project in Oklahoma, as the Indian-Pioneer Histories (bound volumes) in the Archives and Manuscripts Division of the Oklahoma Historical Society in the Wiley Post Historical Building in Oklahoma City, Volume 34, pages 75 and 78-83. Not all the interview has been reproduced here.

The interviewer was James Carselowey, the date September 9, 1937, and the informant was Mrs. Fannie Blythe Marks then of Vinita, Oklahoma, the widow of the marshal named in the narrative. Muskogee was a predominantly black town at one time in its early history, with many black Cherokees, the descendants of freed slaves previously owned by the Cherokees and then freed and adopted into the tribe after slavery was abolished. Belle would have known many Cherokees and black Cherokees who would have sheltered her willingly. The "Legend of Belle and her Black Disguise" is often dismissed as fiction, but this narrative seems to verify the story.

3. Extracted from the Works Progress Administration Writers' Project in Oklahoma, as the Indian-Pioneer Histories, Volume 20, page 473 and 475. Only a small portion of the interview is reproduced here. The interviewer was Ruby Wolfenberger, the date was June 21, 1937, and the informant was Mrs. Gertrude Cooper, then of Sentinel, Oklahoma.

4. Collected from Heather Davis Scott at Red Oak II, in the moved and reconstructed childhood home of Belle Starr, now a museum outside Carthage, Missouri, on August 14, 1991. Mrs.

Scott is the daughter of the owner, internationally known ceramic artist Lowell Davis. The house was originally in nearby Galesburg, and belonged to Sheldon Davis, the artist's brother. The family folklore in the Davis family has always maintained that Belle was born in that house, as well as grew up there, but the land grant of the land on which the house sat, although under an act of Congress of 1847, was not made until June 1, 1850, after Belle was already born. There is general consensus among the locals that she did nevertheless at least grow up in the now-preserved house.

5. Collected in 1990 from George D. Hendricks, who reviewed Hutchins' autobiography/biography, of which Hutchins is said to have written the first fourteen chapters before his death.

6. Extracted from a clipping in a scrapbook, which bore no date. The Carthage Carnegie Library believes the article was written for the *Carthage Press* in 1934, based on other articles glued in around it. The narrator is T.C. Wooten, Company C, 15th Missouri Cavalry, under the command of Capt. Green C. Stotts, then of Carthage.

7. This is a common Belle Starr legend from Fort Smith; the editors have heard it many times, in all its unverifiable splendor.

8. Extracted from the interview with Ike Inman, by Ethel B. Tackitt, done July 18, 1937, at Lone Wolf, Oklahoma, and recorded in Volume 30, page 417 of the Indian-Pioneer Histories of Oklahoma.

9. The subsequent newspaper clipping is from the *Carthage Evening Press* for February 23, 1953, in an article by local historian Ward L. Schrantz, based on his interview with old-timers and his collection of *Press* clippings from the 1880s. This article is difficult for researchers to locate, because Glenn Shirley incorrectly identifies it as being in the *Carthage News* of February 26, 1953. This is the first time this information has been reprinted in its entirety.

10. Collected from Morgan Martin Young, Ed.D., the father of one of the editors, who told this legend in the 1940s and 1950s.

11. Collected from Walker Powell, longtime Stone County, Missouri, resident, in autumn of 1991.

12–15. Collected from Robert Joseph Haswell, of Springfield, Missouri, on July 1, 1991. Mr. Haswell recounted four separate items from his great-grandfather Alanson M. Haswell's memoirs and scrapbook. Each of these items saw limited printing in the local newspapers, and have since been reprinted in the Springfield papers, but these accounts, as retold by Mr. Haswell, are appearing for the first time in national publication. Mr. Haswell is an excellent teller of tales and traditions handed down over three generations.

16. Collected August 12, 1989, from D.A. Calloway of Coon Ridge in Stone County, Missouri. He had heard the story all his life.

17. Collected from Charles S. Hunt at the Powder Horn, his mountain man and Western store in the Commissary Mall in Casper, Wyoming, in April of 1991.

18. Collected from Kerry Chester, a Seneca, Missouri, native, in July 1989. Modern-day residents of the town are largely unaware of its frontier-outpost early days.

19. Extracted from *Hesperothen: Notes from the West,* by W.H. Russell, LL.D., published by Lowe, Masten, Searle and Rivington, London, 1882, Volume II pages 167-168 of an original edition lying in the special collection of the Lead Library, Lead, South Dakota.

20. Ibid. Volume II, page 127.

21. Collected prior to January 1, 1991.

22. This is a well-known anecdote in Dodge, and appeared as a true event in the *Dodge City Times* of July 27, 1878.

23. Provided by George D. Hendricks from his book *The Bad Man of the West,* in the late 1980s.

24. Heard in childhood by Richard Young from his father, Dr. Morgan Martin Young (Ed. D.).

25. Collected by Charles E. Avery of San Antonio, Texas, and supplemented by his research; provided to the editors December 3, 1989. Mr. Avery is an author, historian, and dealer in Western and Confederate memorabilia.

26. Collected from Dick Luntz of the Hill City Mercantile in Hill City, South Dakota.

27. Transcribed from the *Dodge City Times* of April 20, 1878.

28. Collected from Earl Riley from Coffeyville, Kansas, as told by his grandmother, Louella Riley, who lived all her life in Coffeyville. Mr. Riley told this in October of 1989.

29. Provided by Carl Rauch of Coffeyville, Kansas, one of the most authoritative tellers of the Daltons' story, in January 1992.

30. Provided by Cindy Price of Coffeyville, Kansas, in January 1992. Ms. Price is an organizer of the Dalton Defenders Days honoring the town's pioneer marksmen-heroes.

31. This very short account was told by F.E. Gimlet, known locally around Leadville as "The Hermit of Arbor Villa," as though he was present for the events; he almost certainly was not. Provided to the editors by Jim Andrews, the best darn storyteller and unofficial historian of Leadville, Colorado. Gimlet died in the 1960s. Andrews is retired, a molybdenum miner, collector, and Western historian.

32. Provided from a typewritten memoir of their ancestor by a young family from the Muskogee, Oklahoma, area prior to January 1, 1991.

33. Collected from Grover Smith on June 28, 1991. Some versions of this urban-legend-precursor have the sound of the axe falling being the sound of the previous victim being chopped up by the teenage son before disposal.

34. Collected from more than one informant from southeast Kansas prior to January 1, 1991. Some versions have a posse of vigilantes surrounding the home, capturing and summarily trying the Benders, lynching them in the barn (or from a tree), and burying the bodies (or throwing them in a river), all in the same night.

35. Collected from a family of Topeka residents in the summer of 1990. The complete account, with contemporary moralizing, was printed in the Topeka *Daily Commonwealth* of August 4, 1877. In his explanation, the son did not admit or deny that his family murdered a dozen people and buried them on their property, and few, if any, Kansas residents accepted this incredible explanation for the fate of the Benders. One resident we spoke with, however, suggested that Frank Baum may have gotten one of his Oz/Kansas ideas from reading or hearing this fantastic tale.

36. This and other Malcolm Campbell stories were provided by Janey Wing Kenyon, of northern Arkansas, in 1990. Sheriff Campbell was her great-grandfather, and she heard stories from her grandfather about him.

37. Collected from a Kansan who visited Silver Dollar City before January 1, 1989. The anecdote is fairly well-known in Kansas, and was reported in the *Wichita Beacon* of January 12, 1876.

38. Collected from Jim Andrews, local historian and former molybdenum miner in Leadville, Colorado, at the wonderful old Western Hardware Company's Museum and Emporium on Harrison Avenue, on November 24, 1990.

39. Copy provided by the Wyoming State Historical Research and Publications Division, Cheyenne, Wyoming, WPA

Subject 56, a clipping preserved in the home of a Works Progress Administration Writers' Project writer, from the *Wyoming Press* of January 15, 1898. We assume that the writer isn't really the religion editor, but rather "got religion" from the holdup. Although suspects were apprehended rather quickly, the editors have trimmed the clipping to its humorous content. Lacking "funny pages," the frontier newspapers treated their readers to humor in the articles themselves. This is one of the rare instances when a reporter was the victim of a robbery and then wrote about it, thus preserving his thoughts for posterity.

40. From the *Fort Smith* Weekly *Elevator* of August 8, 1877. The Fort Smith in the article is in South Dakota. This is the famous "Hat Creek Gang," not Sam Bass' gang, the latter never making stage robbery pay in South Dakota. The sense of humor displayed by the Deadwood Stage robbers is legendary, and the newspaper articles of the day confirm this.

41. Collected from Alpha Bilyeu, formerly of Stone County, Missouri, in winter 1980.

42. Provided by George D. Hendricks of Denton, Texas, in 1991.

43. Collected from Judy Stroope of Harrison, Arkansas, March 5, 1992.

44. Collected from Rodger Harris, oral historian of the Oklahoma Historical Society Archives in Oklahoma City, in August 1991.

45. This unverifiable legend contains some facts. The Devil's Den area is scheduled to open again as a resort, just as it was in the 1940s and 1950s, and even in the 1880s, making it unlikely as a permanent hide-out.

46. Collected from Dr. Morgan Martin Young, father of one of the authors of this collection, in about 1953. This was one of the first outlaw stories heard by the authors in their lifetimes. Local area historian Gary Schilling of Davis, Oklahoma, says that the Turner Falls area was already touted as a resort by the

Chickasaw Indians, and there was enough traffic there in the 1880s to make it an unlikely hideout. Other caves in the Arbuckle Mountains may have had their lore transplanted to Turner Falls for tourism's benefit.

47. Collected from the Reverend John Morgan Young, grandfather of one of the authors of this collection, back in about 1953. This is one of the first outlaw stories the authors have heard in their lifetimes.

48. This story was learned from Dr. Morgan M. Young in the 1950s, and was probably heard by him while a student at Austin College in Sherman, Texas, in the late 20s and early 30s. The "Quantrill brother" story is apparently not true, though repeated over and over through the years, and still believed by many. No brother appears on the census records. The event (a killing by jayhawkers) might still be true, with the brother element added in as part of the "Quantrill method."

49. Collected from JoAnne Sears Rife of Harrison, Arkansas, originally from Bentonville, Arkansas, March 13, 1990.

50. Collected from Charles Avery of San Antonio, Texas, in November 1989. Mr. Avery is a collector and dealer in Western and War Between the States stories and memorabilia.

51. Told to the editors by Topeka residents before January 1, 1989.

52. Collected from Marty Garrison of Harrison, Arkansas, at a meeting of the General J.O. Shelby Camp No. 1414 of the Sons of Confederate Veterans.

53. Collected from Troy Massey at a meeting of the Sons of Confederate Veterans in October 1989.

54. Collected from Robert Meeks at a meeting of Camp No. 1414 of the Sons of Confederate Veterans in October 1989.

55. Extracted from *Life of the Notorious Desperado Cullen Baker*, "edited" by Thomas Orr, who killed him, printed in Little Rock in 1870, page 49.

56. Extracted from the *Van Buren Press* of Van Buren, Arkansas, in the edition of February 2, 1869, quoted from the *Jefferson Jimplecute* of Jefferson, Texas.

57. Provided by the Ellis County Historical Society, Hays, and the Kansas Heritage Center, Dodge City, on April 12, 1991.

58. Collected from Dodge City residents 1979-1991, and from the newspaper files of the Kansas Heritage Center in Dodge City.

59. Collected from conversations and Western books 1970-1991, and from the newspaper files of the Kansas Heritage Center in Dodge City.

60. Extracted from "Recollections of a Swedish Buffalo Hunter, 1871-1873" by Carl Ludvig Hendricks, translated by his descendant Henning V. Hendricks, published in the *Swedish Pioneer Historical Quarterly*, 32:3, July 1981, 190-204, by the Swedish-American Historical Society of Chicago, Illinois, reprinted by the kind permission of Raymond Jarvi, the editor. This is the only known eyewitness description of a burial on Boot Hill in Dodge City, Kansas, and this reprinting is the only western book to contain this grim but remarkable narrative.

61. Transcribed from "A Burial on Boot Hill" by *Dodge City Times* editor N.B. Klaine, published in the *Journal-Democrat* on August 24, 1906, written some thirty years after the event but from personal experience. This burial is often mistakenly identified as that of Dora Hand, but newspaper articles at the time of her death show clearly she was buried in Prairie Grove Cemetery. Legend associates this burial with the name Lizzie Palmer, but there is no confirmation. The Boot Hill Museum believes the burial to be that of Alice Chambers, who died on May 5, 1878, because she is the only woman mentioned in separate confirmation: an article in the *Dodge City Daily Globe* of January 28, 1879, noting that Alice Chambers' body had been removed to the new Prairie Grove Cemetery. This story and this annotation were provided by the Kansas Heritage Center and the Boot Hill Museum of Dodge City, Kansas.

62. Collected from various Dodge City residents and librarians during a visit by the collectors in November 1990.

63. Provided by Ms. Darlene Smith, librarian of the Boot Hill Museum Library in Dodge City, Kansas, April 12, 1991, from her personal knowledge, from the *Dodge City Daily Globe,* October 8, 1878 (excerpt in quotation marks), and from the *Dodge City Times* of October 5, 1878.

64. Extracted from an 1894 edition of the *Fort Smith* Weekly *Elevator,* date unrecorded on the clipping, in the possession of a family in Arkansas; originally copied (as was then the custom) from another newspaper, the *New York Herald.* It is interesting to note how the mores of 1894 figure into the article about the 1780s.

65. Newspapers in the 1880s relied heavily on correspondents to provide the news. This clipping is from the *Fort Smith Weekly New Era* of September 29, 1875, page 1; they had copied it from the *Leavenworth* Kansas *Commercial,* who had obtained it from their Virginia City, Montana, correspondent, who remains sadly nameless. The correspondent was apparently an eyewitness to some of the Plummer gang's depredations. While oral stories of the Plummer gang are common, this kind of eyewitness account is rare, and was handed down through a family as a clipping. The owners added, "When the men started getting caught, they turned in others to try to win clemency. 'Red' Yeager fingered Plummer. Plummer begged for his life in a shameless way, considering how bravely his men died and how much suffering he had caused others. He even offered to bring in his weight in gold for the Stranglers if they would only give him two hours and a horse. While everyone believed his sincerity, no one thought it was worth it."

As we have pointed out before, there is still a last word on many of the outlaws; recent research and a new book just out indicate Plummer may not have been as guilty as the press and witnesses to the hanging have indicated.

66. Collected from an oral interpretation of, and then extracted from, the original article in the *Fort Smith* Weekly *Herald,* of Saturday, July 31, 1875, from the microfilm in the Fort Smith, Arkansas, Public Library. It must be noted that some appointees during Reconstruction were, in fact, corrupt, and that was the case with William Story; Isaac Parker was apparently incorruptible, and was greatly admired even by his political antitheses. A prejudiced reader would expect the Democratic press to be critical of Republican Parker's early efforts; exactly the opposite occurred. Some critics later charged that Parker's zeal became a monomania in his later years, but many of those critics were on opposite sides of the law, of the docket, or of the political spectrum from Parker, and their criticism is suspect.

67. Collected from an oral interpretation, then extracted from the *Fort Smith* Weekly *Herald* of May 15, 1875, J.H. Sparks, editor, from the microfilm in the Fort Smith, Arkansas, Public Library, to obtain the judge's own words.

68. Collected from an Oklahoma informant based on his family retelling of the events from a scrapbook clipping; collected before January 1, 1989. The actual text has been extracted from the *Fort Smith* Weekly *Elevator* of September 16, 1881. The "Indian Territory Murderers" were: George W. Padgett (also spelled Padget in some papers), William T. Brown, Patrick McGowen (also spelled McGowan in some reports), Abler Manley (also spelled Manly in some Fort Smith papers, and once misnamed as Abner in one paper), and Amos Manley.

69. This legend is actually true, according to the *Fort Smith* Weekly *Elevator* of February 28, 1877, in a longer article titled "THRILLING INCIDENT—Three Men Doomed to the Gallows—A Leap for Liberty or Death." This story has been told around Fort Smith for years, and dismissed as fiction.

70. Collected from George Maledon's great-grandniece Ruby Yeakley of Fort Smith, Arkansas, in August of 1991.

71. Extracted from an interview with J.W. Rice of Tulsa, Oklahoma, by WPA writer Effie S. Jackson on November 29,

1937, as cataloged in the Indian-Pioneer Histories of Oklahoma, Vol. 113, page 341 and 351 (second interview).

72. Extracted from *Hell on the Border* by S.W. Harman, an original copy of which lies in the Arkansas Collection at the University of Arkansas Mullins Library in Fayetteville.

73. This story is confirmed in the *Fort Smith Weekly New Era* of June 16, 1875; Frank Butler was shot June 14, 1875. This information was provided by Ruby Yeakley, Maledon's great-grandniece.

74. Extracted from the *Fort Smith* Daily *Elevator* for Friday, March 20, 1896; these paragraphs were extracted to show the manner in which one of the Indian Territory's worst outlaw cases spent his jail time. Another portion includes selections from a diary kept by a prisoner in a nearby cell, which read, in part: "[Bill] says his execution is no lesson to him, but it may be a lesson to some other poor boy…At 6 o'clock this evening Bill asked [Belle Starr's son] Ed Reed if he was going up on the Valley train. He replied 'Yes.' Ed asked if there was anything he could do for him. Bill said, 'see that nobody runs over my mother.'" Ed Reed was a deputy United States marshal and resided at Wagoner Switch, now called Wagoner, Oklahoma.

75. Collected from Gary Dierking of Manhattan, Kansas, in October 1990. Rodger Harris, oral historian at the Oklahoma Historical Society in Oklahoma City provided details July 24, 1991, as follows: the park was the Nu-Pike Fun House in Long Beach, California; the corpse had been shellacked to preserve it, and then painted over to make it more lifelike after years of display.

76. Collected June 5, 1991, from a collateral descendant of Big Nose George who refused to permit a name being credited. While we have met dozens of people who proudly claim to be descended from famous outlaws, and almost certainly aren't, this relative of George Parrott does not wish to be identified.

77. Collected in July 1991 from A.C. "Duck" McLean of Reeds Spring, Missouri. This gruesome story is true. The shoes, the manacle and a saw used in an escape attempt were on display in Rawlins, and the skull cap-piece was also displayed at Dr. Heath's office in 1951. Most of what was done to the body of George Parrott would be a crime today. Mr. McLean did not know if the skeleton was reburied in a proper grave.

78. Extracted from a clipping from a Fort Smith newspaper preserved in a family scrapbook. The complete article and facts about the specific newspaper were not ascertainable.

79. Collected from Milton Perry, curator of the James Family Homestead Museum at Kearny, Missouri, on July 2, 1991. The late Mr. Perry was curator for thirteen years, and an expert on the James family. He was kind enough to sit under the locust trees on the James farm one afternoon, beside the site of Jesse's original grave, and take time from his busy schedule to comment on our questions. The statements given here are verbatim extracts from a longer interview.

80. Collected in August 1989 from Cliff Wagner of Reeds Spring Junction, Missouri, a descendant of Henry Clay. The story is told as truth in Mr. Wagner's family, despite the fact that many folklorist would discount this as legend, not fact.

81. Collected from Charles S. Hunt at the Powder Horn in Casper, Wyoming, Thanksgiving, 1990.

82. Collected from Texas folklorist and author George D. Hendricks at his home in Denton, Texas, Thanksgiving, 1989.

83. Collected from Jim Yoder at a meeting of the Sons of Confederate Veterans in 1989.

84. Collected from Paul Stock, Jr., formerly of Saint Joseph, Missouri, in the late summer of 1991. Mr. Stock's family has lived in the St. Joe area for many, many years.

85. For the Malcolm Campbell information and stories we are indebted to Janie Wing Kenyon, the sheriff's great-

granddaughter, who lives in rural northern Arkansas. The Alferd Packer story was told to Richard Alan Young in the 1950s by his uncle, Dr. Homer Harry Young, a Colorado summer resident who did endless research on a never-published book. Dr. Young insisted on the Alferd spelling, since Packer himself signed his name that way (although perhaps out of simple illiteracy). That Sheriff Campbell's account should vary from others in regard to the events on "Cannibal Plateau" is not unusual, since he was not present for the search for bodies. His is the only accurate account of the capture of Packer, however.

86. Collected from J.R. Blunk of near Galena, Missouri, on June 23, 1991. The story is told by many Stone County residents, and they disagree on some of the details, sometimes stating Alf was born to Matilda Bolen right there in Ponce, and was deserted by her in childhood. Some versions of the story spell Alf's last name Bolden, mispronounced as Bolen, and others offer the spelling Bolin instead.

87. Told by J.R. Blunk on June 30, 1991. Mr. Blunk had learned the story from Hampton Holt when Mr. Holt was about ninety years of age and Mr. Blunk was about fourteen. The Holt family has lived in Stone County for over a century and a half.

88. Collected from Ken Holt of Coon Ridge, in Stone County, Missouri, in the summer of 1979.

89. Collected from Bob Cooster of Forsyth, Missouri, in 1989.

90. Collected from dozens of informants from 1979-1992.

91. Collected from Walker Powell, son of Waldo Powell, and grandson of Missouri conservationist Truman Powell, on June 26, 1991. This story has been told by residents of Stone and Taney counties for a century. In some versions an ex-Confederate moves into Taney County and the Baldknobbers come and take him by night. He is seated on the edge of the deep cavern's upper precipice and told to think on his crimes, then he is pushed over to his death. Years later his wife asks to go through

the cave, but no remains are ever found. All of Belle's brothers are accounted for in current biographies of her, so it seems unlikely that she would have been there looking for her brother's remains. Several possibilities exist: the man was incorrect in his identification, or the woman may have only resembled Belle, or, it is possible that Belle did come there and used the technique of misdirection, claiming to search for the proverbial long-lost brother while actually seeking some other kind of information, about a former acquaintance, perhaps.

92. Provided by Douglas Mahnkey, attorney-at-law of Forsyth, Missouri, October 14, 1989. Mr. Mahnkey is a third-generation Taney County resident and a prominent author and historian of the area. The editors extracted the most central line of story from a longer, interesting family narrative. The editors do not consider Mr. Prather to have been an outlaw, but a vigilante lawman. Many of the ellipses in the narrative were placed there by Mr. Mahnkey, and others represent the deletion of sentences that contained only family history. The Wright novel *The Shepherd of the Hills* takes place in 1904, when some Baldknobbers were still active illegally, and were considered at that time to be outlaws, some eighteen years after Mr. Prather had ended his association with the organization, and in fact, the original no longer existed.

93. Collected from Bill Deakins at a meeting of the Camp No. 1414 General J.O. Shelby Camp of the Sons of Confederate Veterans, in October 1989.

94. Collected from Bill Deakins at a meeting of the Sons of Confederate Veterans in 1989. The trick of sneaking up on your quarry by disguising your movement with a cowbell is a standard Ozark ploy, and one the Baldknobbers and anti-Baldknobbers would have both known and used.

95. Collected from Ed Marshall, entertainment director for the daytime amusement park at the Shepherd of the Hills Homestead west of Branson, Missouri, where the story of

Harold Bell Wright's novel, *The Shepherd of the Hills,* is re-enacted as an outdoor drama by night.

96. Collected from Sheldon Wade from Long Pine, Nebraska, now living in Edgemont, South Dakota.

97. Collected by Texas folklorist Dr. George D. Hendricks from *Lic.* Amérigo Perédez, a historian of Old Mexico from Brownsville, Texas. To Dr. Hendricks' knowledge, this anecdote has not been published before this time. *Hadar* means "to enchant," and *hadarse* would mean "to become bewitched," or "to get very drunk." While *tapaderos* are usually covers for stirrups, the term is the noun "covering," and could replace the more common *tapaojos* (eye-cover; blinders).

98. Provided by Katie Wakely of Stone County, Missouri, from the reminiscences of her grandfather, Charles Finis McDowell.

99. Collected from interested parties at a storytelling session in Casper, Wyoming, Thanksgiving week, 1990.

100. Collected from a bookseller in Laramie, Wyoming, in November 1990.

101–105. Collected from storyteller and African-American researcher Tyrone Wilkerson of Tulsa, Oklahoma, in November 1990 and August 1991. Mr. Wilkerson is an expert on the multicultural history of Oklahoma and the West in general.

106. Collected from Charles S. Hunt at the Powder Horn in Casper, Wyoming, Thanksgiving, 1990.

107. Collected from Ken Teutsch and Connie High of Casper, Wyoming, April 1991, from a clipping from the *Cheyenne Daily Leader* of Tuesday, July 23, 1889. Lynching rustlers may not have been as common as Hollywood would have liked us to think, but it did happen; and it did happen to women. "Cattle Kate" was the nickname given to Ella Watson, and her name, and even her nickname, are conspicuously absent from the article. She is dehumanized by the references to her, and

the author of the newspaper article is clearly using a yellow journalistic approach to try to justify the lynching. Mr. Teutsch typified the reporting in the article as "How dare this woman curse at us, all we're going to do is lynch her!" Some versions of the story say the regulators didn't mean to kill Kate, just scare her, but she angered them by not being meek and they went through with it.

108. Collected from Mr. Hunt in April 1991. [Note 17]

109. Provided by Katie Wakely of Stone County, Missouri, from the reminiscences of her grandfather, Charles Finis Mc-Dowell.

110. Collected from Mr. Hunt in April 1991. [Note 17]

111. Provided by Janie Wing Kenyon, Campbell's great-granddaughter, in the fall of 1991.

112. Champion's diary was published in numerous papers at the time (1892), and has appeared in at least one book since. This story and the text of the diary were provided to the editors at the time of a visit to the town of Kaycee, Wyoming, near where the events took place, by Ken Teutsch of Casper, Wyoming. The short excerpt from the recollections of Sheriff Malcolm Campbell was provided by his great-granddaughter, Janie Wing Kenyon of rural north Arkansas.

113. Collected in a storytelling session in Casper, Wyoming, in 1991.

114. Collected from Robert Kammer and Charles S. Hunt in Casper, Wyoming, November 23, 1990.

115. Collected by Mrs. Mary Calhoun Wilkins of Clark, Colorado, from her friend, Mrs. Jean Wren of Steamboat Springs, Colorado, July 3, 1990.

116. Heard by Judy Dockrey Young in childhood in the 1950s. Cheney is a common name in the Wagoner area, and not all the Cheneys are related to the outlaw.

117. Heard by Judy Dockrey Young in childhood, confirmed by Nellie Harris of Wagoner, Oklahoma, in 1991.

118. Heard by Richard Alan Young as soon as he came to Harrison, Arkansas, in 1968, from Dr. Henry V. Kirby, unofficial city historian for Harrison, and eyewitness to many of the events at the end of Starr's life.

119. Collected from W.J. Myers, grandson of the W.J. Myers who shot Henry Starr in Harrison, Arkansas, in January 1992.

120. Collected from Ross Fowler, M.D., in Harrison, Arkansas, as told to him by his father, the late Tildon P. Fowler, M.D., who attended Starr on his deathbed.

121. Collected from Roy "June Bug" Milum, longtime Boone county resident and politician.

122. Collected from Ruth Kirby McCoy, now-retired Boone County educator, in 1970.

123. Collected from Terry Wayne Sanders, television comedian who spent one season on "Hee-Haw," in July 1991. Mr. Sanders had heard the story all his life.

124. Collected by Charles E. Avery of San Antonio, Texas, from his grandfather, R.T. Jordan, during his youth, and from a relative of Tom Slaughter. Provided to the editors in November 1989 in San Antonio, where Mr. Avery operates C.E. Avery and Sons Collectibles.

125–26. Collected from Charles S. Hunt at the Powder Horn in Casper, Wyoming, November 23, 1990.

127. Collected from Jim Waddell of Stone County, Missouri, in 1990.

128. Collected from/by Hank and Becky Hartman of Ames, Iowa, in 1971.

129. Collected from Mrs. Carol Durbin on old Tiger Mountain at the church and stomp dance grounds, in Oklahoma, in the fall of 1989.

130. Collected first as an inaccurate quotation, which intrigued us, then extracted verbatim from page 100-101 of *The Black Hills; Or, The Last Hunting Ground of the Dakotahs,* by Annie Tallent, St. Louis, Missouri, 1899. Mrs. Annie E. Tallent (spelled Tallant by some authors) was a schoolteacher at Hill City, South Dakota (then known as simply Dakota, or Dakota Territory), after the tin strike in 1883. She was alleged to be the first European woman to come to the Black Hills. Although Mrs. Tallent admits in this selection that her wording is not exact (she recalls "substantially"), she appears to have no "axe to grind" about Wild Bill, nor any reason to glorify him. Now, as to the element that intrigued these editors: Hickok says (according to Tallent) that no one ever got the drop on him; the other authors mainly quote how Hickok never shot anyone except in self-defense, etc. If what Mrs. Tallent quotes is the truth, then presumably all the stories about someone getting the drop on Wild Bill are false. One small possibility (other than the obvious possibilities that Mrs. Tallent is mistaken or Wild Bill was exaggerating) is that Bill referred to face-offs or other pistol duels, not to events such as described by Alanson M. Haswell (story note 12). Many claims have been made for "getting the drop" on Bill, notably the one by John Wesley Hardin, who claimed very late in life to have gotten the drop on Hickok by using a road agents' spin when he was a teen-ager and Hickok was the marshal, a story discredited by Hickok biographers.

131. Extracted from *Thrilling Events; the Life of Henry Starr by Himself,* published by R.D. Gordon, Tulsa, Oklahoma, July 1914. Starr wrote this autobiography while in the Colorado Penitentiary at Cañon City. He praised the Colorado honor system, and cursed the court of Judge Isaac Parker at Fort Smith, claiming that false charges brought against him there turned him to a life of crime, essentially as vengeance on society. His harsh

comments on prison life refer to Judge Parker's three-story jail at Fort Smith, not to the Colorado Penitentiary.

132. Transcribed from *The Authentic Life of Billy the Kid* (with lengthy subtitle) by Pat. F. Garrett. The poignant quote is this statement about the many sideshow exhibits claiming to display parts of the Kid's corpse. Interestingly, this one quote has prompted theorists to suggest that the Kid is buried somewhere else, or that the Kid was in fact not killed; how else could Garrett be so sure the grave had not been disturbed?

133. Extracted from a copy of the letter of Longley to his sister in the General Libraries of the University of Texas at Austin, quoted to us as an anecdote ("Hanging is my favorite way to die...") by more than one Texan in recent years.

134. Transcribed from the *Denver Republican,* March 17, 1883, with some grammatical changes and with additions in brackets by the editors. The statement was sworn in the presence of General Adams, Sheriff Clair Smith, and Wyoming Sheriff Malcolm Campbell. Packer stuck to this second confession in spite of heavy questioning by the parties at the time, and later during the trial. He always maintained his own innocence. Investigations led by Professor James Starrs and Dr. Walter Birkby show that he was lying in his testimony, and was almost certainly guilty of the crimes of which he was convicted.

135. Collected from a Fort Smith native in the 1960s, who had learned it from his father. The text is in the original edition of S.W. Harman's *Hell On The Border: He Hanged Eighty-Eight Men.*

136. Extracted from *The Life and Adventures of Calamity Jane by Herself,* ca. 1896, written under her married name of Mrs. M. Burk. On another occasion she said Capt. Egan said, "You're good in any calamity," which might better explain the name. A search of military records and correspondence of Capt. Egan by more than one researcher does not yield any mention of this event.